Comfort Me

Revised and Illustrated

ALSO BY LOUIS FLINT CECI

THE CROY CYCLE

If I Remember Him
Comfort Me
Jacob's Ladder
Leave Me Not Alone

AS EDITOR

Not Just Another Pretty Face

Comfort Me

Book 2 of
The Croy Cycle

Louis Flint Ceci

with illustrations by

Jennifer Rain Crosby

les croyens press

Comfort Me
First Edition Copyright 2008 by Louis Flint Ceci
Revised and Illustrated Edition Copyright 2020 by Louis Flint Ceci
Illustrations Copyright 2020 by Jennifer Rain Crosby

Published by Les Croyens Press
An imprint of Beautiful Dreamer Press
309 Cross St.
Nevada City, CA 95959
U.S.A.
lescroyenspress@BeautifulDreamerPress.com
www.BeautifulDreamerPress.com

This is a work of fiction. Names, characters, businesses, places, and incidents are the products of the author's imagination or are used fictitiously. Any resemblance to actual events, locales, or persons, living or dead, is entirely coincidental.

First published by Prizm Books, a subsidiary of Torquere Press, Inc. (2008: Round Rock, Texas)

Revised Edition with illustrations by Jennifer Rain Crosby
10 9 8 7 6 5 4 3 2
Publication date: January, 2021
Printed in the United States of America

ISBN: 978-1-7347389-2-6
Library of Congress Control Number: 2020939759

Cover Design by Tom Schmidt
Cover Art by Jennifer Rain Crosby
Author portrait by Jennifer Rain Crosby from a photograph by Dot

Contents

For Kris, who was always there and still is.
And Don, who told me Yes, I could.

Comfort Me

PROLOGUE

A NDY SIMMS APPLIED the brakes slowly and brought the car to a gentle stop but left the engine running. His foot rested lightly on the brake pedal. He felt calm at last, at peace.

Susan Jacobs looked at him. "Why are we stopping here?"

Already he could feel the rhythmic rumble, feel it more than hear it as it beat upon the water of the White Horse, reverberating on the long slow river like a drum.

"Andy, we can't stop here. It isn't safe," she said.

"I know what has to be done," he said. "We need to start over. We need to start again."

She sighed. "It wouldn't work. You know it wouldn't."

"No, I don't know it wouldn't. Can't we at least try?"

She turned to him. "Isn't that what we've been doing all summer?"

He could see over her shoulder, see the light moving among the cottonwoods, coming closer. "I know I wasn't all I should have been last night. God knows, I didn't mean to hurt you."

"You didn't hurt me," she said. "It's just— I knew the moment I saw the look on your face, I shouldn't have . . ." She dropped her eyes. "It was wrong."

"It was a judgment. But we can fix that. We can make it right. Then everything can go back to the way it was, the way it should be." He looked away. "I can't go back there the way things are now. I couldn't face your father. Not with the whole town knowing."

"They don't know anything."

"What they're thinking, then."

She looked at him fiercely. "Who gives a damn what they think? There's more to life than this town and its small-minded bigots and gossips."

"But don't you see? This is where my heart is, my soul. I

wouldn't know what to do with my life without the church, without music."

"Andy, you're talented. You could make a living anywhere. Get out of here. Go to Dallas or Los Angeles or someplace. Don't go back. Go on."

"Matthew—"

"To hell with my father."

"If you loved me—"

She closed her eyes. "Oh Andy, don't you see? I do love you. That's why I can't—"

The blast from the train whistle cut her off. "Andy!" she cried. "The train!"

"Marry me, Susan," he said.

"Move the car!"

"Marry me."

The whistle blew again. Her eyes went wide with panic. She twisted back and forth, looking at the on-coming train, looking at him. The train's headlight framed her hair, making it glow from within like a halo. She was screaming at him but he was calm now, certain. "I'm not leaving here until you say you will," he said.

"Are you crazy?" Her hand fumbled for the door latch, found it, flung it open. "Get out, Andy!" she yelled. "Get out!"

The whistle was blowing almost constantly now. A great metallic screech began to fill the night. "I'm not leaving here without you," he said.

She dashed out of the car and ran as fast as she could a hundred feet or more, then spun around. "Andy!" she yelled. She could still see him inside the car, his lips moving. She must have been screaming but she couldn't hear her own voice. The night was full of desperate blasts from the train whistle, the throbbing diesel engines, the scream of steel on steel.

And then the full force of the train hit him, glass exploding from the car as it was flipped on its side, pinned to the cab of the engine and dragged down the tracks, spraying white sparks and burning embers deep into the heart of the sleeping town, and she collapsed in the ditch where she stood.

They said it was a miracle, that she had been thrown from the car and saved, and that God must have been watching over her for her father's sake. She was too numb to speak. Then, when she began to show, they said it was a shame, and how maybe it had been a judgment after all, and what a cross it was for her father to bear. The lies were too thick by then for her to say anything.

One Sunday afternoon, she heard them talking outside the church. One of them said, laughing, "I guess we were wrong about that boy after all," and the other said, "Still, it's a poor reflection on the church. A pastor should be able to govern his own house." Then her anger found its voice. She told them all what she thought of their Christian charity and their high moral values, and she swore she would leave their God-forsaken town and never set foot in it again, neither she nor her child.

It was a promise she kept longer than any other, nearly fifteen years.

Chapter 1

THE NEW KID

T HIS WAS A bad idea. His first day and already he was late.
He had taken the shortcut Mrs. Oldfield had told him
about, "Just cut across the field on Allen Street. You'll save
yourself three blocks. There's a walkway that starts halfway
down the street and leads to the back door." That's what had
decided him: not only was it shorter, but he'd avoid the crowd
that was sure to be around the entrance to the school, avoid all
those eyes and questions.

But the early autumn day had dulled his usual sense of urgency and it had taken longer than he'd planned to walk the mile
across town. As he started down the walkway, he could see that
first period had already started. The marching band was out practicing on one side of the field, and the boys' PE class was on the
other, playing some sort of football. He would have to walk that
long walk right between them to gain the back entrance to the
school. Everyone would be looking at him. He should turn
around and go back home, make up some excuse to tell his
grandfather, and try again Monday.

Mally took a deep breath, hugged his books to his chest, and
started down the sidewalk. He kept his eyes focused on the back
door. If he didn't look at them, maybe they wouldn't look at him.

He was almost right. Randy Edom noticed a small figure walking down the sidewalk to the back entrance to Croy Consolidated
High School, but only because it momentarily blocked his view
of the band. The football team he "coached" for first period

boys' PE was handily beating the team "coached" by Red Conner, his best friend and fellow varsity football player, so he didn't really need to pay much attention to it. He was sprawled lazily along the bench at the side of the football practice field while Red paced up and down the sidelines, working up an agitated harangue of his team.

"Come on, come on!" Red yelled with disgusted desperation. "What are you, a bunch of cripples? Marcus! Let's go!"

Randy smiled. Red was big and broad, as befits a linebacker, where Randy was short and more compact, "Like a fireplug," Coach had said once, "small but immovable," a handy attribute for a center. They would both put their builds to use tonight when the Croy Cowboys hosted the Holdenville Warriors. So by rights, Randy ought to be thinking about the game, but Holdenville didn't seem like much of a challenge—in fact, no more a challenge than Red's team was putting up against his. He was more interested in watching the arc of Candy Sullivan's baton as she tossed it into the air while the band tooted and honked in loose formation behind her. And then there was Candy Sullivan herself to consider.

"Oh, for the bleeding love of Christ!" Red yelled. And with good reason. His team had yet to score at all, while Randy's had scored three times.

Randy shook his head and smiled at his blustering friend. He really took this too seriously. "It's hopeless, Red," he said. "You're going down for another five bucks."

Red did not appreciate being reminded about their little side bet. Marcus Longacre, the boy Red had picked to quarterback his team, was calling a play. There was a slight shift in the defensive line, the ball snapped, and Red's offense crumbled as Randy's defense poured over them and buried the quarterback.

Red smacked his forehead and spun away from the field. "Jesus!"

"That was the third play Coach taught us this summer,"

Randy told him. He got up and put an arm on Red's shoulder in consolation. "And the first one I taught them."

Red glared at him, then turned back to the mess on the field. "C'mon," he called, "off your cans!"

If this was meant to rouse his players, it didn't work. Longacre in particular glared at him as he was helped to his feet.

Red continued his motivational speech, "Half the period's gone and we still ain't got a score!"

"We do," Randy reminded him.

"Shut up."

Out on the field, the two teams faced each other over the line of scrimmage. "If he thinks it's so easy," muttered one of Red's linesmen, "why ain't he out here?" The boy across from him grinned. "Whatsa matter?" he drawled, "Too tough for you?"

Now that kind of speech truly *was* motivational. The ball snapped, the offensive line held, and for a moment it looked like there might actually be a receiver open. Marcus looked quickly this way and that, then the offensive line began a slow, clumsy collapse. The very awkwardness of it gave him the opportunity he needed, and he took off through a brief hole pried open by the almost accidental toppling of two defensive tackles in opposite directions.

On the sidelines, Red was stunned. "Hey," he said, meaning to be angry. "That's not the play I taught them . . ." But as Marcus's sprint gained momentum his expression changed. Most of Randy's defense was tangled up in the line or spread out to cover the now abandoned receivers. Marcus had a clear shot for the goal line and charged toward it.

"Go, go, go!" Red yelled.

Randy had to admit Marcus was making a good run for it, his black curly hair flapping against the sides of his head like wings. He crossed the goal line easily before any of his squad got near him. "Wow," Randy said softly. He hadn't known Marcus was a runner. Maybe if he had cut his hair like Coach told him to, he'd have made the team after all.

Red let out a rebel yell. Marcus was being swamped by jubilant teammates.

"Lucky," Randy said.

Red turned to face him, grinning like a sunrise. "Luck?" he said. "Randy, my boy, that was strategy."

"Bullshit."

"Like hell. We're gonna whomp your butts."

"No you ain't."

"And who's gonna stop us?"

"Coach Tucker."

Red's face fell as quickly as it had brightened. "Huh?"

Randy pointed over Red's shoulder, where the assistant football coach stood at the other side of the field, his whistle in his mouth, looking at his watch. Just as Red turned around, he blew the whistle and all commotion on the field stopped.

"All right," Coach Tucker said, his voice carrying easily across the field. "Let's get on in." Then he turned and strode steadily toward the boys' gym.

"Aw, shit," Red said and kicked the ground. "We had you, too. We'da nailed you."

"Oh, gimme a break, Conner, huh?" The two of them started following the rest of the boys.

"Y'all were on the run," Red insisted.

"*You*-all were two touchdowns behind."

"And comin' on fast!"

"Just save it for the ladies, huh?" Randy said. "I hear Mary Kay Halliday really eats that stuff up."

"Oh-ho!" Red said. "Now it comes out."

"The way she tells it, you'd think the Cowboys couldn't win a single game—"

"Envy is a terrible thing."

"—without Mister Red Conner, All-American linebacker."

"It must be sad," Red said.

"What must be sad?" Randy said. "Besides your pathetic bragging."

"It must be sad not having anyone to brag to," Red said. He stepped in front of Randy and turned to face him, forcing Randy to stop and wait to hear the rest of the ragging he knew was coming. "And how is the lovely Sheila these days?"

"Get off it, Conner. Sheila's not the only girl in Oklahoma."

"Mebbe so, mebbe so." Red could lay on a real thick Okie drawl when he wanted to be a complete jackass. "But who else is gonna go out with a sawed-off runt like you?"

Randy looked him in the eye, which was all the more annoying because he had to look up some. He set his jaw. "Anyone I choose."

"Like who?" Red spread his arms, inviting Randy to choose from all the girls in the world. As it happened, just over Red's shoulder Randy could still see the marching band. They were still practicing, but Candy was off by herself. She tossed her baton in the air, spun around once, and caught it deftly. She was pretty good at it, actually. "Candy Sullivan," Randy said, almost without thinking. He was ready to take it back until he saw the look on Red's face. That alone was worth it.

"You're out of your gourd," Red said. And he was serious. Randy smiled.

"Edom! Conner!" Coach Tucker yelled from the door to the boys' gym. Everyone else was already inside. "This ain't a church picnic. Let's move it!"

Red turned to the coach. "Yo!" he yelled and turned back to Randy. The two of them started toward the gym again. "You have flipped your ever lovin' lid. And you know why?" He slapped Randy on the back and broke into a jog. He turned around and continued to jog backward as he yelled out, "Because you haven't had any in more'n a month! It builds up, y'know! You go cuckoo!" He laughed and sprinted for the door before Randy could reply.

But Randy didn't reply. He just smiled and shook his head. More than a month? he thought. How about ever? And he looked again at Candy, spinning in the morning sun, her blond hair perfect, gleaming, barely moving, then he turned toward the gym and the showers.

Candy wasn't happy with that last catch. She tried it again. The baton flew from her hand and she pirouetted. She could sense where she was in space and where the baton was arcing through the air and knew just when to reach out her hand and the baton would be there. And it was, but it hit her hand at a painful angle. She didn't drop it, though. She wouldn't drop it. Not in front of these kids. That's how she thought of them, all of them. Just kids. Going nowhere. All excited by the big game tonight, as if that mattered. It was all so trivial, so small. But she would be perfect, just like she knew she could be. Those trophies on the mantle proved it: the Drums along the Canadian first place, the Spirit Award, the three consecutive county blue ribbons, and the State trophy.

Thought of that last one made her wince. It was the biggest trophy on the mantle, silver with metallic blue columns, spread-winged eagles on either side, and on top a drum majorette perched on a ruby ball. But it was a second place trophy. Second! That wasn't going to happen again. She had a whole year to make sure it didn't happen again. She took a deep breath and began the routine again, oblivious of the band behind her.

Joanie Tibbits, marching in formation with the rest of the woodwinds, was all too conscious of the band and the mess they were making of their drill. She was having trouble concentrating on her music. Unlike the football field where they would play at halftime tonight, the meadow on this side of the field behind the high school was little more than a pock-marked lump of prairie. Just as she would get her concentration right, holding the clarinet so her thumb wouldn't fatigue, focusing on the music, hearing the not very distinct or regular rhythm from the drum section, her foot would catch on some uneven clump of the grass or step in a gopher hole. *This isn't music,* she thought. *This is torture. We're being tortured and the music's being tortured and tonight we'll have the pleasure of torturing our parents and fellow students.* Here, a darker thought intruded, one she wished hadn't sprung up, and she hastily chased it away. Of course her father would be there; he wouldn't have to work late at the pharmacy again. Tibbits Rexall would close at the time posted on the front door and her father would be home for supper and they would all go to the game together and after the halftime show maybe they could all go home because the game wasn't going to be all that interesting. It never was. Even if the team was supposed to be unusually good this year, even if . . . And she suddenly stumbled and nearly fell. Damn! Why couldn't they march on the practice field on the other side instead of this lump-ridden plot? Why did the boys' PE class always get it instead of the band? Let the boys play dodge ball or tiddlywinks or whatever inside so the band could get in some decent time on a level field. Did the school want them to look like idiots tonight?

There. The anger helped her concentrate. And here was Mr. Hansen now, calling them in, the period over. As she and the rest of the band straggled toward the back door to the school, she noticed Candy, still out in the field, still twirling.

The coaches' office was cramped and hot and filling with steam from the boys' shower room. Coach Ardmore was leaning back in the wooden desk chair, swiveling it slightly from side to side. Mally felt awkward and out of place. He didn't want to look at Coach Ardmore, who wasn't paying much attention to him, anyway. He was reading the small bunch of papers Miss Saunders, the guidance counselor, had given Mally to show each of the teachers whose classes he would be joining. Mally's eyes slid over the desk, littered with sports magazines and a coffee-stained newspaper, then snuck over to a little window halfway up the side wall. It was perfectly square and had no way of being opened, the glass crisscrossed with fine wire and completely sealed within its frame. Mally was wondering what it was for when Ardmore spoke, startling him.

"What year are you, son?" Coach Ardmore said.

Mally was afraid he'd been caught looking at the window, but Ardmore hadn't looked up from the papers he held. "A sophomore, sir," he answered.

The coach shook his head. "Well, it's usually just upperclassmen in the first hour class, you see."

"Yes, sir." Ardmore didn't say anything more. Was he expecting Mally to explain? He offered, "Miss Saunders said it was the only one they could fit me in this late in the year."

"Mm-hmm." The coach was non-committal. He slid the papers aside and looked Mally squarely in the eye. "It's a safety issue, son. Most of the boys are bigger'n you."

Mally dropped his gaze. What was he supposed to say? He hadn't picked this class. The guidance counselor had.

Perhaps this occurred to Ardmore, too. He took a breath, and with a small shake of his head said, "Well, we'll just have to squeeze you in." He slumped forward in his chair and reached for the grade book. "What's the name again?"

"Malachi Jacobs," Mally said. He saw a scowl pass over Coach Ardmore's face, his hand with the pen hesitating over the grade book. Mally took a deep breath and started spelling, "M - A - L - A - ..."

By the time Randy got to the showers, Red was already lathered head to toe, the soap churned into a froth on the coppery hairs of his chest. Randy used to marvel at his friend's hairiness, which had come on suddenly and thickly, way before any of the other boys in their class. He'd been envious and disappointed when nothing sprouted from his own chest, but it didn't bother him now. Just part of his Indian heritage, he figured, plus he dried off quicker. He turned on the shower next to Red and stepped under the hot stream. "You still owe me five dollars on that game," he said.

"And you're still pining over Sheila Green."

"Oh, I think Candy can take my mind off that."

"Bull," Red said and spat out a mouthful of water. "There's no way she's gonna dump Freddy Crawford for you. He's two years older than you and nearly a foot taller."

"No sweat," Randy replied coolly. "Look, everybody says she's looking around."

"Yeah, but at you?"

"Hey, give me a little credit, huh?"

"Sure, sure, Big Man," Red said. "But what's Freddy Crawford gonna say?"

Randy turned off his shower and faced Red. "Well, it ain't him I'm gonna be asking out, now, is it?" and he turned and headed for the lockers, leaving Red open-mouthed. As he passed Ardmore's office, he noticed some kid standing inside.

Ardmore frowned at the line in his grade book where he'd just entered Mally's name. "That's a kinda unusual first name," he said. "Biblical, isn't it?"

"Yes, sir."

"Malachi." Ardmore could see that might cause some trouble with the other boys. "Is that what your folks call you?"

"My Aunt Margaret calls me Mally," the boy in front of him said, looking him in the eye for the first time. "That's who I was living with. In Oklahoma City. Before coming here."

"Uh-huh." He tried to draw the boy out more, put him at ease. "Well, how do you like Croy? Not as exciting as OKC, I'll bet."

"Oh, I like it fine," Mally said. "My mom's from here, but—" A wall seemed to descend and the kid retreated behind it. He gave a little shrug and finished lamely, "She left."

Ardmore wasn't ready to give up. "So, where're you going to live?"

"I'm living with my grandfather. I've kinda come to take care of him."

"Oh, yeah?" Suddenly, something clicked. "Say, that wouldn't be Reverend Matthew Jacobs now, would it? Used to be minister at the . . . uh . . ."

"Mount Hermon Bible Church," Mally nodded, enthusiastically. "Yes, sir, that's him. He's retired now."

"Yeah, I remember. You know, I think he married my wife's brother. I mean," he had to chuckle, "you know, he performed the marriage ceremony *for* him and his wife. That was nearly fifteen years ago. Just about the last thing—" But Tucker entered the office just then, clipboard in hand, and there was more important business to attend to. "Hey, how'd it go?" he asked the assistant coach.

"Edom's team over Conner's, 20 to 6," Tucker replied, going straight for the filing cabinet and opening the top drawer.

"Ah-ha, what'd I tell you?" Ardmore grinned at Tucker and held out his hand. Tucker turned around and ruefully pulled out his wallet. Ardmore looked at Mally and winked conspiratorially, his arm outstretched until Tucker had placed a fiver on it. "So, how's the old Reverend doing?" he asked, pocketing the money. The other coach turned back to the filing cabinet, continued rummaging in it.

"He's okay, mostly," Mally said. "But he doesn't get around too well."

"I'm sorry to hear that. But we'll soon get you settled away." Ardmore settled into the business of running his classroom with some confidence. He was pleased with the way he had systematized the PE classes so they practically ran themselves. "Class is divided into six squads, with a varsity ball player in charge of each squad." He picked up the grade book again. "Let's see, your last name begins with 'J.' That puts you in group two." He ran his finger down the left-hand column, looking for a name. "Your squad leader is . . ."

"Edom," Coach Tucker said, dropping the papers from his clipboard into the proper file and closing the drawer. He turned around. "Your star, Randy Edom," and he strode out of the office.

While Coach Tucker may have been willing to grant Randy Edom some measure of stardom, out in the locker room Red was having none of it. "My boy," he said as he walked up behind him, "you haven't got a chance with Sullivan."

"I'll just use my sophistication and charm," Randy said, pulling on his jockey shorts.

"Ha! You'll still be dancin' with your own hand a month from now."

"Yeah?" Randy turned to face him.

"I'd bet on it."

"How much?"

"Five dollars."

Randy had to admit this was a very clever way to welsh. "Shit," he said, "I ain't seen that first five yet."

"It'll make us even," Red said, getting into his clothes. "Five dollars says you won't even have her hooked by the Halloween Dance."

Randy didn't like the pressure of a time limit. He didn't really like the notion of asking Candy Sullivan out at all, actually. It was more of a bluff, something to rub in Red's face. Now Red was turning the tables. "You're crazy," he said, "that's six weeks from now."

Red spread the fingers of his right hand in Randy's face. "Five dollars," he said, drawling the words slowly.

"Edom!" a voice barked from Ardmore's office.

Randy didn't take his eyes off Red, who stood there, grinning. "Yeah, coach," he yelled over his shoulder.

"Step over here a minute," Ardmore called.

"Yeah," he answered. He was still holding his towel and

dressed only in his shorts, but he wasn't going to let Red get the better of him. "You're on," he told him and turned and walked to Ardmore's office.

That kid was still there, hugging his books against his stomach, which looked kind of lame, and staring at the floor. "You wanted to see me, Coach?" he asked.

"Yeah," Ardmore said and nodded toward the kid. "This is Mally Jacobs, just moved down from Oklahoma City. He's going to be in your squad."

Randy gave him a short smile and a nod. Mally looked up in time to see the nod and nodded back.

"Give him . . ." Ardmore paused to consider a moment, "Is one of the Joiner boys' lockers still empty?"

"Yes, sir. Joe's is."

"Okay, give him Joe's locker, and give him the drill on the rules, dress code, equipment, all that, okay?"

"Sure," Randy said. He actually enjoyed this bit, being a kind of coach in his own way. "C'mon," he said to Mally and they walked back to the row of lockers where Red was finishing dressing. All the other boys except Red and him had dressed and cleared out by now.

The fifth locker down the row on the other side from his had been Joe Joiner's. The Joiners' dad had moved the family to the Texas panhandle just before school started, depriving the Croy Cowboys of two of their senior varsity ball players. Fortunately, that had allowed star talent from the junior varsity to move up— talent like Red and Randy.

"This is it," Randy said, showing Mally locker number 65. "You can get a lock from Miss Melanson—that's the secretary in the main office." He turned and faced Mally and noticed the boy still had his eyes sort of downcast. Not at the floor, but not looking him in the eyes, either. More like chest-level. He noticed that he and Mally were the same height. They'd be eye-to-eye if the kid would just look up. He launched into the drill: "You'll need to supply your own towel. And, of course, we're required to shower after each class. Coach's kinda strict on that." He grinned, hoping to get some response. The coach's crusade for daily showers was almost a private joke among the boys. But Mally still wasn't looking him in the eye, and his smile faded. He started delivering the rest of the speech to the air above Mally's head. "You'll hafta dress every day, even if you've got a doctor's excuse. It's a good idea to bring a jacket until we're playing indoors for sure. Mornings get cold . . ."

Mally was mortified. The guy was standing in front of him wearing nothing but his underwear. He hugged his books a little more tightly, as if they could protect him from the other boy's nakedness. This guy, Randy, was rattling on about yellow and white reversible shirts and maroon shorts—the school's colors, apparently—and gym shoes and where to get them. When he stopped, Mally looked up. The guy was looking at him.

"And a jock strap," Randy said. They looked at each other for a fraction of a second. "You got that?" he said.

Mally nodded and swallowed. "Yeah," he said.

"Well," Randy said, "that's all." The other boy just stood there. "I guess I'll see you tomorrow."

Mally shrugged and nodded and didn't know what to do next. "Thanks," he said. His heart was pounding and he felt like he wanted to run out of the room and out of the school and back down the long walkway and all the way back to Oklahoma City. Awkwardly, he turned, nodded again at Randy, and left the locker room.

Randy watched him go, then returned to his own locker. Red was dressed already and spinning the combination on his lock.

"Better hurry, Big Man," he said. "You'll be late for chem."

"Yeah," Randy said, distracted.

"Who's the twerp?"

"Some new kid from OKC," Randy said. "Jacob or Jacobs or something like that."

Red snorted. "Jack-off, more like."

Randy laughed, "Yeah." He finished dressing but was slow about it. Something about the new kid irked him.

By the time lunch hour came around, Randy had forgotten all about Mally. He hung out with Red and Al (Albert, but don't call him that) and Tom on the steps that led to the gymnasium balcony just off the main hallway. Red was stuffing his face with a Snickers bar, as usual, and Tom Hansen had his nose in a book, as usual. All you could see of Tom were the tops of his black-rimmed glasses and his wiry blond hair exploding out in all directions.

"He must have some Jew in him," Red had once said about Tom Hansen.

"What?" Randy had said. "Because of his hair? You're nuts."

"And those eyes of his—"

"Oh now *there's* a give-away. Blue eyes is a sure sign of a Jew."

"Like Paul Newman," Red had said. "In *Exodus*. And he's reading all the time."

"Literacy is not a racial trait, dumb ass."

"I dunno," Red said. "Look at Longacre. He can hardly read at all, and you know what they say about him."

Randy had just rolled his eyes and shook his head. Looking now at the top of Tom's head, he had to smile. If he knew half the things Red said about him a fight would break out for sure, right here in the main hall. But Randy knew a good part of being Red's friend was keeping Red's careless comments to himself.

The other member of their crew, Al Mattingley, was rattling on about something or other that Randy wasn't really interested in, though he found it entertaining to watch Al talk. His face seemed to be in constant motion, all animated freckles and thin eyebrows that moved independently above the unsteady anchor of his nose. Al's nose had led him to be called "Eagle" at one point in his life, but then he'd broken it in freshman football practice and the moniker no longer made as neat a point as it used to. Al wasn't really cut out for football, Randy thought, but when basketball season came around his thin frame of springs and wires would really shine, and Randy's more stocky build would become a handicap. Maybe he shouldn't be thinking so far ahead, what with football season barely started, but he wasn't looking forward to basketball this year. Sitting on the bench game after game was pointless, but what else was there to do from January to March? Wrestling, maybe. He sighed with unearned discontent and, leaning on the railing, surveyed the main hall.

The "lair on the stairs" was as good spot as any for such an occupation. The school had been considered innovative when it opened in 1965, which was sooner than the city fathers had anticipated. The ceiling on the boys' gym of the old school, a WPA relic, collapsed during an Oklahoma-vigorous spring storm. The school administrators had wanted more time to consider the delicate social fabric of the town as Croy become one of the state's first "consolidated" school districts. But the kids proved more flexible than the school administrators and city fathers put together, and they took to their new school with gusto. With all deliberate speed, they set about the business of establishing eternal enmity between under- and upperclassmen, defining and defending territorial hang-outs, creating air-tight cliques, and inventing spontaneous traditions. By the time Randy and his classmates entered these halls, they were already deemed hallowed and seemed always to have been so.

To Randy's way of thinking, the varsity football players commanded the best turf of them all. From the small landing off the main hall, he could survey much of the real life of the school, the life that took place outside the classrooms. He could see Joanie Tibbits and Bobbie Littledeer, nearly always inseparable, come out of the sophomore English class and head for their lockers. He could see Mr. Maxwell, the chemistry teacher, hurry to the teachers' lounge for a quick smoke before lunch. He could see the pathetic Mr. Noyes, looking baffled and annoyed as usual, heading for the cafeteria for lunch duty—not that he would be the least bit effective if a fight or something broke out. He'd probably just faint. You could even see through the glass window in front of the principal's office from here. That window was probably a real mistake. Randy was sure it had been put there so the principal and secretaries could look out and watch the kids in the hall, but the office was better lit than the stairwell where he and his buddies hung out, so it was more like the guys were keeping an eye on the principal's office than the principal was keeping an eye on them.

Randy watched as Joanie Tibbits approached her locker and opened it. He'd had his eye on that part of the hall since the start of lunch hour. Not that he was interested in Joanie, but her locker was next to Candy's.

Red's voice rode over Al's, cutting through the hall chatter despite a mouthful of peanuts and caramel. "So how's the passionate affair, Randy old boy?"

Randy shrugged. "I haven't seen her since first hour."

Red shook his head. "Excuses, excuses."

"What passionate affair is this?" Al asked. He was suddenly curious and just as quick to forget what he had been talking about as everyone else.

"Ask Big Man, there," Red said.

Randy shrugged, "It's nothing." He sort of resented Red's having brought it up.

"I bet him five dollars he couldn't get a date with Candy Sullivan."

"That's nothin'?" Al exclaimed. "Man, I'd like to get some of that nothin'!"

"I'd just like to be introduced to her," Tom said, looking up from his book. "Both of her." He pounded out a rhythm on his books. "I want Candy!" he sang. That was good for a laugh.

"Yeah," Randy said, "but she hasn't even been past her locker all day."

Red opened a bag of peanuts. "If you're going to hunt quail, my boy," he said, grabbing a handful, "you can't just sit in the bushes and expect them to jump in your lap."

Randy regarded his friend, smirking with a mouthful of peanuts. Jeez, didn't Red ever eat a normal lunch? But the point had been made and Randy wasn't going to let Red win it. With an "Okay, Mr. Smart-ass" look at Red, he got up from his slouch against the railing and headed out into the hall.

"Isn't Sullivan already going out with Crawford?" Al asked.

"That don't bother him," Red said, still smirking.

"They kicked him out his senior year for punching a teacher."

"It wasn't a teacher," Tom said. "It was Noyes."

"If that fairy tried to paddle me, I'd deck him, too," Red said.

"Have you seen Crawford's car?" Al said, falling into his favorite topic. "I'd run over my grandmother for a set of wheels like that."

"Tsk, tsk," Tom said, nose back in his book. "Remember the tenth commandment, my son. 'Covet not thy neighbor's ass.'"

"Do wha-a-a-t?" Al felt like he'd been insulted in some weird way.

Red giggled at the two of them. "I think Randy's got that department covered," he said as he watched his friend make his way down the hall. He gave out a rebel yell just to make sure Randy knew he was being watched. Randy turned and grinned back at them.

Joanie turned when she heard the yell. She was crouched before her open locker, getting her books in order for the second half of the school day. When she looked up, she saw Randy Edom walking her way. Great, that's all she needed. Cat-calls from the football rowdies. She turned her attention back to her locker but could tell the Edom boy had stopped at the locker next to hers and was leaning against it.

"Hey," Randy said.

"Hello," she said, not looking at him. She would be civil, but she wasn't interested in being polite. She took out her history book and put the heavy literature anthology under the biology book.

Edom was still there. "Uh . . ." he said articulately, "Candy been around?"

She yanked out the biology book and shoved the history book in its place. "No," she said, "she hasn't."

"Oh."

Joanie's long brown hair curtained either side of her face, shielding her from him. There wasn't much more she could do at her locker except stare into it.

"She go home for lunch?"

"I wouldn't know."

"Well, her locker's right next to yours."

"Yes," she said and stood up to face him. "But we're not Siamese twins. We aren't joined at the hip from birth, you know."

He straightened up at that, no longer the easy slouch against the locker and the lazy grin on his face. "Yeah," he said, "well, that's obvious." She continued to look at him, almost daring him to say anything else. "Well, uh . . ." he finally stammered, "thanks for the . . . um . . . information."

"Don't mention it," she said. And meant it. She turned back to her locker. She could hear Randy let his breath out and walk away. She made sure he was a good ways down the hall before she turned and looked at him again.

Chapter 2

BIG PLANS

ECAUSE THEY KNEW they could get away with it, Randy and Red decided to duck out of seventh period. All the varsity boys got out of seventh period anyway to get ready for the game, so they hopped into Randy's Chevy Impala and drove over to the Conners' split-level in the new subdivision southwest of town, out where the streets were called "avenues" and followed curves and circles instead of the flat grid of the rest of town.

Randy's Chevy was a good enough car despite it being an automatic transmission. He'd bought it at Sullivan's over the summer for a pretty good price—better than the one scrawled on the windshield, but he knew the car had been in a roll-over near Vanosa that had killed the driver, and the salesman knew he knew it, and the crash had tweaked the frame a bit and they both knew that, too, even though neither of them mentioned it.

Red was oddly quiet on the drive to his house and Randy thought he knew why. "You're not thinking about the game, are you?"

"Naw," Red said.

"Holdenville's nothing,"

Red nodded, tense. "It's just that . . ." he started. Randy glanced at him. "We've got to be good. I mean, not just good."

"Hey, we *are* good. They moved us up to varsity."

"But we *should* be varsity," Red said. "I mean, . . ." and he trailed off again.

Randy could guess what he was getting at. Red's dad was not a mean man, but he could be awfully demanding, like nothing Red could do, no matter how good it was, was good enough. It hadn't always been like that, at least not that Randy remembered. He and Red had been friends since the fifth grade, when the Conners had come to Croy and moved into the house down the block from his. Randy liked Red right away. His friend had dark moods from time to time, but Randy was usually able to cheer him up. And the Conners had been a good refuge, a place to go when things had started falling apart at the Edoms. Mr. Conner seemed quiet and steady, and Randy had needed that, and when Randy's mother and father had finally split, Red's father had been a reliable substitute for Randy's.

But just about the time the Conners moved into their new house, there'd been a change. Randy couldn't put his finger on it, but he knew Red felt the pressure.

They got to the Conners and went in through the garage door. Mr. Conner was in the spare bedroom that he used as an office, which was kind of surprising in the middle of the day. His thick briefcase lay open on the floor and insurance policies spread out over the table. "Hi, Randy," he said, looking up and over the rim of his glasses, and he nodded at Red, "Son."

"Hi, Dad," Red muttered.

"Howdy, Mr. Conner," Randy said cheerfully.

"So, you're finally going to play some real ball," Mr. Conner said.

"We did pretty good last week," Red said. "We beat Dibble City."

"Dibble City ain't in the conference," Mr. Conner said. "It's those Warriors you've got to watch out for. It always is."

"Yes, sir," Red said. "I've got to get my mouth guard." He headed off for his room upstairs.

"You should keep that in your locker at school," Mr. Conner called after him. "I didn't pay for those braces for nothing, you know."

"Holdenville's not going to be much of a problem," Randy said, leaning against the wall.

"They've a lot of seniors on their offensive line," Mr. Conner said. "That's going to make defense pretty tough."

"Aw, Red'll break through, you'll see. He always does."

"Hmm." Mr. Conner turned back to the forms in front of him.

Mrs. Conner came in from the den where a television was playing softly. "Is that you Randy? I thought I heard your voice."

Randy straightened up. "Yes, ma'am."

"Would you like a bite to eat?"

"No, thank you. I've just dropped off Red and then we're going to my place and then back to the school."

"That's a bit of a round trip, isn't it?" Mr. Conner said, looking up again. "Tell you what, you go on to your place. I'll drive Red back to school."

"It's no trouble," Randy said, but Mr. Conner continued to look at him. "Sure, fine," he said, backing toward the door. "Thanks." He turned and yelled up the stairs, "Red? I'll see you back at school."

It steamed him a little, getting shooed away like that, but he took that out on the accelerator as he drove down Caddo then Choctaw, cutting across the south end of town. Mr. Conner was turning into a real hard-ass and Randy couldn't see any reason for it. Oh well, at least he wasn't *his* father. Sometimes, no father at all (to speak of) was better than what some guys get.

He was still going at a pretty good clip when he made the turn off Choctaw onto Front and then into the alley that ran behind his house. Hitting the gravel, the back end fishtailed a bit, which was the effect he was aiming for. No one had lived in the house on the corner since the Conners moved out, so there was nothing to worry about there, but Old Lady Oldfield was out in her back yard as always, dressed to kill in a sun hat, weed puller, and scowl. He gave her a good show and threw up more gravel as he passed her back yard and the tiny granny house at the bottom of her lawn. Pulling into his own back yard was kind of a let-down, really. It seemed a shame to hit the brakes and lose all that energy. But it was that or go slamming into the back porch and up the steps into the kitchen. Impressive, maybe, but Virginia wouldn't take kindly to it (plus she'd smack him for calling her "Virginia"). So he brought the black Impala to a rough stop, hopped out and bounded up the porch steps.

Virginia was standing there in the kitchen in her bathrobe, the ironing board set up in front of the sink, a cigarette in her hand.

"Hi, Mom," he said nonchalantly.

"Hi, yerself," she said. She took a long drag on her cigarette. "Did you raise enough dust to cover the back yard or are you gonna hafta go out and do it again?" The smoke drifted out of her mouth with the words.

"Aw, naw," he said, heading for the fridge. "Just enough to excite old lady Oafield." He liked to pronounce it that way, Oaffield, and it was something his mom let him get away with—if she noticed at all, that is.

"Hmph. Probably the high point of her day," she said, flicking her cigarette ash in the sink. She picked up the iron again.

"Yep." Randy got the grape jelly and bread out of the fridge and took the peanut butter down from the cupboard and proceeded to make himself a sandwich. His mother was ironing a dress, he noticed. The one she usually wore when she went out. She was being pretty careful about it, too.

"We got new neighbors," Virginia said.

"Oh yeah? Who?"

"Don't really know." She turned the dress on the ironing board. "Moved into the granny house behind Mrs. Oldfield's. One of them's old Reverend Jacobs."

Randy stopped chewing, a lump of unswallowed peanut butter in his mouth.

Virginia continued, "Me and his daughter used to be quite the wild bunch. We lived near by to the Jacobses when you was a kid. In that big stone house, remember? Across from the Holy Rollers? Naw, you probably don't remember that."

Randy got up and walked to the kitchen window. From here, he could look over to Mrs. Oldfield's back yard and the low, narrow green house at the foot of the lawn. A lot of back yards in Croy had "granny houses," built to house ancient mothers-in-law who were too meddlesome to keep in the house and too useful to send off to the old folks home. In size and layout, it resembled a twenty-four foot trailer, but it was made of wood and covered in green asbestos siding. Randy could see several cardboard boxes stacked on the side of the house. He swallowed and took another bite of his sandwich.

"He retired or something, years ago," Virginia was saying. "You wouldn't know about him." She took another drag on her cigarette. "Don't know who the skinny kid is with him."

Right on cue, the skinny kid appeared, lugging a sack of garbage to the trash bin. It was Mally Jacobs.

"Shit," Randy said to himself.

It didn't escape Virginia. "What did you say?" she asked sharply.

"Aw, I got jelly on my jacket," he said, which was true.

"Well, don't throw that stuff around. It ain't free, y'know."

"Yeah," he said and walked over to the sink to get the dish rag and wipe it off.

"You always put too much jelly in it."

"Yeah." He could tell she was looking at him. He got a glass out of the drying rack and went back to the table.

Virginia started ironing again. "I saw a sign in Tibbits today," she said without looking up.

"I know." He reached behind him and got milk from the fridge.

"You don't turn eighteen for another year."

He poured himself a glass and drank it. "I reckon we're doin' all right."

"Now," she said, still ironing. "We're doin' all right, now.

And maybe we'll still be fine when you get that trust money. But that's a year away. I don't know what it'll be around here come December."

Randy stared at the empty glass. "You could sell another piece of land."

Her head snapped up at that. "I'm not letting go of one more acre, not one damned square inch."

"Yeah, okay." He put the glass in the sink. "I'll get on it as soon as football's over."

"Oh. You think Mr. Tibbits is just gonna reserve it for you for a couple of months?"

"Okay, okay." He started putting stuff back in the fridge. "I'll talk to him Monday. Maybe I can start on weekends or something."

"And there's other jobs . . ."

"Okay!" He got the point already. She seemed to think so, too. She threw her cigarette into the sink and unplugged the iron. She picked up the dress and held it against herself to see how it draped. He watched her a moment. "Not goin' to the game tonight, huh?" he said.

"All the way to Holdenville? No, thank you. Besides," she said, "got a date."

He nodded and waited. "Paul?" he finally asked.

"No-o-o. Kenny."

The dumb one. He drew circles on the countertop. "Y'know," he said, "if you played it right, I bet Paul'd really go for you."

"Well," Virginia said, smoothing the dress against herself, "the question is, do I really go for him?" Then she suddenly looked up at him. "And what's this with the advice for the lovelorn? Let's not forget who's the parent around here, young man."

"Yes, ma'am," he said. He could tell she wasn't sure if he was joshing her or not and looked like she had half a mind to start in on him again. "I gotta get back to school and suit up," he said. "See ya later."

He went out the back door. Virginia watched him, a scowl on

her face, as he climbed back into the Chevy. When he didn't tear up the alley on his way out, she reached for her cigarette again, only to mutter a curse when she discovered she'd already tossed it in the sink.

"Jacobs!"

The shout froze him in his tracks. Mally turned toward the open door to the coach's office. "Yes, sir?" he asked.

"I didn't see you take a shower today, son." Ardmore was reclining in his chair.

"No, sir," Mally admitted. "I haven't gotten a towel yet, sir."

"Any store in town'll carry them," Ardmore said. "I'll expect to see you take a shower like all the other boys tomorrow."

"Yes, sir."

He stood there in the doorway, waiting. It took a while for him to realize Ardmore was done with him. Finally, the coach rocked forward, saying, "That's all," and reached for his grade book.

Mally nodded and slipped out of the doorway. When was he supposed to go shopping for towels? By the time he walked home, it was time to fix supper. And Mrs. Oldfield had his time pretty well laid out otherwise. He'd spent Saturday with a push mower pacing every square foot of the impeccable lawn, and she had lined him up to clean out the gutters and downspouts next weekend. It was in place of rent, he knew, and he supposed he should be grateful. He could bring a towel from home, but he saw how the other guys treated theirs and he hated asking his grandfather for anything. Maybe he could get to the TG&Y after church on Sunday, if it was open, or make a detour on his way home from school. He'd figure it out somehow. He always figured things out eventually, just like he'd figured out what that little window in the coach's office was for.

Al was so excited he was practically walking backward to tell them the news. The three of them strolled down the hall, heading for the "lair on the stairs."

"No shit," he exclaimed to Red and Tom, "it musta rolled over two times. It's a complete wreck. And he just gets out of it and walks away as pretty as you please."

The guys made sounds of amazement and admiration.

"Hey," said Tom, "that ought to make things a little easier for our boy, Randal." He grinned at Red. "Better kiss your five bucks good-bye."

"I haven't got a thing to worry about," said Red. "The bet's for the Halloween Dance, not for what he can pick up on the side." That was a lie, actually, but these guys didn't know that. "Freddy'll be back in commission in a week." He spotted the Jacobs kid walking toward them down the hall. "Hey," he said to Al and Tom, "get this."

Mally was walking pretty much on the other side of the hall, but Red veered subtly so their group couldn't help but pass him. Just as they did, he caught Mally square in the chest with his forearm, knocking loose the books he clutched there. That was hilarious. Then Tom clutched his own books to his chest and stuck his nose in the air and minced hurriedly to the stairwell. That was hysterical.

Mally didn't see this little caricature, but Joanie, standing at her open locker, did. "Creeps," she muttered. The kid picking up his books looked pathetic, but she had bio labwork to check, and she wanted to do it over lunch hour. She started sorting through her books for the right one as Candy walked up to the locker beside hers.

"Did Randy Edom see you Friday?" Joanie asked her, digging through her books.

"Nope," Candy said. She jiggled the handle on her locker, which wouldn't budge. "C'mon!" she said irritably.

"Well, he was looking for you."

"Yeah? What about?" She tried the combination again; still no luck. "Shoot!"

"Don't know."

Joanie had looked through all the books in her locker and not found the right one. She started searching the ones in the crook of her arm.

Candy wasn't having any luck, either. With gathering violence, she tugged at the handle, kicked at the bottom of the door, then finally smacked it three times with her open palm. Then she spun around and collapsed against it, her arms folded tight across her chest. "Oh, I think I'm going crazy!" she exclaimed.

Joanie gave the locker an appraising look. "They work better if you treat them nice," she said.

"It's not just the locker," Candy said and let out a sigh. "First, Daddy takes away the car because of that stupid ticket. Then Freddy—" She turned to Joanie. "Two weeks ago, he promised me we'd go to the drive-in over at Tyrola before it closes. The first weekend, he had some silly excuse, I don't even know what. Then last weekend he just had to go to Dallas for the weekend, and of course he couldn't take me."

Joanie's eyes widened. Did she even know what she was saying? But Candy wasn't really paying attention.

"So what does he do this weekend?" Candy continued. "He wrecks his car! Just smashes it up in some stupid drag race with some creep from Dibble City."

The news of Freddy's accident was about to reach Randy, too, as he approached his customary perch on the stairwell.

"Hey, Big Man," Red greeted him.

"Hey, yerself," he said.

"This may be your big day."

"How's that?"

"Freddy Crawford totaled his car Saturday," Al said, proud of the news.

"So?"

"So guess who's without wheels?" Red said.

"And hasn't had fun-fun-fun since Daddy took the T-bird away?" added Tom.

Randy smiled. "Yeah?" He looked down the hall and saw Candy at her locker.

"Well, Ace?" Red prompted.

"'Nuff said," he said and strode off down the hall.

"Anyway," Candy continued to Joanie, who was now trying the top shelf of her locker in a final attempt to find her lab book, "I'm stuck at home all week. If I don't get out of the house before Friday, Daddy and Mommy and Darling Little Sister Beth are going to drive me straight up a wall."

Candy's exasperation was contagious. "Oh-h-h!" Joanie said, finally giving up. "I bet I left my lab book in the lab." She put her books on the floor and turned to Candy. "Would you watch my stuff while I run after it?"

"Oh, sure," she replied. "I'll probably be here all noon hour."

"Thanks," Joanie said and quickly dodged around her and ran smack into Randy Edom. "Oh!" she said.

"Excuse me," he said. He didn't move.

She got the point of his "apology" but didn't have time for this nonsense. She stepped around him and hurried down the hall.

Candy was spinning through her combination for the third time and barely noticed Randy's arrival.

"Hi," he said.

"Hi," she said, concentrating on the lock. She jiggled the handle violently, but the door still refused to budge. She glared at it.

Randy took a look, too. Calmly, he reached over and banged the door hard once about two-thirds of the way up. It popped open.

A smile of genuine surprise spread over Candy's face. "Why, thank you," she said. "Chivalry is not dead."

He smiled back. He smiled so much he was finding it hard to talk. Finally, he put on a serious face. "Hey, I heard about Freddy's wreck," he said. "Was he hurt?"

"Him? Good Lord, no." Candy turned to her locker and started changing her books. "A sack of bricks could fall on him from the sky and he'd barely grunt."

Randy's smile faded. He didn't need yet another reminder of how "tough" Freddy Crawford was.

"I nearly wish he had been, though," Candy was saying. "I thought he'd given up these childish games of his."

That was more promising. "So," he said, "you're without wheels then, huh?"

"Yes," Candy said, disgustedly. "Stuck like a bump in the mud. And I do believe I am going stir-crazy."

"Well, maybe I could help you out. Again."

"Hmm?" She didn't bother to look up.

"I said, maybe I could take you out."

That was so unexpected it nearly took her breath away. She looked up at him, open-mouthed, but fortunately didn't say the first thing that popped into her head. Instead, she smiled again. "Well, isn't that sweet of you?" she said. She saw the grin broaden on his face. Really, he was in serious jeopardy of splitting his ears if he grinned any more. She'd better let him down easy. "But, I . . . uh . . ." Then inspiration struck. "Oh, say, I know what."

"What?"

"Why don't you and Sheila and me and Freddy go double— in your car?"

The smile disappeared. "Ah . . . Sheila and I aren't . . ." and he shrugged.

"Oh," she said and looked down at the floor. At Joanie's books. She barely had to think about it. "Well, listen," she said, "I know Joanie's just been dying to go out with you. Why don't you ask her along?"

"Well," Randy said, getting lost somehow, shifting from one foot to the other.

She put a hand on his shoulder to steady him. "And I'll keep next weekend free. I promise." She looked him straight in the eye. He stopped shifting and in a moment the smile seemed in danger of coming back. "Okay?" she said.

"Okay. Sure." The smile was back now in full. He started backing away from the lockers. "I'll . . . uh . . . I'll see you later then, huh?"

"Yep," she said, giving him a perky smile.

He backed off completely then, grinning like an idiot, and turned and ran down the hall to the stairwell. She turned and faced her locker, rolling her eyes and letting out her breath. Sometimes this was really too much work. She took out her compact and started touching up her makeup using the mirror in her locker door.

Edom was back at the stairwell with his gang when Joanie got back from the lab, the whole bunch of them huddled together. They burst into laughter just as she passed, but she ignored them.

"Did you talk to Randy?" she asked Candy when she got to their lockers.

"Yep," she said, applying some lipstick. "What do you think of him?"

"Randy Edom?" she said.

"Mmm-hmm."

She was surprised Candy would want her opinion about any-thing. She shrugged. "Oh, he's okay, I guess. Not as bad as some."

"He's kinda cute, you know. For being so short. Kinda like an elf."

"Hmph," Joanie said. "Looks more like an ape, if you ask me." She stooped down to pick up her books.

"If you ask me," Candy said, "I think he's sweet on you."

She nearly dropped her books.

"In fact," Candy said, closing her locker, "I wouldn't be sur-prised if he asked you for a date."

She should have said no. If fact, she would have said no if he had had the nerve to ask her to her face. But instead he had to telephone her house and her mother had to answer it first and somehow manage to wheedle out of him the purpose of his call and she was so excited for her daughter and so delighted by the time she handed the phone over to her that she really couldn't say no. Really, it was so embarrassing. It wasn't like she'd never gone out on a date before. She just hadn't gone out on one lately. Well, okay, not since the junior high graduation dance, but she'd been busy. She was serious about her studies, and there was a lot to think about.

Unlike the movie itself, which wasn't worth thinking about at all. It was stupid, some drunken priest getting all moony over a girl half his age and crashing about in the Mexican jungle. She wished it would end. She thought of a dozen ways it could end, a dozen ways to end this nightmare date with Randy Edom sitting silent as a carrot in the driver's seat and her sitting equally poised in the passenger's seat and the muttered rustling and friction going on in the seat behind them that they were both trying to ignore (though she caught Randy glancing in the rear view mirror more than once). Despite the ferocity of the late autumn mosquitoes, they had to keep both front windows open just to keep the windshield from steaming up. Not that blotting out the picture would be any great loss. Who needed to look at those enormous alcoholic faces anyway? Maybe a tidal wave would roar up out of the Mexican Riviera and wash the whole silly lot of them out to sea. Maybe flaming hail could smash down on them from a clear sky, like in *The Ten Commandments*, and then sweep out of the screen and rain damnation on them all. Or an earthquake. There'd been earthquakes in this part of Oklahoma before. She could imagine the drive-in movie screen toppling forward and crushing the first two rows of cars. Or maybe a giant snake would rise up out of the Canadian River and swallow the entire outdoor theater, screen, cars, kiddie slide and all and put an end to it.

"I wish," she said, not meaning to say it aloud.

Randy looked over at her. "Movie not to your liking?" he asked quietly.

"Not really," she said. "You?"

"I dunno," he said. "I keep hoping maybe a giant snake will suddenly show up and eat the bunch of 'em."

She gave him a funny look. She hadn't said that out loud too, had she? He turned and smiled at her. She smiled back.

"No, not there!" Candy's harsh whisper came from behind them.

They both turned their stony eyes back to the picture. After a minute, Joanie said, "Randy?"

"Yeah?"

"I know the movie isn't quite over yet, but would you mind . . . ?"

"Sure," he said. He unhooked the speaker from his window, its thin voice still plaintively reciting, and started the engine.

"Hey," said Freddy, his face appearing above the back of the seat for the first time in an hour. But Candy's arm coiled around his neck and dragged him back down.

They left them on the sidewalk outside the Sullivans' house. There were no lights on inside and they just stood there on the sidewalk in the dark, wrapped around each other, apparently just as comfortable standing up as they had been lying down.

The lights were on at the Tibbitses' when Randy pulled up in front, both in the front room and in the hall. He turned off the engine and they both sat there a moment.

"Well . . ." Joanie started. There wasn't really much to say. "Thank you for taking me to the movie."

"Sure," Randy said. "My pleasure."

She turned and looked at him, then turned to look at the house. The porch light went on. She looked at her hands in her lap. They looked strange to her.

"Well, I guess I'll see you in school on Monday," Randy said.

"Yes," she said. "Well . . . good-night." She knew that was

the right thing to say, and she knew what was supposed to happen next, but she didn't know how to make it happen.

He looked at her for a moment. Then he slid over on the seat and leaned toward her. She turned her face to him and he bent forward and kissed her on the lips. She closed her eyes, and when he pulled away she dropped her head. "Good-night," she said softly, then opened the car door and stepped out.

He watched her go, puzzled. She was halfway up the walk before he remembered he should have gotten out and opened the car for her. He wanted to call out an apology or something, but she was already at the door. Feeling like a real jerk, he started the engine and pulled away.

"Home so soon?" her mother called from the front room before she was halfway up the stairs. "How was the movie?"

"It was stupid," she said and hurried the rest of the way up to her room.

Ruth heard the door to her daughter's bedroom close and wondered if something was wrong. She cast a worried look at her husband, John, but he was oblivious behind his paper. She sighed and picked up another sock to darn. Things were always so tough for Joanie. Maybe the two of them would have a heart-to-heart about it tomorrow.

Mally wasn't really asleep when the car lights swept across the thin curtain. It was a small room and the head of his bed was right below the window. He rolled over and got up on one elbow. He could move the curtain aside just a bit and see out pretty well without being seen.

It was Randy Edom's car, rolling quietly into the cinder-packed driveway behind his house. He saw Randy get out and walk past the basketball hoop on a rusty pole and start up the back steps. But then he stopped. He was looking into the house. A faint light was coming through the window beside the back door, but Mally couldn't see into the house from this angle.

Randy stood still a moment, one foot on the top step. Then he changed his posture and just stood there. Finally, he turned around and came back down the stairs and went around to the trunk of his car. He got out a carton, closed the trunk, and sat on it. He fished in his letter jacket for something and pulled it out. Mally could hear the church key opening the can of beer from across the alley.

Randy scooted back on the trunk and leaned against the rear window. He looked up at the stars. They were pretty bright tonight, like they sometimes are in the fall. There was a particularly bright one right overhead, part of a bunch that made a sort of V. Or maybe a W. He took a long pull on his beer— well, it *was* his beer now, anyways, its original purchaser having gone on to better things. "Thanks, Freddy," he said and raised his can in a salute. "It's been a helluva night." He downed another gulp.

What he had seen from the back porch was the light coming from the living room. He had heard music, softly, a country-western waltz. And then, briefly, the kitchen doorway had framed two figures, dancing. One was Virginia, of course. It took him a second to place the man, but when they turned before waltzing out of sight again, the light played across the man's face. It was Kenny.

He settled against the rear window of the car, his left arm crooked behind his head. He might just stay here, at least until the 12:04 rumbled through town on the old Santa Fe tracks. He didn't think he'd drink the whole six pack, but it was a comfort to know it was there if he felt like it.

Chapter 3

FRIENDS AND ENEMIES

"HEY, NOW, THIS ain't exactly fair," Marcus said as the two teams of boys approached the line of scrimmage. His blue eyes glittered at a chance to goad the others. "You've got one more'n we got."

"Yeah," said one of the boys on the other side, "but we've got Jack-off."

Mally took his position in the vague backfield, turning red and trying to stay out of the way. He was getting no direction from Randy, who, as usual, was busy talking to Red on the sidelines.

"Time's running out, Big Man," Red needled.

Randy was trying to sound self-assured and not doing too well at it. "I tell ya, it's all set for this weekend. Just have your ten dollars ready, 'cause in four weeks, it's mine."

"Su-u-u-re," Red drawled. "Provided Freddy-boy doesn't wear her out by then." He flicked a thumb at the field. "I hear from Marcus the fun didn't really start till after you dropped them off."

"Aw, hell, what could they do without Freddy's car?"

"My boy, there are some things for which you don't need a car."

A play went down on the field, but neither boy much noticed.

"All set for this weekend, huh?"

"Yup."

"But you haven't spoken to her since Friday."

"Nope."

"And here it is, Wednesday already."

"Well, what'd'ya expect? She hasn't been to school for two days. I ain't gonna chase after her."

Red grinned. "Sure."

Randy shrugged. "Why should I? She practically guaranteed me a date this weekend."

"Oh-ho," Red said, nodding sagely. "'Practically.'" He patted Randy on the shoulder consolingly. "Well, you just hold that thought in mind, there, Randy-boy. You just hold that thought in mind."

Tucker blew the whistle then and ended the taunting, but Randy lingered on the field. The band was out like it had been when this whole thing started more than two weeks ago, and Candy was there, back in front, tossing her baton in the air. No word why she'd missed Monday and Tuesday. It was like those two missed days hadn't happened, like the double date Friday night was something he'd made up. As he drifted toward the gym, he took another look at the band. That was funny. He hadn't noticed Joanie Tibbits in the band before. But there she was, at one end of a line of clarinets, wearing slacks, which didn't much flatter her. Candy, on the other hand, was in her full regalia. You could see the full length of her thigh, all the way up to the hip.

He had to check himself at the door. He didn't want to go into the locker room looking like that.

There was plenty going on in the locker room as it was. The guys were playing a game of keep-away with somebody's towel. He saw pretty quick it was Mally's. The kid was in a circle of guys, some from his squad, some from Red's, and Red was egging them on. Marcus had the towel at the moment. Mally made a grab for it, but Marcus tossed it to Red.

"What'd'ya need a towel for?" Marcus yelled. "You ain't never took a shower."

Mally spun around and Red dandled the towel in front of him. Mally hesitated, then lunged, but Red passed it from one hand to another, faking Mally out. Then he held real still for a moment and Mally did, too. Just as Randy stepped up to the group, Red gave a whoop and tossed the towel back to Marcus. Mally whirled around again. Randy could see his face was flushed. Maybe he ought to do something. The kid was in his squad, after all.

Just then, Marcus tossed the towel to him. Instinctively, he caught it in mid-air and held it aloft. Just as Mally was turning to him Red yelled, "Hey, Jacobs!" and instead of facing Randy he turned to Red.

It was expertly timed. The gob hit him square on the forehead. Mally just stood there, frozen.

"Now you need a towel!" Red yelled and guffawed.

Mally turned to Randy, who was still holding the towel in the air. The spit was beginning to trickle down one side. It seemed fun before, but with Mally looking at him, he couldn't keep his smile. His arm came down of its own weight. "Here," he said and handed him the towel.

"What's the ruckus in here?" Coach Tucker bellowed from the end of the row. All the boys were suddenly facing their lockers, busy minding their own business. Nobody said anything, but Red's shoulders were quivering and Randy knew he was giggling. Even Mally was quiet in front of his open locker, his face hidden by the door.

"Nothing, Coach," Randy said.

"You boys hurry up now," Tucker said. "This ain't a country club."

Red was still giggling. Mally was the first to finish dressing and left quickly. Randy could see his eyes burning.

"God, what a fag," Red said.

"Yeah," Randy said and headed for the showers.

They were studying poetry in sophomore English and Joanie was intrigued. There was this one poem by William Blake about a sick rose that was both disgusting and beautiful at the same time. Mrs. Gregory had asked for their reactions to it and what they thought it was about. Bobbie Littledeer went for the obvious, of course.

"It's about rose canker," she said. "I see it all the time in my mother's roses. The buds get eaten and it kills the flowers."

Joanie disagreed. "That's not caused by flying worms," she said. "And what kind of worm could fly through a 'howling storm'?"

"That's a good point," Mrs. Gregory said. "The poem does make sense on Bobbie's level, of course. It could literally be about a rose and the parasite that feeds on it. But that flying worm suggests maybe there's something more going on. Anybody else?"

She looked hopefully around the room. Joanie was hopeful, too. She was sure this was about something more than gardening, otherwise what was the point?

She was amazed when she saw Mally's hand rise up two chairs in front of her. Mrs. Gregory seemed amazed, too, and maybe a little pleased. "Yes, Mally?" she said.

"Isn't the rose also used as a symbol for Christ?" he said.

"Yes," Mrs. Gregory said. "Christ is sometimes called the Rose of Sharon. But then what would the worm be?"

"It could be Satan, the Great Worm," Mally said.

"But the worm is killing the rose," Bobbie objected. "Satan can't kill Christ."

"Maybe that's what Blake was afraid of, or what he found really interesting about it," Mally said.

On the way to lunch after class, Bobbie was in a temper. "How can he say things like that?" she said. "It's disgusting."

"Well, the poem is kinda disgusting, too," Joanie said. "That's part of what makes it so good."

"I don't think it's such a good poem. I don't think it's good at all," Bobbie said. They each grabbed a tray and started through the cafeteria line. "And if it's about what he says it is, then it's not just a bad poem, it's blasphemy."

"Bobbie, not everything is an attack on Christian life," Joanie said. Sometimes her friend could be more than a little irritating. She reached for a dish of chocolate pudding.

"Oh, you think not?" Bobbie said. "You just don't have your eyes open, is all."

"Well, I have my eyes open enough to see Mally Jacobs sitting over there all by himself. Why don't we go over and ask him if it's blasphemy?"

Bobbie was horrified. "You wouldn't!" she said, wide-eyed. They were already walking in his direction.

"Nobody else is sitting there."

"There's a reason!" Bobbie hissed.

"And what would that be?" But they were too close to where Mally sat for Bobbie to say anything. "Hello," Joanie said as she sat down across from him. Bobbie sat down next to her, but looked like she was tied to a spring that could jerk her back at any moment.

"Hi," Mally said, smiling.

"You're Mally Jacobs, aren't you?"

"Yeah."

"I'm Joanie Tibbits and this here is Bobbie Littledeer."

"Hi," Mally said, nodding to Bobbie. Bobbie gave the briefest possible smile and then started to study her lunch tray.

Okay, thought Joanie, *if I have to carry this all by myself, I will.* "How do you like Croy?" she said. "It's not much after O. City, I'll bet."

Mally shrugged. "It's all right, I guess. I haven't seen much, really. I have to stay home most of the time."

"Oh?"

"Yeah. Grandfather's got arthritis real bad. I gotta take care of him. Fix meals, clean up, stuff like that."

Joanie turned to her friend. "Mally's granddad is the Reverend Jacobs, you know."

Bobbie gave her a look. "Yes, I know," she said, and went back to eating her lunch. Of course she knew. It was Bobbie's church he used to be pastor of.

"He doesn't call himself Reverend anymore," Mally said. "He's retired."

Bobbie looked up at that. "You can't retire from a calling."

Joanie glared at her.

"Well, you can't," she insisted. "Anyway, how's he live if he doesn't preach?"

"My mother sends him checks from time to time," Mally said.

"Where's she now?" Joanie asked.

"In Los Angeles. She's working in television."

"Your mother's on television?" Bobbie asked, incredulous.

"Well, not exactly," Mally frowned and seemed at a loss for words.

Joanie decided to rescue him. "And now you're living with Mrs. Oldfield."

"No, not with her, thank God," he blurted out. He suddenly looked as if he was afraid he might have said something wrong. Joanie laughed, but Bobbie was tight-lipped. "I mean," he said, "we live in the little house behind her place. And she's real good about it. She hardly charges any rent."

That seemed to mollify Bobbie. "Well, he may have stopped preaching, but I bet he hasn't stopped being a Reverend."

"My mother says he used to be a really fine preacher, and a scholar, too," Joanie said.

"Yeah?" Mally said, breaking into a smile.

"Yeah. She says they called him—"

"Bobbie!" someone called out from across the cafeteria. Joanie turned to see who it was. "Bobbie, c'mere a sec! I've got something to tell you." It was Mary Kay Halliday.

Bobbie swiveled around in her chair, a spoon still in her hand. "Okay!" she yelled, then turned back to them and started picking up her things. "Y'all don't mind if I leave just now, do you? Mary Kay's got something to tell me and, uh, it's been real nice talking to you, uh . . ." and then she just left.

Joanie couldn't believe it. She just abandoned her here with this strange boy. She watched Bobbie's too-long skirt disappear across the cafeteria. When she turned back around, Mally was looking at her. He flashed her a smile.

Well, what could she do? She smiled back. Then she started in on her lunch. She'd done so much talking she had hardly touched the whatever-it-was. She remembered it had been plopped out onto her tray with an ice cream scoop, though it had meat in it. What kind of meat is served with an ice cream scoop? And right next to it was a perfect little ice cream scoop of mashed potatoes. She was sure the lunch ladies could serve the entire meal out of ice cream scoops—the vegetables, certainly the pudding, even the milk. Except, of course, if there were real ice cream. They'd serve that with salad tongs.

This was ridiculous. She was pretending Mally wasn't even there. She looked up and saw for the first time what he was eating. It was a bag of potato chips. There wasn't anything else in front of him. She watched as he took a single chip out of the bag and put it in his mouth. He still had his fingers to his mouth when he noticed she was looking at him. He blushed a little and put his hand down.

"I like to make them last," he said sheepishly.

"Is that all you have for lunch?"

He shrugged. "It's enough."

She looked down at her own plate, at the food she had just been mocking. She bit her lower lip, then she took a deep breath and straightened up in her chair. "I don't know why I got this old pudding," she said. "I hate chocolate. Would you do me a real favor and take it off my hands?"

"Uh . . ." he said.

"Good," and she passed the bowl over to him. "Haven't even touched my spoon," she said and passed him that as well.

"You sure?" he said, looking from the pudding to her.

"Oh, yeah," she said, crossing her arms in front of her. "What I really wanted was the Jell-O."

"Thanks."

"Sure." He tied into it, eating a little too quickly for good manners. Embarrassed by his eagerness, she turned and looked across the cafeteria. She could see Bobbie and Mary Kay chattering away. They both glanced her way and she turned back around.

Her jaw dropped in surprise. The pudding was entirely gone. The bowl looked like it had actually been licked. She was glad she hadn't seen that. But when she looked up, Mally was smiling happily at her. She closed her mouth and he dropped his eyes, still smiling.

She didn't know where the thought came from, but it was as obvious as daylight. "Hey," she said, "do you have to get home right away after school?"

Mally shrugged. "I have to be back in time to fix dinner. It's usually time to start by the time I walk home."

"You *walk*? All the way to Mrs. Oldfield's? That's gotta be five miles!"

"Naw. It's not that far."

"It's clear t'other side of town! Isn't there a school bus?"

He shrugged again. "They don't pick up kids in town."

"Well, that's just silly." And just typical of Croy Consolidated High School. "Listen. My mother's coming to pick me up today. Whyn't we just give you a ride?"

Mally was fidgeting. Why should this make him nervous? "Oh, well," he was saying, "I wouldn't want you to—"

"Oh, it's no trouble," she said. "Really."

She had to dash to the pay phone to squeeze the call in before lunch hour ended, but she made it. "Hello, Momma? Could you pick me up after school today? Oh, good. And could we give another kid a ride? His name's Malachi Jacobs. Yeah, his grandson. Oh, it's pathetic, Momma. I'll bet he hasn't eaten lunch in a month." She didn't even have to make the suggestion herself, her mother did. "You would? Oh, thanks, Momma. Yeah, that'd be swell. Thanks. Bye."

See? No trouble at all.

It just wasn't working out with Freddy and she was going to have to face that fact. Candy sighed. It had been fun at first, and a bit of an adventure, but last Friday night was the last straw. He had been all over her like some overgrown puppy. And the way he kissed! It was like he was trying to turn his mouth inside out all over her face. It lacked finesse. It was all about his eagerness and his urgency, his hands and his arousal, and in the end she had felt nothing, though Lord knows she had tried. It depressed her, and she spent all Monday and Tuesday at home, trying to lift herself out of her mood. But being home hadn't helped at all. Her mother had been too cheerful, bringing her glasses of water every five minutes, as if the problem were in her kidneys and needed to be flushed out. She finally had to escape to the school, but there was nowhere to think here, either. Just a bunch of noisy kids. Their silly posturing and trite gossip are what made her look for someone with more maturity in the first place. But she had made a mistake; Freddy Crawford just didn't have it.

No, it was over. Now what was she going to do?

"Hey, Candy."

The voice startled her, coming up from behind as she walked down the hall. She turned around with what she was sure must be a stupid look on her face.

"Hey," the boy said again. "About this weekend . . ."

"Oh," she said. What was this boy's name? "Oh, I'm so glad I ran into you, Rickie. Listen. I'm so sorry, but Daddy's going to

Tulsa this weekend, and he's taking all of us—I mean *all* of us—with him."

The kid's face fell. "Oh."

"I'd get out of it if I could," she said, talking as fast as she could while still being polite, "believe me, I would. I know it just messes everything up, but . . ."

"Oh sure," he said. "I know how it is."

She glanced at her watch. "Oh, gosh, the planning committee for the band trip is meeting. I gotta go."

"Well, how about next weekend?" he asked.

"Well, gee, I . . ." Couldn't this dork take a hint? "Listen, Rickie, I tell you what. Y'all call me after school today, huh?"

"Yeah," he nodded, a little uncertainly. "Okay."

"Okay. Talk to you then!" She flashed him a smile and headed toward the band room, where she had absolutely no intention of sitting through some boring old committee meeting.

Randy watched her go. "Randy," he said after she turned the corner. "Not Rick. Randy."

It was fascinating just watching him eat, fascinating enough to capture both Joanie's and her mother's attention. The afternoon sun was streaming in through the dining room window, softly filtered by the sheers behind the floral print curtains and glinting off the glass in the built-in china cabinet. The only sound in the dining room was Mally's spoon dipping into the bowl again and again.

A pot of stew simmered quietly on the gas range in the kitchen, filling the house with the warm smell of beef broth and cooked vegetables, but there was no sign of the quick work that had gone into making the meal. Mrs. Tibbits kept a clean house. She and her daughter now sat at the dining room table, leaning slightly forward, and didn't relax until Mally put down his spoon.

"That was real nice, Mrs. Tibbits," Mally said. "I haven't had stew that good in a long time."

Ruth smiled. "I'm glad you liked it," she said. "I tell you what, why don't I just put some of it in a little dish for you to take home for the Reverend?"

Mally looked concerned. "Oh, really, ma'am," he said. "I don't want to put you out in any way."

"Oh, no bother a-tall," Ruth said. "The Reverend and I go back many years. Why, I even remember when you were born, young man."

Joanie noticed Mally blushing. "How come I never met Reverend Jacobs, Momma?" she asked.

Her mother gave her an odd look, and then glanced at Mally, who was still looking down, embarrassed. She smiled at her daughter. "Well, he retired just about then, dear." She got up from the table. "And your Daddy and I didn't take to the new pastor at Mount Hermon. Plus we'd just bought this place—to make room for you, as a matter of fact," now it was Joanie's turn to blush, "so, we moved and started going to Antioch Baptist." She smoothed out her apron. "Well, I'll get a casserole dish for the stew. I won't be but a minute," and she left for the kitchen.

"That'll be a break for you, won't it?" Joanie said to Mally. She called out to her mother, "Mally does all the meals at his house."

"Oh?" she said from the kitchen.

"It's no big deal," Mally said, trying to be loud enough for Mrs. Tibbits to hear in the kitchen without shouting. "I'm not really good at it. I can never get it all to the table hot."

"Me, neither," Joanie said. "I've tried once or twice, but it was a real disaster. I think you've gotta be a mother of five for about a hundred years to get it all to come out right."

"It's mostly suppers throw me," Mally said. "Breakfasts I do fine. Pancakes, omelets, waffles—"

"Anything with eggs, right?"

"Right!" The two of them laughed. "But we don't have them that much. All Grandfather seems to want for breakfast is Cream of Wheat."

"Ugh! Can't stand the stuff. It doesn't taste like anything. 'Cream of What' I call it."

"Huh?" Mally didn't seem to get it.

"You know, cream of wheat—cream of what."

"Oh. Yeah." He smiled and nodded. He still didn't get it.

And then it was quiet again, like it had been in the cafeteria. Joanie wrapped a strand of her hair around her index finger. Mally seemed suddenly interested in the light fixture above the dining room table. It had a big red globe in the center with clear circular windows. Four smaller red globes sprung out of the center on curving arms hung with cut glass.

"Gaudy, isn't it?" she said.

"Huh?" he said, startled.

"Daddy got it at an auction. Momma doesn't care for it. Says it looks like it came from a bordello."

"I kinda like it," Mally said. "It's neat."

"What's it like in O. City?" she asked. "Was school different from here?"

"Not really," he said. "Well, kinda. I went to a Catholic school."

"You're Roman Catholic?" she said, wide-eyed. This was getting interesting.

"No, not really." Mally squirmed a little. "My Aunt Margaret is, though. We lived with her."

"She your mother's sister?"

"No, she's my . . ." Mally had to think about it a little. "She's really my mother's aunt. My mother's mother's sister."

"So, your great-aunt, really."

"Yeah," he smiled and nodded. "I never really thought of it that way."

"You have to think like that among the Tibbits," Joanie said. "We've got family all over town."

"Do you have a lot of brothers and sisters?" Mally asked.

"Naw, it's just me and the Bean."

"The Bean?"

"My little brother. I wanted to call him Little Stinker, but Momma wouldn't let me, so I just call him the Bean."

"Where's he now?" Mally said, looking around.

"Oh, Lord knows. Out burning down a church with that Rafe Hamilton, most like."

"You're kidding!"

"No, I'm not. Last summer, he got caught throwing firecrackers in the window of the Assembly of God church. They'd've locked him up, too, if he hadn't been but six years old." They both laughed. "What is it with boys and blowing things up?"

Mally grinned. "It's fun!"

"Oh, not you, too," she groaned. "Did you have fun like that with your pals up in the city?"

That seemed to throw a bucket of cold water into the room. Mally looked down. "Naw," he said.

Shoot, things were going so well! Joanie thought.

"I miss Mr. Anderson, though," Mally said, looking up.

"Who was he?"

"A meteorologist. He worked in Norman, but he lived next door. He got my mom her first job."

"Oh. Was he and your momma dating?"

"Oh, no," Mally said quickly. "He was just a neighbor, you know, being neighborly. And he was an amateur astronomer, too. He had a telescope and all. He used to come out at night in his back yard and set it up. I'd go over there and he'd point out the brightest stars and the nearest ones. Sometimes he'd go out in the country, away from the lights, and take me with him. And he'd let me look through his scope."

As he talked, Joanie saw a change come over Mally. His face brightened, his eyes took on a sparkle, and his hands no longer flopped around like pieces of paper he was trying to shake off the ends of his arms. "What was it like?" she asked. The way he was talking, it was almost something she wanted to do herself.

"Oh, like nothing else! Millions of stars." He looked at her. "You think you see millions of stars from here, but with the scope—I never dreamed there was so many. You look up and—they're just packed together. Each one a star, or sometimes a whole galaxy! With billions of suns. Each one with its own worlds, probably, its own planets. Millions and millions. And this one we're on is just one of those, just one of those millions."

Joanie thought about it a moment, then shuddered. "That's kinda scary."

"Oh, no," Mally said, looking concerned. "It's not. It's . . . I don't know . . . it's beautiful. Somewhere out there, there's got to be, for each of us, someplace called home."

They sat for a moment, quiet. The doorbell rang.

"Joanie, would you get that, please?" her mother called from the kitchen.

"Sure, Momma," she said and walked to the door full of thoughts. Someplace called home? But this was home, right here, planet Earth, Oklahoma, Croy. Surely everybody already had a home.

All the interesting thoughts flew straight out of her head when she opened the door.

"Oh, hi," Randy Edom said, lurking on their front porch.

"Hello," she said stiffly.

"Umm . . . your dad home?"

"No, he's still at the store." What was Randy Edom doing here?

"Oh," he said informatively. "Well, I just . . . "

"Who is it, Joanie?" her mother called from inside the house.

"It's Randy Edom," she called back.

"Well, invite him in, dear!"

Well, now she had to, so she did. Her mother had sounded dangerously cheerful. If she started fussing like she had when he'd called Joanie for the date, she'd just die. She walked Randy through the living room into the dining room where Mally still sat. "You know Mally Jacobs, don't you?" she said. She made a point of sitting in the chair beside him.

"Uh, yeah." Randy nodded at Mally. "Hey."

Mally just nodded back. She could tell he was rubbing his hands against his pants under the table. He looked scared. Was Randy one of the football jocks who had been bullying him? She decided she wouldn't ask Randy to sit down.

"So," Randy said. "Haven't seen you around much, Joanie. Where you been at?"

"School."

"Oh."

That seemed to exhaust his social repertoire. She'd have liked the awkward moment to stretch out more, but her mother came in from the kitchen.

"Well, what brings you up our way, Randy?" she asked.

"I've come to see Mr. Tibbits about that job he's got posted," he said.

"Oh." Her mother smiled, but Joanie could tell she was disappointed. *She* wasn't, though. "Well," her mother said, "I suppose the best place to find that out would be at the store."

Randy shrugged. "I went by, but it looked closed."

"Oh?"

"I figured he closed early for something."

"Yes, I suppose that's it."

Mally had felt like an egg caught between two snakes since Randy entered the room. Now he felt the tension rise another notch. He noticed Mrs. Tibbits was wringing the towel in her hands.

"Yes, that must be it," she repeated. "He must've had a delivery over to Liddle. That's what the job's about, anyway. He's either got to become a permanent delivery service or just give up the business, one."

She gave a short laugh, but there didn't seem to be any humor in it. Mally looked to see if Joanie noticed, but she was staring at Randy.

"Won't you sit down?" Mrs. Tibbits was saying. "He's sure to be home any minute now."

"Oh!" Mally said, suddenly remembering. "It's getting late. I'd better be getting home. Grandfather'll want supper."

"Just a minute, Mally," Mrs. Tibbits said. "Let me get that dish and I'll take you."

"Oh, wait a second, Momma," Joanie said, rising. "Randy, you live right across the alley from Mrs. Oldfield, don't you?"

"Yeah."

She smiled at him. "Well, then, you could take Mally home, couldn't you?"

Randy's face froze, his eyes locked on Joanie's.

Mally looked from one of them to the other. "Uh, no," he said, "look, if it's out of the way . . ."

Joanie wasn't even paying attention to him. "But it's just across the alley."

"Well, he is really waiting for your father," Mrs. Tibbits put in.

Something came over Randy. "No, that's all right, Mrs. Tibbits," he said. "I can come back some other time."

"Oh, that'd be a real favor, Randy," Mrs. Tibbits said.

"Sure," he said. But he didn't say it to her. Or even to Mally. He said it to Joanie, who smiled.

Chapter 4

Strange Alliances

R ANDY DROVE ON automatic, trying to forget who was in the car with him, so they were already coming up on Herman's Drive In before he saw Red's flaming hair and letter jacket perched atop Al's convertible. A dread came over him. "Uh, look," he said, keeping his eyes on Red as they approached Herman's parking lot, "maybe that would ride better down on the floorboard, y'know?"

"Huh?" Mally said, holding the stew in his lap.

"That stuff she gave you." He waved in the direction of the casserole dish. "It'd ride better on the floor."

"Okay," the kid said and stooped over to put it down. He was straightening back up just as they drew abreast of the lot.

Randy's hand caught him on the back of the head. "Lid's come loose," he said and forced him back below the dashboard.

Just in the nick of time. Red stood up in Al's back seat. "Hey, Edom!" he yelled and Al honked his horn.

Randy waved and honked back.

There was a thump from below the dashboard. "Ow!" Mally yelped.

"You okay, there?" Randy said, reasserting his hand. He didn't let up until they turned the corner and entered the town's central square. The county courthouse sat in the middle, its red bricks sharp in the setting sun. This was Croy's main "downtown" and all the major stores faced the courthouse around the square. Randy noticed Tibbits Rexall still looked locked up and closed. He was determined now more than ever to get that job, and he gunned his engine as he took the corner that led to his side of town. That caused the casserole to start sliding, and Mally, alarmed, reached down to steady it. But this time, he did not tuck his head under the dash.

Mrs. Oldfield was pulling tomatoes from the vine and dropping them into a blue Tupperware bowl when Randy's Impala pulled into the alley and dropped Mally off.

"Thanks," Mally said, stepping out and clutching the casserole dish safely to his chest.

"Sure," Randy said without looking at him.

Mally closed the car door and Randy pulled away, turning into the cinder-packed driveway behind his own house just a few yards away. Mally watched him as he got out and ran up the back stairs into the house.

"They'll be picking pieces of him out of a ditch some day," Mrs. Oldfield said, standing by her plants.

Mally turned to her. "Ma'am?"

"The way he drives," she said and shook a weed puller in the direction of Randy's house. "He's a menace to the town. Look at the way he's torn up the alleyway there."

Mally pretended to look. "Yes'm," he said. He turned and headed toward the granny house.

"What's that?" Mrs. Oldfield asked, pointing to the casserole dish.

"Some stew," he said. "Mrs. Tibbits heated some up and sent it over."

"Mrs. Tibbits?" Mrs. Oldfield made the name sound like an accusation. "And what call did she have for doing a thing like that?"

Mally stopped, puzzled. "Ma'am?"

"What in heaven's name does she think?" Mrs. Oldfield was advancing on him, the bowl of tomatoes forgotten. "That I can't look after the Reverend myself? She should get her own house in order before she starts calling others to shame."

"I don't think she meant anything by it," Mally said.

"Maybe not. But you haven't lived in this town as long as I have. Mrs. Tibbits would do well to take her nose out of other people's business and try sticking it into something useful. Like First Corinthians, Chapter 6."

"Ma'am?" Mally repeated. He was getting further and further lost in this conversation. But before she had a chance to answer, he heard the screen door to the granny house swing open.

"Malachi?" his grandfather called out. "Is that you?"

Mrs. Oldfield halted. "You just ask your grandfather," she said, then turned and gathered up her tomatoes.

"Malachi?" his grandfather called again.

"Yes, Grandfather," he said and headed for the open door.

His grandfather was standing just inside, lost in the gloom of the unlit interior. "I was beginning to worry," he said.

"I was over at Joanie Tibbits's," he said. "Her mother made this and sent it over."

"Tibbits?" Matthew Jacobs said. "Mrs. John Tibbits? Ruth?"

"Yes, sir," Mally said.

A ghost of a smile wandered over the old man's face. "Well," he said, "let's see what she's cooked up for us."

Randy had something to settle—two somethings, really. He took care of the easy one first. He called the Sullivans. No, Mrs. Sullivan said, Candy wasn't home yet. On a hunch, Randy wished them well on their trip to Tulsa. Mrs. Sullivan hadn't the faintest idea what he was talking about. That was okay, he told her, never mind, it wasn't important.

He'd liked to tell Candy Sullivan to her face just how unimportant it was, but when he got in his car and headed back to town, he decided it just wasn't worth it, even if he could track her down.

He wouldn't have had to go far. In fact, he had already passed by her twice, had he known where to look. But no one would think to look for her here. That's why she liked it. The store was quiet and cool. Almost no light came in through the sun shades drawn across the windows, and the lights over the rows of cosmetics and cold remedies hadn't been turned on. She could sit at the fountain and sip her milk shake and let the rest of the world slide away.

"It's so nice of you to let me stay after closing," she said. "It's peaceful here."

John Tibbits looked up from behind the pharmacy counter. "Just take your time, honey," he said.

Joanie's mother only made her feel worse by praising her. "That was so thoughtful of you, dear," she said. "He really needed that meal. And it was sweet of you to get Randy to take him home."

Joanie could just crawl into a hole. She'd only spoken to

Mally on a dare, and that Edom jerk had had it coming. Now she was being congratulated for embarrassing her best friend and getting even with a boy who had humiliated her by using some hapless kid as a weapon. What was she going to do for toppers? Murder her little brother?

The doorbell chimed. "I'll get it," she said and sprang for the door, saved from her guilty conscience by the bell.

Not quite. Randy Edom was on their front porch again.

"Oh," she said. "Daddy's not home yet."

"Oh, that's okay," he said, nodding with his chin thrust out a little. "I just came by to say thanks."

"Thanks for what?"

"Thanks for fishing me into driving Jack-off home."

Joanie stepped outside and closed the door behind her. "That's not his name and you know it," she said sharply.

"What was that, anyway," he said, angry himself. "Some kind of test or something?"

"Well, you passed, didn't you?" she said. "I mean, your reputation isn't ruined in the tri-county area from having shown him a little kindness, is it?"

"Listen," he said, "the kid's a loser. He practically invites it."

"Oh, and what does that make you for rising to the challenge? A winner?"

"Now hold on—"

She had no intention of stopping now. "Just because he's a little different—"

"A little?"

"—doesn't give you and your jock friends the right to harass him. Is that the only way you guys can feel big when you're off the field? Big time junior varsities—"

"Hey, we're not *junior* varsity—"

"—tricking some hapless sophomore, stuffing his locker—"

"I didn't have anything to do with—"

"—and playing mean and spiteful jokes on him?"

They stood there on the porch a moment, their hands locked on their hips, glaring at each other.

Randy broke first. "Oh, hell," he said, turning away and scratching his head. "This ain't what I come here for."

"Well, I already told you," Joanie said. "My father's not home yet."

He turned around. "That ain't it either."

"Well, what then?" She looked him up and down.

He faced her for a moment, his weight on one leg and his head cocked to one side. Finally, he said, "I came to ask you for a date."

Her jaw dropped. He saw that and his eyebrows raised a little. She recovered quickly and closed her mouth, but she couldn't think of anything to say.

"After the game. Friday," he said.

"If this is another one of Candy Sullivan's super deals—" she started.

Randy raised a hand in denial. "No, ma'am. I swear to God." He looked at her and sort of smiled. "Well?"

She bit her lip.

"This is a test," he said. And definitely smiled.

A car pulled into their driveway just then and the front door opened behind her.

"Is that your father?" her mother said from the doorway. Then she noticed Randy. "Oh, hi, Randy," she said and smiled broadly at him, then at Joanie.

Joanie turned to speak to her, but her father stepped out of the car and Ruth stepped around the two teenagers to greet him. Ruth put an arm around John's waist and gave him a peck on the cheek. He was looking up at the two of them on the porch.

"Well, well," her father said. "A visit in person from the football star!"

Randy straightened up and unhooked his thumbs from his pockets. "Evening, Mr. Tibbits," he said.

Joanie's mother muttered something to her father as he stepped forward. He nodded and turned to Randy. "I understand this is purely a business call," he said, then he looked at Joanie. She tried to fade into the siding. "Well," he said, "maybe not." He turned back to Randy. "What can I do you for?"

"Well, sir," Randy said, "I saw your sign, and I thought maybe I could do the job you had in mind."

"It's two jobs, actually," John Tibbits said. "I need someone to run the fountain and be apprentice. That's pretty much full time."

"Oh." Randy's face fell. "Well, I've got football another two weeks at least."

"Ah-ah," John said, wagging a finger at him. "There's the second job. Delivery boy. You need come only around 4:30 or 5:00 each day Monday through Thursday—Friday evenings off, see?—and be stock boy on Saturdays. How's that sound?"

"Terrific." Randy broke into a broad grin. "I think I can talk Coach Ardmore into letting me out in time."

"Well, if you're a couple of minutes late these first few weeks," Mr. Tibbits said, expansively, "I'll understand. It's mostly farm deliveries, or over to Liddle or Daggs Valley. Not much, just far." He turned to his wife. "That's where I was to-night."

"Well," she said, smiling warmly, "you must nearly be famished."

"That I am." He put his arm around her and they headed toward the door. He turned to Randy. "I'll expect to see you . . . let's see, tomorrow's Thursday but I don't expect to need you then, and the next day's Friday . . . on Saturday, then. Deal?" He stuck out his hand.

"Deal!" Randy said and shook Mr. Tibbits's hand.

Mr. Tibbits turned and gave his daughter a peck on the cheek. "Hey, Angel," he said and went inside.

"Don't be long, dear," her mother said. "Dinner'll be right

soon." She went inside and discreetly closed the door behind her. Once inside, she could see her husband loosening his tie before sitting down in his favorite chair in the living room. He was chuckling to himself.

"That boy's no better a horse trader than his father was," he said to her.

"What do you mean?"

"He never even asked what I'd pay him," he said, laughing.

"Now, you treat that boy right, John Tibbits," she said, heading for the kitchen. "A lot more than a job may be riding on this."

Out on the porch, Randy was still waiting for his answer. "Well?" he said, "what'd'ya say about Friday night?"

Joanie was taken by the speed of events. It was funny how your perspective could change. That off-center stance of his, for example, standing with his weight on one foot. It had seemed so cocky before. Now it just looked kind of playful, like he knew he wasn't the big man his stance claimed him to be. She smiled and lowered her gaze.

"You could make my day complete," he said.

She looked up at him and smiled and gave a little shrug. "Sure," she said.

Mally took the pot of stew off the two-burner stove and brought it over to the table. The kitchen was also their dining room in the small wooden trailer, and all that separated the kitchen from the living room was a flimsy set of floor-to-ceiling shelves, meant to hold books but deep enough only for paperbacks and strong enough only for light-weight knickknacks. Mally dished the stew into a blue ceramic bowl in front of his grandfather and put the pot on a hot pad in the middle of the table and sat down. They bowed their heads, Mally making the sign of the cross as they did so, and prayed silently. Then his grandfather straightened up and picked up his spoon.

"Aren't you having any?" he asked.

"I had some at Mrs. Tibbits's," Mally said.

His grandfather nodded and started eating. After a moment, Mally asked, "Would you like some bread?" His grandfather nodded again, so he went and cut a slice from the loaf in the kitchen. He cut himself a slice, too, and sat down to put butter and salt on it.

"This is very good," his grandfather said, getting to the bottom of his bowl. "You must remember to thank Mrs. Tibbits for me. It was very charitable of her to send it over."

"Mrs. Oldfield didn't think so," Mally said, tearing into the chewy crust. "She seemed to think Mrs. Tibbits was doing it to shame her. And she said something about Mrs. Tibbits keeping her nose out of other people's business, too, and paying more heed to Corinthians, Chapter 6. What's that?"

"You mean you don't know?" his grandfather said, looking up. Mally shook his head. "Well, I suppose you wouldn't. Not much Bible study in a Catholic household, is there?"

Mally thought his grandfather might be scolding him, but there seemed to be a twinkle in his eye as well.

"No, I suppose not," his grandfather said, leaning back in his chair, satisfied. "And none in that school you went to, either. Too busy turning you all into good little Papists. Have you never looked into the Good Book yourself?"

"No, sir."

"Probably a good thing. All Margaret would have had around would be some lame version of the Douay, a translation full of apocrypha and errors and based on a squabble. Still, you've got to hand it to the Catholics. Without their little additions to Holy Scripture we might never have had the charming story of Judith and Holofernes. Now, there's a lesson in what not to do on a first date. And the story of Elijah just isn't complete without Ecclesiasticus and that neat little ride in the fiery chariot. All that's missing from our Bible."

Mally was surprised. "Our Bible? You mean, there's more than one?"

His grandfather laughed. The stew, a hearty supper for once, had put him in a good mood. "Open that cabinet, there," he said, indicating the space below the bookshelves. Mally crossed the room and opened the doors. There were more substantial shelves inside, and they were full of books. "Those are all Bibles."

Mally was astonished. "Why are there so many?"

"Why do so many people claim they're God's chosen people?" his grandfather said. "Or, more to the point, want to claim that certain other people *aren't* God's chosen people? They've each got their own way of looking at Christ, and they've each got to have their own way of being right. So, there's the Hebrew Bible, the Greek Bible, the Latin Vulgate, the Douay-Rheims, the King James—that's the big black one, there—and all the other translations from Hebrew, and Greek, and Aramaic, and Latin, each one touting a different angle, each one claiming a special toe-hold on the slippery face of salvation."

Mally looked at the books in wonder. "I had no idea."

"Why'd you think those boxes were so heavy?"

Mally laughed, then looked at the bibles more seriously. "Which one's right?"

"It's not in the words, Mally," his grandfather said, "it's in the spirit that comes through the words. You sometimes have to read several different versions to get to the heart of what God was trying to whisper in our imperfect ears."

"Which one should I read first?" He was interested tracking down that quotation from Mrs. Oldfield.

"Well, the King James has its faults, but its voice rings through our language like a bell. Our highest thoughts and most serious sentiments are in that voice. When we dream of God, we dream in the King James version. But the language can be tricky. Some of the words they used don't mean the same thing anymore." He got up and came over to the cabinet and pulled out a book. "I'd try this one," he said. "The language is closest to our every-day."

Mally held the book like a treasure. He looked up at his grandfather. "Would you teach me how to read it?" he asked.

The wind seemed to go out of his grandfather and he sat down on the sofa bed. "You don't teach the Bible, son," he said. "It's there for you to figure out, on your own. And besides, it's been too many years, too many years since I've tried."

Mally thought he'd said something to hurt the old man and felt ashamed. "I just thought," he said, "with so many to choose from, it might be a while before I figured out what Mrs. Oldfield was trying to say."

That made his grandfather chuckle. "You don't need the Bible to figure out what she's getting at. She's nowhere near as inscrutable as Old Jehovah." He rubbed his chin thoughtfully. "Though they do have certain traits in common."

Mally smiled, relieved that he and his grandfather had a common understanding of their landlady.

"You can get the gist of what she meant just by knowing Mrs. Oldfield," his grandfather said. He looked off into the distance, searching his memories. "Her husband, Gerald Oldfield, was alcoholic when she first got hold of him. And she was determined to break him of it before they married. She held his hand through the DT's. She hauled him out of bars and taverns most women wouldn't have the courage to pass by on the street, let alone enter. She got into his house and smashed every bottle in every cupboard and drawer and hiding place Gerald could think of." He looked down at Mally. "And she did it. She saved that man. And she never let him, nor the church, nor anyone in town forget it." He took a deep breath and let it go. "They were married twelve years. And then he died."

"What of?"

"Oh, lotsa people say things. I don't know." His grandfather looked back toward the kitchen. "Love, maybe." He got up and went to the kitchen table and began clearing his place.

Mally followed and started running the water for the dishes. "But it was right, wasn't it?" he said. "Keeping him from the bottle. What she did was right, wasn't it?"

"Malachi," his grandfather said, "in the hands of some people, the power to do right is a dangerous and cruel thing. That's—" He broke off abruptly and just stood still a moment. Then he handed Mally his bowl and went back to the living room and sat down.

Mally followed him. "That's why you quit preaching?" he asked gently.

"No," the old man said. "I was nearly sixty-one. I was old. I was tired. That's all." He closed his eyes and his head lay back against the sofa. "I needed a rest."

He'd be going to bed soon, and that meant folding out the sofa bed. Mally went back to the kitchen and started quietly doing the dishes. There weren't many; it wouldn't take long.

She was exasperated and angry. Now was not the time to be bringing all this up. She had only a brief break between broadcasts. She had just called to talk to Mally, and now she finds out he isn't even with Margaret anymore, that he's down in Croy with her father. "Well, when did he go?"

"I sent him down there the end of September," Margaret said, sounding tinny over the pay phone.

"You should have told me."

"Susan, I tried," her aunt said. "I tried calling and I tried writing. You keep moving. You're never at home."

"Look, this is the first real break for me," Susan said. "It's real exposure. I'm on every night. It's only a few moments, but I'm out there."

"So, you're not coming back."

"I can't. Not now."

"Is being a weather girl so much more important to you than your own child?"

"Don't be like that." She felt tears beginning to form. "You're the one who encouraged me to come out here and try it in the first place."

"That's before I knew," Margaret said.

"Knew what?"

"What kind of trouble a young boy can get into."

"Well, what did he get into? What was it?"

"Oh, never mind, Susan. I don't want to talk about it. Anyway, when Mrs. Oldfield called—"

"Not that old biddy again. Hasn't she caused enough grief?"

"Now just a minute, young lady," Margaret said sharply. "She found your father in that hospital room and he was none the pretty sight. And his rooms at the Mrs. Chisholm's were even worse. It looked like he hadn't cleaned in two years. She took him in, and then she had the guts to call me. Now I know we hardly see eye to eye, but she was doing something family ought to do. It was the least I could do to send Mally down to help her."

Susan was taken aback. She had no idea things had gotten so bad. Plus it was a shock to hear Aunt Margaret defend Mrs. Oldfield. But then, they had a common enemy now: her. She sighed. "You should have asked, that's all."

"Well, do you want me to send him out to you in L.A.? Because he's not coming back here."

There it was again. What wasn't she saying? "No," she said. "Out here's no good. It's no place for a kid. At least he's safe in Croy. At least there's people there will look after him. And he won't—" she hesitated, "—won't get into trouble."

"Right." Margaret was brisk.

"Listen, have you got a phone number down there?"

"Only Clara Oldfield's. There isn't a phone in that little house."

Susan Jacobs sighed again. "Okay, give me that." But she knew she wouldn't call. There was no way she would come crawling to that dried-up old harridan after all these years. "And give me the address, too."

Chapter 5

THE WORD

THEY WON THEIR next-to-last home game easily, leaving only the re-match against Holdenville between them and the conference championship.

Red was in high spirits. "We're going to clinch it for sure," he said as he got dressed. "And you know what? I'll bet the basketball team goes to state, too. We'll be the first class in the history of Croy Consolidated to win both titles in one year. What do you say to that? Hah!"

Randy was enjoying his friend's enthusiasm, but he had to shake his head. "You'll have to do it without me," he said.

"What'd'ya mean?" Red said. "We're a team!"

"You're a team, maybe," Randy said. "But I'm no good on hoops, you know that."

"Of course you are," Red said, concerned. "Of course you are. You scored—what?—last year."

"Four points," Randy said, holding out his fingers so Red could see just how pathetic that was. "Just four points. And two of those were free-throws. Face it, it's no place for a runt like me. I'm just warming the bench."

"But—" Red seemed to run out of reasons. "You've gotta play. We've always played. What are you going to do if you don't?"

"I've been talking to Coach Tucker," Randy said. "I may go out for wrestling."

"Yeah?" Red said. "Huh." It was as if Randy had just said he might skip the rest of the school year and take a trip to Mars. He couldn't fathom it so he shook it out of his head. "Hey," he said, "do you want to go out to the reservoir tonight? Mattingley's uncle can get us a couple of six-packs."

"Can't," Randy said. "Got a date."

Red was thunderstruck.

"Don't look so hang-dog," Randy said. "It's not with Candy, so your money's safe."

"Who then?" Red asked eagerly.

Randy just smiled and closed his locker. "I'll see you later," he said.

Joanie was waiting outside near the entrance to the boys' gym. "Sorry to keep you waiting," he said as he walked up to her.

"No big deal," she said. "I helped Mr. Hansen put the band stuff away."

They started to walk around to the front of the school where the parking lot and Randy's car was. They walked in silence, Randy trying to figure out how to put what he wanted to say. Finally, he said, "I wasn't sure you'd still be out here when I came out. I wasn't even sure you'd go on a second date."

"You call that fiasco a date?" she said.

"Oh," he said. "So, I guess you figured out what was going on."

"It took me a while," she said. "About seven seconds."

"It was just . . . just something stupid I got into," he said. "A game, kind of. Seems silly now."

"It was silly," she said. "And a little cruel, too, you know. You shouldn't play with people like that."

Randy looked away. He didn't know what to say. This date wasn't starting off any better than the last one. "I guess I'm lucky you were willing to try it a second time."

"Oh," she said airily, "I did it more out of pity than anything else."

"Oh, yeah?"

"I was tired of seeing you beaten into the ground every time Candy Sullivan came up with something new to do on weekends."

He winced. "Yeowch! Yeah, that's pretty pathetic. But that's all done with now, anyways."

They had reached his car. Red and Al came around the corner of the school just then, heading for Al's convertible. When Red saw who Randy was with, he gave out a whoop and Al, alerted, whistled. To get him and Joanie out of sight, Randy opened the passenger door and let her in, then went around and got in the driver's side. Al's convertible tore past them, Red blowing kisses at them over the rear seat. Randy chuckled.

"That clown will never grow up," Joanie said.

"Who?" he said. "You mean Red? Aw, Red's all right."

"Red Conner's one of those people who will never leave high school," she said.

"Are you kidding?" he said, shocked. "You need a C average to be on the team and at least a B to be a class officer. That goes for both of us. And I know he does better'n me in some classes."

She shook her head. "I don't mean grades."

"Well, what then?"

She took a moment to gather her thoughts. "What I mean is, ten years from now, he'll still be hanging around here—hanging around every football game, every basketball game, hanging out at Herman's, going out and getting drunk every weekend. He'll never leave this place."

"Well, I think you're wrong, there," he said. "Red's got lots of ambition. I know for a fact he's planning on going to college, same as me, hoping for an athletic scholarship. We're going to Norman together if we can, the both of us, the Dynamic Duo."

"The what?" she said, half tickled and half appalled. "What are you, Batman and Robin?"

"Naw, we're like brothers. We've always stuck together. When we were kids, people used to think we were twins."

"Oh, come off it. You two are nothing alike."

"Sure we are."

"No," she said, "you're not." She was serious so suddenly that he paid attention. "You can be thoughtless at times, but you're not mean. At least, you don't mean to be."

"What times? When was I thoughtless?"

"Well, like the way you guys treat Mally—"

"Aw, look," he said, not wanting to hash that out again. "I've got nothing to do with that. I don't do anything—"

She cut him off, "No, you don't 'do' anything. You don't do anything *to* him, but you don't do anything *for* him, either. Look, he's got no dad, and his mother's way off in California somewhere. He's living all alone with that old man and Mrs. Oldfield. You of all people ought to know how hard that's gotta be."

Randy looked at her, then he looked out the windshield.

"Look," Joanie said, her voice softening, "I'm sorry I dumped all that on you at once. I mean, it's a fine way to start a date."

"No," he said and turned to look at her. "No, it's okay."

"I must sound like I've been saving it up for years."

"No," he said, "not really." Then he smiled. "Have you?"

She blushed and looked out the window on her side. "Well," she said, "Croy's a small town. We practically grew up in each other's laps."

"But on different sides of the tracks," he said.

"Well, yeah, but," and she turned to look at him, "I've had my eye on you."

"Oh you have, huh?" he said, grinning.

She nodded. "Yup."

"Well, you've sure kept quiet about it. Didn't see anything you liked?"

"Oh, I saw things I liked."

"Like . . ." he prompted.

"Well, you're probably the most intelligent of that bunch of baboons you hang out with—"

"Hah!" He was enjoying this.

"—and you are pretty good on the football field. More patient than most boys I've met, though not much of a talker. And you can be gentle and kind." She paused and her mood shifted. "But not always. Like last time, when you kissed me."

Randy felt a sudden chill. "You mean, you didn't want me to?"

"No," she said, shaking her head, "it's not that. When you kissed me, you did it because you thought you ought to, because it was what your pals expected you to do, but not because you wanted to. Not really wanted."

He hung his head. "Yeah," he said. "I'm sorry."

She looked at him. "A kiss should mean something," she said.

He looked up and met her eyes. "You mean, like this?" He leaned in and kissed her slowly and softly on the lips.

"Yeah," she said, and she leaned a little closer to him. "Like that."

Mally placed his grandfather's King James Version next to the Revised Standard Version he had gotten earlier. The glow from the lamp on the nightstand cast a warm pool of light in the room, embracing the bibles that lay side by side with him in the bed. The King James, bound in black leather with pages edged in gold, gave off an odor that was both sweet and musty. When he opened it, the verses seemed to leap out at him in larger-than-life type, each verse on a separate line. It looked like poetry. By comparison, the RSV seemed about as inspiring as a civics textbook. It had a dull red cloth binding, and there was nothing special about the type face or the paper it was printed on. The verses weren't laid out like verses at all, but like bits of sentences run together into paragraphs. The King James looked like the Word of God, but the Revised Standard Version looked like merely words about God.

He almost got side-tracked looking up the Book of Malachi in the King James, but then remembered his purpose. His grandfather had said the Revised version would be easier to read, so he started there. There were two Corinthians and he'd forgotten which one Mrs. Oldfield had mentioned, but he remembered the chapter. The first part of 1 Corinthians, Chapter 6, didn't make much sense to him: it seemed to be all about lawsuits. "To have lawsuits at all with one another is defeat for you," he read. What did that have to do with Mrs. Tibbits? He looked at the King James Version to see if it provided any help.

> *Now therefore there is utterly a fault among you, because ye go to law one with another. Why do ye not rather take wrong? why do ye not rather suffer yourselves to be defrauded?*

Nope, no help. And grandfather was right: the King James sang, but the Revised Standard made more sense. Maybe he should be looking in 2 Corinthians.

But then he read a little further, and his heart stopped. He couldn't believe what he was seeing on the page. He read it again.

> *Do you not know that the unrighteous will not inherit the kingdom of God? Do not be deceived; neither the immoral, nor idolaters, nor adulterers, nor homosexuals . . .*

He stopped again at the word. He'd only seen it twice before in print, heard it spoken only once. He read on:

> *. . . nor thieves, nor the greedy, nor drunkards, nor revilers, nor robbers will inherit the kingdom of God. And such were some of you.*

And such were some of you. Some of you had been, there had been, such people, people like him, two thousand years ago. Mally felt thrilled and terrified at the same time.

The thrill was familiar. He remembered feeling it the first time he had seen the word in print in the magazine he had snuck out of Mr. Anderson's house. It was like a bolt of lightning, the word that finally named him for what he was, that finally called to him and told him he was not alone, that he had if not a family, at least a tribe, a history. He and his kind were known, named, and recognized.

And reviled. That was there, too. The magazine had made that clear by emphasizing all the things they supposedly were not: not sick, not pathetic, not criminals. It wouldn't have to say those things if most people didn't already believe them.

And so the terror was bound up with the joy, and the word evoked a lightness in his head and a sinking in his stomach. He wanted more and went looking for it. He snuck Volume X of *Compton's Encyclopedia* into a secluded corner of the school library and flipped quickly to its middle. He held the large awkward volume, titled "Heating – Infection," close to his chest, his face flushing as he neared the entry he hoped was there. Once last summer he'd climbed one of the pylons behind the baseball diamond for no apparent reason, his heart racing as he got closer to the thick black cables and their murderous buzz. That feeling was nothing compared to what clamored in his heart now, making the arteries in his neck jump like rabbits. He found the entry but kept his thumb on "The Homestead Act" so he could flip back to it quickly if anyone came by. But the entry for the word he was seeking had been short, dry, and detached. It spoke of a clinical condition, a stubborn disorder, linked to alcoholism and drug addiction. None of that spoke to him or his inner fears, his inner hopes.

Still, the word had been there. It existed. He existed.

Car lights played across the curtains. He quickly reached for the light and turned it off, as if he had been caught doing something shameful. The open bibles lay nestled in his lap, and as Mally strained to peer through the curtains, the King James fell to the floor with a thud. He froze. Had he woken grandfather? No, there was no sound from the living room. Car lights played over the curtains a second time, and he turned to the window.

The first car had been Randy's. It was parked now in its usual spot and Randy was standing beside it. The second car coming down the alley was a convertible with three guys in it. He recognized one of them as soon as he spoke.

"Big Man!" Red Conner declared too loudly from the passenger side of the convertible.

Randy grinned. "Have a good time at the reservoir?" he asked. Randy could see Al behind the wheel and Al's uncle—only three years older, but still an uncle, and old enough—lolling in the back seat.

"'Trific," Red said. "And a good time was had by all. Or was it? Did you finally catch yerself some quail? Get yerself some—"

"Hey," Randy interrupted. "Keep it down."

"Oh, I can keep it down," Red insisted. "The question is, can you? Or, no, the question is . . . the question was . . . what?"

"Hop in," Al said. "We're going over to Herman's for some burgers."

"No, thanks," Randy said. "I just got home."

"What is the question?" Red said.

"Are we going or not?" Al's uncle said from the back seat.

"No, that's not it," Red said.

"C'mon," Al said. "We've still got some in the trunk." He gunned the engine.

Randy saw a light go on in Mrs. Oldfield's house. "Naw, y'all go on without me," he said.

"And y'all can go on without *me*," Red said with abrupt vehemence, and then he tried to vault out of the front seat without opening the car door. He almost made it, too. He landed in a heap at Randy's feet. "Ow!" he said, landing in the cinders on the driveway.

"You all right there, bud?" Al called out.

"Hush!" Randy said, glancing nervously at Mrs. Oldfield's.

"'Hush'?" Al said, indignant.

Al's uncle poured himself into the front seat. "C'mon, let's get outta here," he said. "If I don't get some food in me, I'm gonna ralph."

"He told us to hush," Al said.

"Jesus Christ," Red said, picking cinders out of his hands. "What d'ya pave your drive with, broken Coke bottles?" His left hand was bleeding.

"Oh, great," Randy said. He bent over and started helping Red to his feet.

"Let's move it, Squirt," Al's uncle said and shoved his left foot on top of Al's. The car lurched forward.

"Will you just go?" Randy said, his arms full of Red's unsteady body.

"Well, be like that," Al said, and the convertible tore down the alley. Al gave the horn a shave-and-a-haircut-two-bits for good measure as they turned up Front Street.

Randy looked down at Red's bleeding palm. "C'mon," he said, "let me see that." Red let him get a good look at his hand, at least as good as could be had from the streetlight. It wasn't a big cut, just kind of deep, and it was slowly oozing blood. He shook his head. "I think I've got some band-aids in the car," he said, and the two of them walked around to the passenger's side, where Randy reached in and got a kit out of the glove compartment. "You better wash that out good when you get home," he said, peeling the band-aid onto his friend's palm.

"What?" Red asked, as if he hadn't been paying attention at all to what they were doing.

"You don't want to get that infected," Randy said. "You won't be able to hold on to the ball."

Red inspected his hand with some wonderment. "Too bad we don't still have some of that Jack Daniels," he said. "But we ate it all. Too bad. It was good stuff."

"Yeah, a lot of good it did you."

"Aw, don't be an old lady. You should try it."

"No thanks," Randy said. "I'll stick to beer. One drunk in the family is more than enough."

"I am not drunk!" Red protested. "Well, okay, I am a drunk. No, no. I am *drunk*, but I'm not *a* drunk." He was certain he had gotten that right. "Tonight was just an abner-ration."

Randy smiled. "Yeah, if you say so."

"No shit, you shoulda come with us. It was good stuff. It'll put hair on your chest." Red giggled. "And you could use some." He spread his arms and delcared, "'For my brother Esau is an hairy man, but I am a smooth man.' But you am the smooth man, and I am the Harry."

"All right, that's it. You're going home," Randy said and headed for the driver's side of the car.

Red just stood there and shook his head. "Oh, man, I don't think I can make it," he said

"I'll take you, dumb ass."

Red looked at him over the hood of the car. "Why don't I sleep over here?" he asked. "Your mom won't mind."

Randy glanced at the back of the house. There were no lights on, but he wasn't sure Virginia was home yet—or if she was, that she was alone. "Naw," he said, "I gotta get up early tomorrow. I'm starting my job over at Tibbits."

"No shit?" Red's face lit up with genuine delight. "You got it? Hey, congratulations! Let's celebrate!"

"You celebrate for me, huh?"

"No shit," Red shook his head in wonder. "Hey, why don't I sleep over here?"

"Not tonight, Red."

"We used to sleep over all the time. We'd raise hell way into the night, too. Whyn't we do that no more?"

"Well, you moved, remember?"

"Oh, yeah, I remember. Big, fine house. Split-level. All-electrical chicken. Two cars in every . . . Aw, I like your place better. Can't I stay?"

"I don't think we'd both fit in the bed, fella. You kinda grew on me."

Red started chuckling. "I sure did, didn't I? Yeah, I got my growth spurt." He was genuinely amused by that. "I got my growth spurt. You just got a growth splat."

"That's it. In the car."

Randy got in on his side and Red, with minor fumbling, got in on the other. "Hey, one more thing," Red said. "One more thing, I'm serious. Are you serious about dropping basketball and going out for wrestling?"

Randy nodded. "Yeah, I've given it some thought."

Red nodded, too, and looked out the windshield for a moment. Then he said, "Think Coach Tucker'd take me, too?"

Randy shrugged. "I don't see why not." He started the car engine. "You think Coach Ardmore will let you go?"

Red lowered his head and shook it. "Aw, jeez," he said, "it just won't be the same without you."

Randy backed out of the drive and started down the alley. He wanted to say something consoling to his friend, but when he looked over at him, Red was chuckling again.

Red turned to him and grinned. "Splat," he said.

That weekend began one of the longest and sweetest Indian Summers people in those parts could remember. Even on that first day, it felt as if something special were beginning, full of promise and good humor. The days made people indoors itch to be outside doing something—raking leaves, throwing a football, or just walking in the hills above town. The nights pulled people toward more reckless forms of recreation, long drives to Tulsa or Dallas or nowhere in particular, just to be out in the enveloping, fast thickening dark, feeling the last of the summer magic slip through their fingers and blow through their hair.

Randy found his first day of work at the Rexall kind of satisfying, which surprised him. When Red came by around noon to

razz him for stacking rolls of toilet paper and "feminine products," Randy felt charitable enough to present him with a bit of
good news. It made his friend forget all about the nasty buzz in
his head and grin triumphantly.

"So, you're giving up, eh?" Red said. This was even better
than ribbing his friend about bench pressing sanitary napkins.

Randy shrugged. "It's just not worth it," he said. "If Candy
only wants to go out with guys who are two years older than her,
what do I care?"

"So," Red said, "we're even."

"Yeah, we're even. And I can take whoever I want to the Halloween Dance."

"Someone like . . . ?" Red prompted.

"Oh, no," Randy said. "You're not fishing me into that again.
That's my business, none of yours."

As luck would have it, Joanie passed them in the aisle just
then, bringing her father's lunch from home. Red didn't miss the
little look that passed between them.

"Oh, I get it," Red said. "Sucking up to the boss's daughter,
eh?"

"Get out of here," Randy said. "I mean it," and he hefted a
box of tampons threateningly.

"Yeow!" Red said, retreating. "The big guns." He bought a
Snickers bar at the counter and left, but not without leering and
winking at Randy as he went out the door.

"Hey," Joanie said, coming up behind him.

"Oh," he said, a little startled. "Hi."

"Daddy working you to death?" she asked.

"Oh, no. This is fine."

"Do you get a break for lunch?"

He hadn't really noticed being hungry until she mentioned it.
"I'll check with your Dad," he said.

"I already did," she said. "Let's go across to the square. I
brought you a sandwich."

They stepped out into the sharp daylight and crossed over to the green that surrounded the court house. There had been a chill earlier in the week, enough to start some of the trees turning, and the air was a heady mix of leaf mold, new-mown grass from the court house lawn, and a tang of smoke from someone with the good sense to ignore the law and burn a line of leaves in a ditch a few blocks south.

They ate in silence for a while, suddenly unable to look at each other. Abruptly, Randy remembered his manners. "Thanks for the lunch," he said.

"You're welcome," Joanie replied. "I wasn't sure what you'd like, but I figured I couldn't go wrong with baloney."

"It's great," he said, then lapsed into silence again. After a moment, he said, "Salami's fine, too."

"Oh, good," she said. "I like a man who's broad-minded."

He looked at her and she gave him a perfect deadpan. But she wasn't able to hold it for long and they both broke out laughing.

"Hey," he said, "I was wondering what you were doing to-night."

"Well, I'm actually over to your neck of the woods."

"Really?"

"Yeah, Mally and I are going over the assignment Mrs. Gregory gave us. At his house. It's supposed to be an essay about poetry, a defense of poetry or an attack on poetry, depending on how you take it."

"Oh," he said. The thought of Joanie and Mally flitted briefly through his mind. But that was impossible, right? Right. Un-less . . . He looked down and started fiddling with a blade of grass.

"Do you want to join us?" she finally asked. "That is, if you think you can stoop to the sophomore English level."

"Oh, I can stoop, all right," he said. "I'm plenty stoopid." And he was feeling it, too, right about now.

"Now, don't be like that," she said. "You had Mrs. Gregory, too. Maybe you can give us some pointers."

He plucked the blade from the lawn and started chewing it.

She frowned. "Unless you'd rather not."

"No," he said, "it's not that. It's just not what I had in mind."

"Oh?" she said, arching her eyebrows.

"Well, you know. Two's company and . . ."

"And Mally's a crowd," she completed for him.

"Oh, please," he moaned. "Can't we just have a conversation that's not about him for once?"

She looked at him sideways. "Don't tell me your jealous?"

"Of Mally? Hell, no."

"Well, you needn't make it sound so improbable."

He looked at her. "You know what I mean."

She narrowed her eyes. "Don't you start in on that. He's my friend, and I won't have him mocked or made fun of."

"Your friend."

"That's right."

"But not your boyfriend."

"Well, no, of course not. I mean, yes, he's a boy and, yes, he's my friend, but he's not my boyfriend."

"And I am?"

"Well," she said, "at least on the baloney-sandwich-in-the-park level."

Randy took a deep breath. "It's not enough."

She looked at him. "What do you mean?"

"Baloney-sandwich-in-the-park. It's not enough. I want to take it up a notch. In fact," he took another breath, "I want to take you to the Halloween Dance."

Joanie looked stunned. "Wow," she said. She looked away across the street. "That's quite a notch." Formals and corsages made an unexpected appearance in her mind, followed quickly by an odd feeling of lightness in her heart and a close relative of panic in her stomach. She told her various body parts to hush up so she could think, then smiled and said, "Okay."

"Okay what?"

"Okay, I'll go to the dance with you."

Randy grinned from ear to ear. "Then I *am* your boyfriend."

"Yeah, sure."

"Not just a boy and not just a friend."

"Don't push it, Edom."

"Fair enough. And tonight?"

"I already promised."

"Okay," he said. "I can wait." But just barely. "And maybe I'll drop by after all," he said.

He almost didn't. It wasn't just Mally, whom he'd almost gotten used to seeing next door. And it wasn't that they'd be studying poetry, though that would be about as much fun as watching hay dry and then chewing on it afterward. It was that she would be over here, in his part of town, where some of the streets weren't paved and most of them didn't have curbs or even sidewalks. Where the run-down house on the corner was not an aberration, but more of a signpost indicating which way they were all headed. Where piles of coal clinkers littered the back yards and the metal garbage cans were so rusted through there was hardly any point in saying they had an inside and an outside. Where he and his mother lived with no sign of his father, nor had there been these five—or was it six?—years. How would the four room converted sharecropper's shack he called home hold up against what he'd seen of the Tibbitses' cozy house?

But he talked himself into it. She wasn't coming over to his house, after all, but to Mally's, which was a clear sight worse than his. And Mrs. Oldfield's was the best-looking property on the block with the neatest lawn. (He mowed his own lawn when he got home that afternoon, much to Virginia's amazement.) He watched anxiously as Mrs. Tibbits dropped Joanie off, then waited an excruciating half an hour just so he wouldn't appear too eager, then washed his face one more time and stepped out the back door and crossed the alley.

He knocked on the screen door. "Come in!" Joanie's voice called from inside.

They were spread out on the living room floor, old Reverend Jacobs sitting in a corner reading a book.

Joanie lit up when he came in and she got up. Even Mally seemed pleased.

"Evening, Reverend Jacobs," Randy said, nodding to the old man.

"Randy," the man said. "It's been quite a while. You've grown."

Well, that succeeded in mortifying him.

"Would you like something to drink?" Mally said. "There's ice tea."

"Yeah, sure," he said. "That'd be great."

"I'm glad you came after all," Joanie said as Mally maneuvered around him into the tiny kitchen.

"So," Randy said, "where's this poem we're supposed to attack?"

The evening went pretty well. At one point, Reverend Jacobs excused himself and said he was going to sit outside and enjoy the fine evening. That gave them a little more room to spread out, which may have been his purpose all along.

The assignment, which wasn't what Randy remembered at all from his sophomore year, was to take the question, "What's the point of poetry?" and either attack or defend the existence of poetry.

"All poems?" Randy asked.

"I guess so," Joanie said.

"The Bible is poetry," Mally said.

"I don't think this is about the Bible," Joanie said.

"Why not?" Randy said. "It has verses."

"Mrs. Gregory wouldn't give us an assignment about the pros and cons of the Bible," Joanie said. "What would be the point? There aren't any cons."

"Now you sound like Bobbie Littledeer."

Joanie slapped his leg, which tingled pleasantly.

"I think the Bible has some beautiful poetry," Mally said. "There's a great love poem in the Song of Solomon."

"There's a love poem in the Bible?" Randy said. "Maybe I should read it after all."

"Couldn't hurt," Joanie said.

"Gee, thanks," he replied. "But really," he said to Mally, "all I ever heard about was damnation and plagues. That's why I stopped."

"The Song of Solomon is a series of poems, really," Mally said, "a dialog between a man and a woman. The man keeps saying how beautiful the woman is and how much he wants her, and she keeps saying how she loves him, but she keeps turning him away."

"Huh," Randy said. "Typical."

"Oh, excuse me," Joanie said. "And isn't this beside the point?"

"Give us an example," Randy said.

Mally looked thoughtful, then said, "Okay, this is the woman talking about the man:

'As the apple tree among the trees of the wood, so is my beloved among the sons. I sat down under his shadow with great delight, and his fruit was sweet to my taste.'"

He smiled.

"And what does the man say about the woman?" Randy asked.

Mally closed his eyes a moment, then said,

"Behold, you are beautiful, my love, behold, you are beautiful! Your eyes are doves behind your veil. Your hair is like a flock of goats—"

"A flock of goats?" Randy interrupted.

"Shhh!" Joanie hissed.

"Well, goats were important to them," Mally said.

"I can see why this couple had problems."

"Do you mind?" Joanie said. "Go on, Mally."

Mally nodded.

"Your lips are like a scarlet thread, and your mouth is lovely. Your cheeks are like halves of a pomegranate behind your veil. Your two breasts are like two fawns, twins of a gazelle, that feed among the lilies."

"Wow," Randy said. They sat silent a moment. "So, what happens? You said she keeps turning him down."

Mally shrugged. "Eventually, he gives up and goes away, and she goes looking for him all over the city, but she can't find him again."

Randy gave Joanie a look.

"This is getting us nowhere," Joanie said, suddenly all business. "We all know the assignment isn't about the Bible. So . . ."

They went on throwing ideas back and forth like that for another hour or so. Then Reverend Jacobs came in, saying it was beginning to grow chilly, and Joanie said it was time for her to call her mother to come pick her up.

Randy perked up at that and suggested he drive her home. He smiled and winked at Mally. "Only fair," he said.

Mally didn't get the joke until they were already out the door. He hoped Joanie wouldn't have to crouch below the dashboard all the way to her house. He doubted she would.

The granny house shrank in on him and his grandfather after they left. Mally cleaned up the few dishes, but this petty chore, which he had done automatically so many times before, now seemed to drag on forever. He wished Joanie and Randy were back in the house with him, he wished his grandfather weren't, and then scolded himself for thinking that. He hoped to make up for the unkind thought by sitting up with his grandfather, but the old man seemed to tire quickly tonight and said he'd like to go to bed early. Mally knew that meant he would have to confine himself to his bedroom so his grandfather, stretched out on the sofa bed, could have some privacy, but he hated going back to his room. He knew he'd just lie there on the bed, staring at the ceiling, waiting to see the flash of lights on the curtains and hear the crunch of tires on the gravel. By now he could even tell the difference between the sound the tires made in the alley and the sound they made when Randy turned into his drive.

He lay on his back and looked into the night. It seemed to him that he would never get out of this room. Small as it was, its flimsy gray green walls would be the boundaries of his life forever.

His hand wandered between his legs and he thought for a moment he could get to sleep that way. But then the argument started again, his Aunt Margaret holding him by the shoulders, her eyes glaring inches from his own. "Did he touch you, Mally? Did he do anything to you?" "No," he'd said, so frightened tears were running down his face. "I'll kill him," she said, fiercely. Her eyes weren't even his Aunt Margaret's anymore. "I'll by God kill him!" Her anger was charging through her, running down her arms, digging her fingers into his shoulders. "No!" he'd said, not understanding but understanding all too well. "It wasn't anything like that! He never touched me, never!"

But his Aunt Margaret had stopped listening. She had stormed out of the house and across the yard, her hair like a wildfire on her head, and he had heard the yelling clear inside their house. It rang through the windows, hammered on the door to his room, tunneled through the pillow he held tight, tight over his head, so tight he thought he might suffocate, wished he would suffocate. Then the outside door slammed shut and footsteps came up the stairs and the door to his room had opened and Aunt Margaret stood there, panting. "You will never go over there again, do you hear me?" He had said nothing, sobbing. "Never!" And she closed the door to his room and his only hope of ever finding out about himself.

It was his fault. Somehow, Aunt Margaret had figured it out. Maybe she had found the magazine. Maybe someone from the school had called, someone who had seen him looking through the encyclopedia. He had ruined everything. Now he would never get to talk to Mr. Anderson again, never look through the telescope and dream about the stars. But he'd told the *truth*. He had *never* been touched. No one had touched him, and what Mally found out he could do he had found out all by himself, with a nightshirt between his hand and his dick so that, faithful to what the nuns had taught him at school, even he didn't touch himself.

He'd rubbed himself raw the first couple of times, but he had gotten better at it, and now he knew how to be more careful, slower. And the reversible tee-shirt, the spare one he had gotten for gym class, was softer than the nightshirts he used to wear. It was always handy, tucked beneath the mattress. Just touching it was reassuring.

Chapter 6

LOYALTIES

S HE HADN'T BEEN exaggerating. Things really were going better for her. The weather spots were only two or three minutes in a half-hour local news show, sandwiched between some heart-rending human interest story and the almost explosive enthusiasm of the sports reporter, but people now recognized her when she went on auditions. "Oh, yes," they'd say, "Susan Jacobs, the weather girl." She was afraid she was getting typed, but an older woman at one of the casting calls had told her, "Honey, types always get cast. That's the whole point of this business."

So she really couldn't leave just now. But Margaret's words continued to gnaw at her. They kept her up at night, dredging up old memories and running old accusations through her head. There was only one kind of trouble she could think of that would have set her aunt off like that, and she hoped to God it wasn't that. Anything but that. But she had to find out for sure, so she made the call.

The phone rang several times before someone picked up. "Hello?" a cold male voice said on the other end.

"Hello, Sammy?" she said uncertainly. It didn't really sound like him.

"Suzie-Q, is that you?" The old warmth flowed back into his voice, turning his words into laughter. "Oh, honey, it is so good to hear your voice!"

"Hi, Sammy. It's been so long. I just wanted to talk."

"Oh, I'm so glad you called," Sam Anderson said. "Another

two days and you wouldn't have gotten through. I'm having the number changed. I'm getting an unlisted one."

"Why?" she asked.

"Oh, it's just been awful. You don't know how good it is to pick up the phone and hear a friendly voice. It's been hell, Suzie-Q, pure hell."

"Why? What's happened?" She caught herself biting her nails and hastily put her hand behind her back.

"Didn't Margaret call you?"

"She's . . . she's had trouble getting ahold of me," she said, not exactly lying. "I've moved around a lot."

"Well," Sam let out a big sigh. "You know that bar I took you to once, the one outside of Tulsa?"

How could she forget? "Yeah."

"Well, they raided it last August. There wasn't anything go-ing on, not really. Well, there were a couple of guys dancing, but they took down all our names, even people like me. I was just sitting there, having a drink! And they took all our names and published them in the police column, in the newspapers."

"Oh, Sammy!"

"It's just been hell ever since. Harassing phone calls, obscene stuff scratched into the hood of my car. I lost my teacher's aid position."

"No!"

"But I've still got friends at NOAA. Thank God for Dr. Michaels!"

"Oh, Gosh, Sam. I had no idea."

"I thought for sure Margaret would have told you. She stormed over here the day after the papers came out and raised one hell of a stink. She accused me of all sorts of things. It made me furious. After all I've done for her and for you and for Mally, for her to say those things was just . . ." he seemed to run out of words.

The silence stretched uncomfortably. "Just what?" Susan said at last.

She heard him sigh again. "You think you know a person," he said at last. "We've been neighbors for nearly twenty years, since before you and Mally came to live with her. And still, she came over here, and in the same kitchen where we used to have coffee and gripe about the city council, she stood there and accused me of doing filthy things and . . . and getting Malachi mixed up in it, too."

There was a pause. She couldn't bear it, she had to know. "And did you?" she asked.

"What?"

"Did you . . . get Malachi mixed up in it?"

The silence on the other end was like a deafness, like the dead air in a room after something has been snapped in two.

"I thought, Susan," Sam said at last, "that you of all people would know the answer to that."

"I had to ask," she said.

"No, Susan," he said. "No, you didn't." His voice was that cold, empty voice that had first answered the phone. "But since you did, the answer is no. I wouldn't harm a hair on that boy's head. He was like a son, and although I could never take the place of a real father, I was honored to be a part of your family. I thought you knew that. I thought you knew how much it meant to me. I thought it meant a lot to you, too. I guess I was wrong."

"I'm sorry, Sam," she said.

"I'm sorry, too, Susan," he said. "Don't bother calling again. I get enough calls like this as it is." He hung up.

She put the receiver gently back on the cradle. She felt the sudden, nauseating grip of a familiar guilt close in around her, and her small rented room turned into a hot, confining place. She got up and headed for the bathroom to take off her makeup. She had meant to put her mind at rest so she could sleep, so she could stop the fretting that was beginning to show in her eyes and cut into her auditions. Now she wondered if she would sleep at all, or spend the night wandering along the twisted railroad tracks of her dreams looking for the body of a lost friend.

Red's dad was in the downstairs office, where he seemed to be spending more and more time. Papers were spread out around him in an arc and his briefcase lay open on the floor. Red approached the table and sat down across from his father and waited. Mr. Conner was busy changing something on one of the forms. When he still hadn't looked up in over a minute, Red decided to speak.

"Whatcha doing there, Dad?" he asked cheerfully.

"I'm working, Richard," Mr. Conner said. "Please leave me be."

Red sat quietly, watching his father. Maybe now wasn't a good time, but he'd need an answer pretty soon. He decided to risk it. "I've been thinking about going out for wrestling," he said.

Mr. Conner looked up. "Now, who put that idea in your head?"

"No one. I just thought . . ."

Mr. Conner laid down his pen and sighed. "Do you want to go to college, Richard?" he asked. When Red didn't answer right away, he prompted, "Well, son, do you?"

"Yes, sir."

"Well, your grades alone aren't going to do it, now, are they? We know that from past experience." Red dropped his head at the reminder. "So it's got to be an athletic scholarship or nothing. And how many of those do you think they give out for wrestling?"

"I don't know," his son said, still not looking up.

Mr. Conner sighed. "Look, son," he said. "Your mother and I can't afford it. You know that. Football and basketball are your best shots."

Red looked up. "It's just that Randy's going out for wrestling—"

"What's that Edom boy got to do with it?" he said, beginning to sound angry.

"Well, we've kinda done all our sports together," Red said. "He and I are a team. You know, the Dynamic Duo." He grinned and hoped his father would get the joke, but Mr. Conner just sat there with an expression like dark stone on his face. Red shrugged. "We've been buddies since fifth grade," he said, "ever since we moved to Croy."

"Well, maybe it's time the two of you went your separate ways." Mr. Conner picked up his pen again and turned to the form in front of him. "We didn't move out to this part of town for you to hang out with white trash."

Red's jaw dropped. "Don't say that!" he blurted out.

Mr. Conner's head rose slowly, crimson beginning to cover his face. "I beg your pardon?" he said, cold and furious. He took off his glasses. "Who do you think you're talking to, boy?"

Red was in a panic. Why was his father being like this? "Randy's my best friend. We've always done stuff together. He's practically the only guy I can hang around with, and talk to, and—"

"Talk to about what?" his father barked. "You haven't been shooting off your mouth, have you?"

"No, sir," Red said, a sudden chill in his stomach.

"Did he put you up to this?" his father asked, pointing his pen at him.

"No—"

"I don't want you hanging around him anymore, do you hear?" his father said. "All you two do is get drunk and hot rod around town in that car of his. And I don't want him coming up to the house."

"Dad! No!" He sprang to his feet. "You can't do that!"

Mr. Conner rose slowly, taller than Red, towering over him. "What the hell do you mean, I can't do that? Whose house do you think this is? Who do you think pays for this place? Who do you think puts three square meals a day on your table? Who buys your clothes, pays for the dentist, paid for your mother's new car? Where do you think all that comes from? If I say you'll do it, you'll do it, and that's final. Is that clear?"

They stood facing each other, silent.

"I asked you, boy, is that clear?"

"Yes, sir, it's clear," Red said, but he didn't drop his eyes and they stood there a moment longer. Then Red turned and walked stiffly away, through the dining room, past the curio hutch, up the stairs of their split-level home to his room.

Mr. Conner felt the heat rise from his head as he glared after his son. Then with a muttered curse he sat down and faced the stack of forms again.

Mrs. Conner breezed in from the den. "What was all that shouting about?" she asked.

He shuffled the papers in front of him. "Nothing," he said tersely.

"Well, it didn't sound like nothing," she said. When Mr. Conner didn't speak again, she shrugged and left.

In his room, Red punched his pillow again and again and again. He was by God not going to cry, not going to let that bastard get to him. Was it clear? Oh yes, sir, Daddy Sir, Poppa Asshole, it was clear. Very clear. Mr. Conner had said no to Randy, no to his best friend, no to hanging out with his buddy after school. But he hadn't said no to going out for the wrestling team. And there was nothing his father could do to keep Randy from being on the same team with him.

"Joanie will be down in a minute, Randy," Mrs. Tibbits said, smiling as she led him into the living room. "Won't you sit down?"

"Thank you, ma'am," he said. He made his way over to the sofa where a boy of about six in a cowboy outfit was playing with a toy pistol.

The boy gave him a suspicious squint. "Who're you?" he asked.

"Now, Kyle," his mother said, heading for the dining room, "be nice. He's here to see your sister."

"I'm Randy," he said, sitting down.

"You Joanie's boyfriend?" the boy asked.

"Must be," Randy said, smiling.

"I heard about you." The boy frowned and returned to inspecting his pistol.

"How about you, sheriff?" Randy asked. "Who are you?"

"I'm Kyle," the boy said, as if that should be obvious.

"Oh, yeah," Randy said, nodding sagely. "I heard about you, too."

"Head what?" Kyle said, suddenly interested.

"Heard you threw a stink-bomb in the Assembly of God church."

Kyle smiled and looked down at the floor. "Yeah," he said. He was kind of proud of it.

"Whatcha plannin' on doin' next?" Randy asked.

"Me and Rafe is gonna blow up the statue of General Longstreet."

"What for?"

"He's a traitor to the South."

Randy nodded. "That seems fair enough. What're ya gonna use?"

"Penny crackers."

"Oh, I don't know, Stinker," Randy said. Kyle looked up at him, ready for a fight. "I don't think penny crackers are gonna do it. You need a cherry bomb or two."

Kyle's eyes went wide. "You got some?"

"For heaven's sake, don't encourage him," Joanie said, walking into the room.

Randy stood up. Her dress was a dark green that made a brisk sound as she walked, and she carried a pink sweater over her arms. She looked—well, she looked really pretty. He was kind of surprised by how pretty she looked. He felt a little shabby by comparison, but it was the best he could do. And it was way too late to back out now.

"Are you kids off to the dance, then?" Mrs. Tibbits said, reentering the room.

"Yes, Momma," Joanie said, leaning over to give her mother a peck on the cheek. "'Bye, now."

"You get her back by ten-thirty, hear?" Ruth said to Randy.

"Sure will," he said. He made a short, stiff bow. "Good night, Mrs. Tibbits." He turned to Kyle. "See ya, Stinker."

"'Night!" Kyle yelled.

The Tibbitses' house wasn't but a few blocks from the school, but Randy made a point of driving them there anyway, and he was very certain to open the car door for Joanie as she got in.

"How come you get to call him Stinker?" she said on the drive over.

Randy shrugged. "It just seems natural. He's a neat kid."

"You can say that. You don't live with him. Heaven only knows why Momma and Daddy want another one. You'd think they'd learn."

"Your folks expecting?"

"No, but Daddy wants a large family. He's always said he wanted six kids."

"How about you?"

She gave him a look. "You're getting a little ahead of yourself, aren't you?" she said. "We're just going to the Halloween Dance."

Randy turned bright red. "No, I—" He got so flustered he missed the school parking lot and had to make a U-turn. "That's not what I—" Then he looked over at her and saw the mischief in her eyes. He started to laugh. "You've done it again, haven't you?" he said. "Man, it must be like shooting fish in a barrel."

"Well," she said, "you do kinda take the challenge out of it."

They had a swell time at the dance.

Mally got used to the showers, and after the first time, when someone had snatched away the towel he'd wrapped around himself, he even got used to walking through the locker room naked. All he had to do was remember that first humiliation and he was able to stay loose. He just had to watch his timing, that's all. If Randy was in the showers, he waited until he came out; if he was in the showers and Randy came in, he rinsed off quickly and coldly and left. He dressed facing his locker, keeping his back to the lockers and the boys on the other side of the aisle.

He was lost in a dream under the hot water when he heard Red and Randy enter the shower room. He turned up the cold water and finished up.

"So, it's official?" Red's voice boomed across the tiles. "You and the boss's daughter?"

"Her name's Joanie. And where was Mary Kay, anyways?" Randy asked, wanting to change the subject. "I didn't see her around."

"Oh, she was, you know," Red said vaguely, looking embarrassed.

"So you decided to go stag?"

"Well, I wasn't going to sit at home," Red said. "Besides," he punched Randy on the arm, "I thought you and I might hang out after. I didn't know you would be 'busy.'"

Randy gave him a look and turned off the shower. The two of them headed for their lockers.

"Just tell me this, Big Man," Red said. "Can you still do this?" He got in front of Randy and crossed his fingers and crossed his arms.

"What the hell is that?"

"Well, can you?"

"Buzz off," Randy said and brushed Red aside.

"Just as I thought, just as I thought," Red said, coming up behind him. "My boy, you are pussy-whipped."

"Oh, get off it, Conner," Randy said, opening his locker.

"Hah!" Red laughed. "I'm right!" He glanced across the aisle and gave Randy a nudge in the ribs. "Hey," he said, "get this." And he wound up his towel in a tight spring, taking a bead on Mally's butt.

Randy turned around just in time to see it. Red let fly with the towel, intending to give the Jacobs kid a smart smack on the ass, but just as he did, for some reason the guy turned around. Instead of landing a hit square on that skinny butt, the towel went "Crack!" right in the boy's genitals.

All the color drained from Red's face. The whole front of Mally's body was turning bright red. "Jesus," Randy whispered.

"Jeez, I'm sorry," Red stammered. "I didn't mean, I mean I . . ."

Mally was looking at them with an expression of pure fury. He took three steps across the aisle and was two inches from Red's face. Even looking up at him, he seemed taller. Mally's jaw was so tight he could barely speak, but he hissed, "Why don't you leave me the fuck alone?"

"What in God's name is going on here?" a voice thundered from the end of the row. Randy turned to look. It was Coach Ardmore, standing with his hands on his hips, looking angrier than he could ever remember. Coach Tucker towered behind him, silent and dark as a thundercloud. "Edom? Conner? Jacobs?" The boys were silent. "I asked you a question!"

Nobody spoke. The whole locker room was silent, listening.

"All right, listen up!" Coach Ardmore barked. "Everyone. When you get dressed, you fall into formation, is that clear? Nobody leaves until I tell you to. Got it?" He turned and went back to his office, but Coach Tucker stayed, looming over the aisles, making sure just by his presence that nobody left.

They all turned to their lockers and dressed in silence. "Jesus," Red whispered, "how was I to know he was gonna turn around?"

Dressed, they all stood in a row by height. Coach Ardmore came out of his office, a rolled-up magazine in his hand.

"Y'all think this is pretty funny, don't you?" he said. No one was smiling. "Y'all think it's just one big game, isn't it? Just fun and games. Well, what do you think we're here for, huh? Just for laughs? Have a good joke?" He walked up to Marcus. "What about you, Longacre. You having fun?" Marcus didn't say a word. The Coach moved down the line. "And you, Conner. I expected more out of you. I bet you're laughin' right now. Is that what you're here for?" Red opened his mouth, but nothing came out. "Well, I'm not!" Coach suddenly roared and smacked the magazine against the nearest locker.

"What do you think is going on out there?" he said, jerking his thumb over his shoulder. "Do you read the paper? Watch the news?" He looked up and down the row of boys. "Well, I'll tell you what's going on. Our boys are dying. Our boys, boys from our state, from this town, are out there, fighting, dodging bullets and bombs and God knows what. And dying. For you. For you pack of glad-hands. They're out there, in the real world, getting shot at and blown up, facing booby traps and land mines, am- bushes, little kids on bicycles riding up to them with hand grenades in their pockets, women with dynamite strapped to their chests. And if one of our boys gets caught, one of them gets ahold of them, do you know what they do? They cut their nuts off and stuff them in their mouth, that's what. And that's what they'll do to you. That's what you're facing. And that's why this is not about fun and games. This is about discipline, and loyalty, and looking out for your buddy. Because without that, you are just meat. Dead meat!"

The end of the period bell rang. Nobody moved.

"There will be no more horsing around in the locker room," Coach Ardmore said. "There will be discipline in my class room or you will be ten times sorry you ever came in here." He gave them all another long look. "Now, get out of here."

The line broke hesitantly, then the boys hurried toward the door.

"Jacobs!" Ardmore called out just as Mally was beginning to move. The thin kid froze. "My office."

The boy followed him to the office. When they were both inside, Coach Ardmore closed the door and sat down behind his desk. "Do you have something you want to say to me?" Ardmore asked.

Mally looked him in the eye. "No, sir," he said.

Ardmore looked at him. "I said it would be rough, son. Do you want out?"

"No, sir."

"I could transfer you to study hall."

Mally shook his head. "I'm fine."

"Okay," Ardmore said, nodding. "Okay. Better go, you'll be late." He scribbled a note. "Here's a hall pass in case you need one."

The boy nodded and left.

Ardmore sat in his chair a while. He had trashed the magazine. It was all crumpled up and the sweat on his hands had peeled the ink off the cover. He threw it in the waste can.

Still, he thought, the kid had looked him in the eye. He hadn't blinked even once. That's some progress.

Chapter 7

FAMILY TREE

MALLY DIDN'T UNDERSTAND how boys work at all. For two months, no one except Joanie Tibbits had spoken two words to him. Now, Marcus Longacre comes up behind him in the hall, claps a hand on his back, and says, "Pretty cool, Jake," and walks off. He was still puzzling over that on his way home when Randy Edom's car pulled up alongside him.

"Hey," Randy called from the driver's seat.

The car was cruising slowly to keep up with him. Mally gave it a glance and continued walking.

"Wanna ride?" Randy called.

"No thanks," Mally said.

The car continued to keep pace.

"I'm going that way," Randy said.

Mally stopped and faced the car. "Don't you have football practice or something?"

The car stopped. "I left some of my gear at home," Randy said. "I gotta go anyway, so . . ."

Mally looked down the sidewalk. It would cut twenty minutes or more off his walk home. He looked back at Randy. "Do I have to hide under the dash again?" he asked.

Randy regarded him steadily a moment. "No," he said.

They stayed like that, Mally on the sidewalk, Randy in the car. Finally, Randy said, "So, do you want a ride or what?"

Mally nodded. "Yeah," he said, "thanks," and got in.

"Look," Randy said after they'd ridden in silence a while, "I don't know if it means anything to you, but, uh . . . I think Red was . . . Today I think he was way outta line."

Mally looked at him. Randy wasn't looking at him, but keeping his eyes focused on the street.

Randy continued, "And, uh . . . I don't know . . ." He seemed to come up short of words. Then he shrugged and said, "I guess I want to apologize." He glanced at Mally.

Mally looked at him then looked out the windshield. "You didn't do anything," he said.

"Yeah," Randy said, "that's been pointed out."

They rounded the corner of the town square and headed east over the railroad tracks, then south along Front Street.

"Look, it's none of my business," Randy said, one hand hanging on the steering wheel, the other resting on the open window, "but if I were you, well, I just wouldn't put up with it, that's all." He looked over and could see Mally shaking his head. "Well, I wouldn't," he repeated.

"Well, what am I supposed to do," Mally said, "call him out behind the school some day?"

"Well," Randy said, "that's where I'd start."

"He'd beat the living crap out of me!" Mally said with surprising heat. "And that's probably just what he wants. I won't play at that game. I'm not gonna fight Red and I'm not gonna rat on him. Either way, he wins."

"Huh," Randy said. "Well, I don't know if I could take it."

"Oh, I can take it all right. I learned that at St. Albert's. No matter how much it hurts, you never let them see you suffer."

"Well, I don't know how you even managed to walk. I'd've been rolled up in a wad on the floor, bawling my eyes out." He looked over at him. "You're pretty tough."

Mally made a disgusted sound and looked out the window.

"What?" Randy said.

"For a sissy," Mally said, still turned away.

"Come again?"

Mally turned to face him. "Pretty tough for a sissy. That's what you mean."

"Oh, hey, I didn't say—"

"No, but that's what you're thinking. That's what you're all thinking."

"Well, maybe we were wrong."

"Well, maybe you were right. Ever think about that? Does that give Red Conner the right to smack me in the balls?"

"No," Randy said, pulling back, "not really. 'Live and let live' is my motto."

"Oh, now, that's a comfort. It's good to know I'm riding through town in a car with someone who will let me live."

"Hey, I'm trying to be nice, here. Cut me some slack."

"I'm sorry," Mally said, settling down, "but I'm still pretty sore. Both ways."

"I can see that."

"Maybe this ride wasn't such a good idea."

"Now hold it right there, buster. This is my car and I get to decide who rides in it."

"You don't have to try to be friends with me just because of Joanie."

Randy smacked his steering wheel. "Oh, now this is just too much. I try to talk to Joanie and all she wants to talk about is you. I try to talk to you and you start talking about Joanie. When do I get my turn?"

Mally looked appalled. "She talks about me?"

"The only way I'm going to get in on this little chat fest is if I take on the both of you."

Mally looked alarmed. "What? Take on—what?"

"Look," Randy said, "I hadn't told Joanie this yet, but I was planning on taking her on a little picnic this weekend. I may as well take you along. We'll just end up talking about you anyway."

Mally shook his head. "No. No, I couldn't. Three's a—"

"Do *not* say 'three's a crowd'! My god, what do the two of

you do, rehearse?" Mally looked at him. The words sounded angry, but Randy was grinning. "So, what'd'ya say?"

"I don't know," Mally said honestly. "I have to take care of grandfather—"

"Aw, c'mon," Randy said. "Old Lady Oafield can look after him. We'll only be gone an hour or so."

"You sure Joanie won't mind?"

Randy's grin turned wicked. "It would serve her right if she did. So, are you in?"

Mally shrugged, grinned, shook his head, shrugged again. "Sure," he said.

"All right!" Randy felt in high spirits as they came up on the alley. "Hey. Watch me spook Old Lady Oafield."

He pulled his classic maneuver, the fish-tail on the gravel, the burst of speed through the alley, the abrupt stop at his driveway. They looked back and could see Mrs. Oldfield, frozen in her tracks, half bent-over her vegetable garden, a tomato stake in her hand and her mouth hanging open. The two boys burst out laughing.

"What'd I tell you?" Randy said.

Mally got out of the car. "Thanks for the ride," he said, still smiling.

"Don't forget your books," Randy said, chucking them across the seat.

Mally grabbed them and said thanks again, and the car took off down the alley. Mally was partway to the granny house when he suddenly remembered. "Hey!" he called after Randy's car. "Hey, you forgot your . . ."

But Randy was gone, headed back to school. *Huh*, Mally thought. *Maybe that's how boys work.* He hefted his books in his hand, then brought his arm down to his side. They felt kind of natural that way, hanging on the end of his arm. He turned and headed for the granny house.

Mrs. Oldfield didn't let the matter pass idly, especially once she heard Mally was going on a picnic with Randy. She spoke to his grandfather about it. Mally heard them talking as he did the dishes Friday after supper. His grandfather was outside, enjoying the evening again, when Mrs. Oldfield came down from her porch. Mally didn't hear all of it, but by being really quiet with the dishes, he could hear some.

"I just don't think it's safe," Mrs. Oldfield said. "You see the way he tears through this alley."

"That's just his way of making a point, Clara," his grandfather said. "He doesn't mean anything by it."

"If you let him take Mally, you're encouraging his wild behavior."

Mally's heart started pounding. Could Mrs. Oldfield really keep him from going on the picnic?

"I think," the Reverend Jacobs said, "by allowing him to take Mally, I'm encouraging his responsible behavior."

"You're putting that boy's life in jeopardy."

"Clara," his grandfather said, "don't be so harsh. Joanie Tibbits is going, too. I'm sure Ruth wouldn't agree to that if she thought her daughter's life were in danger."

"Well, we all know how well Ruth Tibbits looks after her family."

"Now, that's enough," his grandfather said, and there was a hardness to his voice Mally had never heard before.

There was a silence. Mrs. Oldfield's voice was so small and soft when she spoke again that Mally barely caught the words. She said, "I just don't want him to end up like his father."

What his grandfather said then he couldn't make out. It was all low murmurs and quiet words. Eventually, Mrs. Oldfield went back up to her house, but before she left, Mally thought he heard something that might have been from her, something like a sob.

The next morning, he was up earlier than usual. Randy

wouldn't say where they were going, but they were set to leave his place at ten o'clock to pick up Joanie. By nine o'clock, Mally had all his morning chores done plus he'd made the potato salad that was his contribution. He sat on the sofa with the Tupperware bowl in his lap, staring into space, his right leg jigging up and down a mile a minute.

"Mally," his grandfather said from his chair in the corner.

"Hmm?" he said, barely able to focus on the old man.

His grandfather simply pointed to his leg, which continued its wild ride.

"Oh," he said and quieted his leg, then turned to stare out the window. Within minutes, his leg started up again on its own.

"Perhaps," his grandfather said, putting down his book, "you might prefer to wait over at the Edom's."

Mally looked eager. "You sure you'll be all right?" he asked.

"I'll be fine," his grandfather said, "if Mrs. Oldfield will have the charity not to talk me to death. Go."

With barely a muttered, "Thanks," Mally shot out the door and across the alley and up the back steps to the Edom's house. When he got to the back door, though, he was suddenly cowed. He'd never been this far on their property before. Should he knock or ring the doorbell? He looked. There was no doorbell. Maybe he should go around the front.

"Don't just stand there like a peddler," came a woman's voice from inside. "Come in."

He opened the screen door and stepped into the kitchen.

Randy's mother was standing beside the stove. "Sit down, Mally. Randy's not ready yet," she said. "Big surprise."

"Oh, it's not his fault," Mally said. "I'm early." He sat at the table in a chair that looked like it came from a diner. It didn't match the other chairs.

"Did you have breakfast?"

"Yes'm."

"Want some coffee?"

Mally was unprepared for such a question. "Uh, no," he managed to say, "thank you."

"No," Virginia said, pouring herself a cup and sitting down, "I don't suppose you would." She eyed him long enough for him to get uncomfortable. "You don't remember me, do you?" she said.

"No, ma'am, I don't."

"Well, that's hardly surprising," Virginia said. "You couldn't've been more than two when I visited you and your momma in Oklahoma City. We used to be neighbors, you know, here in Croy."

Mally looked out the door to the granny house. "You mean, here?" he said. "At Mrs. Oldfield's?"

"Oh, no," Virginia laughed. "We were in much better shape back then. We lived across the street from the Holy—from Mount Hermon church."

"Mom?" Randy's voice called from a room nearby. "Have I got clean socks?"

"If you washed 'em, you've got 'em," Virginia yelled back. She turned to Mally and smiled. "We used to hear the music from the church every Sunday and on Wednesday nights, too. It was one of the nicest things about living in that part of town. And the Tibbits used to live nearby, too, before John bought the Rexall. So in a way, this little picnic y'all are going on is a sorta reunion." She reached into her house dress and pulled out a pack of cigarettes.

"So, you knew my folks?" Mally said.

"Your momma and I were thick as thieves," Virginia said, lighting up. "And I had great respect for your daddy. He's the one made the choir sound so good and played the piano. Oh, say!" she said, pulling the cigarette out of her mouth so abruptly Mally could almost hear it pop. "I never thought of it before. He used to live in that little house where you are now. Seems we've been neighbors even longer than I thought."

Randy came into the kitchen carrying his shoes. "Hey, Mally," he said. "Morning, Mom."

"Oh, now it's 'Morning, Mom,' is it? Not 'where's my socks?'"

"Mom, please," Randy said, sitting down to put his shoes on. "Guests?" He nodded toward Mally.

"Oh," Virginia said. "I get it. Well, Mally," she said, rising, "if your being around means I get some manners out of this one," and she flung a gesture toward Randy, "you're welcome to come over any time."

Mally and Randy headed out the back door. They had just reached the car when Mally said, "Oh, shoot!" and handed the potato salad to Randy. "Can you hold this a sec?" he said. "I forgot something."

"Sure," Randy said. Mally took off across the alley. "Hey," Randy called, drifting after him, "need any help?"

"No thanks," Mally said, "it's just a book," and he disappeared around the corner of the granny house.

Randy continued to drift across the alley. The morning air was soft and carried just enough scent from a few late mimosas not to be sickening. He rounded the corner Mally had just disappeared around and stopped in his tracks. Ambushed.

"Randy," Mrs. Oldfield said with a grim smile. "Well, it's been a while since we've seen you over on this side of the alley."

"Yes'm." He felt defenseless holding the Tupperware bowl in front of him.

"So," she said, advancing, "what have you been doing with yourself?"

"Oh, nothing much," he said. She waited. "I got a job over at Tibbits," he conceded.

"Oh?" she said. "I didn't know people with inheritances needed to work."

Randy set his jaw. "I didn't need to," he said. "I just wanted to."

Over Mrs. Oldfield's shoulder, Randy could see Mally come out of the granny house, a slim book in his hand. Mally stopped when he saw them.

Mrs. Oldfield was continuing, "I haven't seen your mother yet this morning."

"Then I guess she hasn't been out yet," he said.

"I would like to speak to her. A little matter of neighborhood disturbances I'd like to talk to her about."

"I'll tell her when I see her."

Mrs. Oldfield raised her eyebrows. "Then she isn't home this weekend?" she asked.

At that, Mally reached behind himself and opened the screen door and let it go again, giving it a push so it made an audible slam.

"I gotta go now, Mrs. Oldfield," Randy said. "We gotta pick up Joanie."

"Thanks for looking after Grandfather, Mrs. Oldfield," Mally said, all cheerful smiles.

"My pleasure," she said. As the two boys headed back across the alley, she called out, "And don't forget to tell your mother, Randy. When you see her."

As soon as the car left the alley, Mally let out a sigh of relief. "God, what an old bat."

"Amen!" Randy said.

Joanie sat in the window seat of the living room, scanning the street. The morning had not gone well. Her mother and father were engaged in some sort of silent, wordless fight, and the tension had filled the house to the snapping point until the Bean had finally done something worth being yelled at, which had sent him into a fit of yowling, and that had only made them all feel worse by giving voice to how they all felt. What was it with her folks, anyway? Parents were supposed to get along, and if they couldn't get along they should keep it to themselves, which meant more than just stalking around the house like a bunch of unexploded fireworks. She was glad when her father left for the store, but that left her with a mother who was giving off black clouds of misery and a little brother who was so cross he could make pitch boil. She was shooing him out the front door when she saw Randy's car coming down the street.

"They're here!" she yelled back into the house to her mother. "'Bye, Momma."

"Joanie?" her mother called, coming toward her from the kitchen. "Remember your jacket, dear."

"Yes, Momma," she called, though in fact she didn't. Who needed a jacket on a day like today? Forget it was November—everyone else had.

Randy's car pulled to a stop and Mally hopped out and got in the back seat.

"Hey, Stinker," Randy yelled to Joanie's little brother as she got in the front seat.

"Hey, yerself," he yelled back.

"How's the campaign against the General?" Randy asked.

"Do what?"

"Could we just get out of here?" Joanie asked.

"Sure," Randy said. "See you later, alligator," he yelled to Kyle.

"Not if I see you first," the boy yelled back.

"I'm sorry to be in such a rush," Joanie said as they headed out. "I just couldn't stand it around the house one minute longer."

"Yeah," said Randy. "We've had a real delightful time ourselves this morning."

"Oh? What's up?"

"Guess," said Mally. "What's old and rhymes with 'nasty'?"

"Oh, that old bat," Joanie said.

"My words exactly," Mally said.

"I suppose you get that every day?" she asked.

"Yeah," Mally said. "I think it's included with the rent."

"Boy, do I pity you."

"Hey, what about me?" Randy put in. "I've been living across the alley from her since forever."

"And you haven't been warped for life?" Joanie asked.

"Not so's you'd notice."

"Um, some do, some don't," Mally said nonchalantly.

"You kids keep quiet back there or I'm turning this car around."

Joanie laughed. "Where're you taking us?"

"Oh, it's not far," Randy said. "You can see it from here. Just a little piece of property we've kept in the family." He made the jog at Ninth street that led to the county road west of town. "There it is," he said. He pointed to a small house on a hill covered with feathery Indian grass and bluestem gone dry and reddish in the autumn sun.

The house was much like the one Randy lived in now, but all trace of paint had peeled off it years ago and now it was a uniform, weathered gray. It sat alone on its hill, kept company by a small tree too distant and stunted to offer the house any shade. They pulled off the county road at a spot that seemed almost arbitrary—there was no driveway or road or even a set of ruts. The wheels of Randy's car cut through the weeds, making their own temporary trail.

They parked a little distance from the house and began to get out the picnic things. Mally kept glancing back at the house and the tree. The tree especially caught his eye and he wandered over to it. It looked as if the wind passing over this hill had never failed to take a swipe at it, twisting its trunk into a slow corkscrew, snapping off a limb here and there, giving the whole thing a tormented look. Short, stubby branches stuck out at odd angles where older, heavier limbs had snapped off.

"Well, what do you think?" Randy asked as he took hold of the picnic basket.

Joanie shifted the blanket in her arms. She looked over at the house and at Mally staring at the tree. "Looks kinda desolate . . . for a picnic, anyway," she said.

"What kind of tree is this?" Mally called out.

"That old thing?" Randy said. He and Joanie walked over to him. "It's an apple tree, or what's left of one. There used to be an orchard up here, but old Granddaddy Alquist cut 'em all down. This was his land then; now it's my mom's. My dad and I tried to clear it once, but the soil is no good and the spring's dried up." He walked up to the tree and patted the trunk. "Don't know why this one's still standing. A twister came through here a couple of years ago."

"Yeow," Joanie said, "I remember that."

"You mean it tore through here and missed the house?" Mally asked, amazed.

"Well, you can't blame it for trying," Randy said. "And it's not really a house." He turned away. "More of a shed."

"Oh, it'll do," Mally said. He was going to say it looked like Randy's house in town, but thought better of it.

"Well, where should we have the picnic?" Joanie said. "I'm getting tired of lugging this old blanket around."

Randy brightened at that and pointed to the crest of the hill. "Right up there," he said. "That's why I took us out here."

The three of them topped the hill and stood staring down at the town. The dry grasses of the prairie rolled along the hills to the north and west of town; ranchland quartered off by rows of blackjack oak spread south and east. Compared to the blond and sepia of the surrounding countryside, Croy lay like an oasis in the valley of the White Horse River. Some of its trees had the barest touch of autumn color in their topmost branches. A few church steeples poked up here and there, and the red brick and white cupola of the court house rose from its center. You could see the railroad tracks cutting across the east edge of town, isolating a strip of homes from the rest of the community. The rail yard was a barren patch in the northeast, empty now with most of its spur lines torn up; beyond that lay the cemetery. A meandering line of cottonwoods and tamarisk marked the gully of the White Horse and the town's easternmost edge. That barrier had forced most of the recent expansion of the town west, where the subdivision sprouted and the tin roof of the high school shone bright like a soda can. Seen from here, the water tower rose on a line with the court house, but you could not see the oil pump beside it that ran constantly, rocking slowly up and down, eking out the last drops of revenue from beneath the city.

"Oh . . ." Joanie said.

"You see?" Randy said, grinning.

"Well," Joanie said, covering her amazement, "I always knew it was small . . ."

"This is probably the only hill in the county where you can get a good look at it."

Joanie lifted her hand in front of her face. If she held her palm out at arm's length, she could blot out the entire town. It gave her a chill. "Well," she said, "here we are, masters of all we survey. Shall we at least eat before we starve to death?"

They spread the blanket and got the picnic plates and chicken from Joanie's basket and opened Mally's potato salad.

"There," Joanie said when all the food had been distributed, "just like a real family."

"Sure!" Randy said. He got into the act with a real hillbilly accent: "Ah'll be Poppa-Daddy."

"And Ah'll be Big Momma," Joanie said. The two of them looked at Mally.

"And Ah'll be Buford, the family dawg," he said.

"Aw, no," Randy said, dropping his drawl. "You gotta be something."

"Way-ull," Joanie said, "he's too big for the baby."

"Right," Mally said. "I mean, 'woof.'"

Randy turned to Joanie in amazement. "We-all's gonna have a baby? Why warn't Ah told?"

"It jest plumb slipped mah mind."

"Don't fret none, Poppa-Daddy," Mally said, laying a consoling paw on his shoulder. "It hain't got nothin' to do with you, anyways."

"Down, boy," Randy said. "Well, now let's get this here thing settled. First off, we gotta give the young'un a name. He's gotta have a proper name."

Joanie raised her eyebrows. "What if he's not a him? What if he's a she?"

"Then we'll give him two names," Randy said authoritatively.

Mally dropped his act. "Whatever you do, do not name him after a prophet of the Old Testament. It'll mark him for life."

"How on earth did you end up with Malachi, anyway?" Randy asked.

Mally raised both hands. "I had nothing to do with it. Happened before I was born."

"Was it maybe a name on your father's side?" Joanie offered.

"No," Mally said. "He wasn't around by then." He saw Joanie and Randy exchange glances. "As I guess everybody's figured out."

"Hey," Randy said, "we didn't mean to—"

"Aw, it's all right," Mally said. "We're all family here, right?"

"Right!" Joanie said with a bright smile.

"And I've been curious myself," Mally said. "I wonder if my grandfather had a hand in it, him being an Old Testament sort. The name means, 'messenger of God.'"

"Yep," Randy said. "That'll mark you for life."

"How do you know what it means?" Joanie asked.

"I looked it up," he said. "Everybody's name means something."

"Really?" she said. "What's my name mean?"

"Joan. Feminine form of John. I'll bet you were named after your father."

"Well, of course she was," Randy said. "He was born at least twenty years a-fore she was."

They booed him and threw wads of napkins at him. When

he'd been sufficiently chastised, Joanie asked, "So, what does John mean?"

"'The Lord is gracious,'" Mally said.

"What's Randy?" Randy asked.

"Randolph. Means, 'protector, shield.'"

"Not Randolph. Just Randy."

Mally shook his head. "Dunno."

"Aha!" Joanie said, raising a chicken drumstick like a diadem. "My superior intellect rises to the fore."

"It's about time," Randy said.

"Randy is a five-letter word meaning bawdy or drunken and lewd."

"Bingo!" yelled Mally.

"You're kidding!" Randy said.

Laughing, the three of them started in on the picnic. The sun warmed the hill and soon they were sprawled out on the blanket, enjoying the heat and listening to the occasional calls of scissortails.

"Is there anything more beautiful than Indian Summer?" Joanie asked of the sky.

"Thank you very much," Randy said, a length of Indian grass in his mouth. "It's nice to know our efforts are appreciated."

"Who gave you all the credit?" she asked.

"Hey, I'm one-quarter Chickasaw."

"So's half the town."

"Really?" Mally said, intrigued. "On your mother's side?"

"The Alquists?" Randy snorted. "Good lord, no! Old New York Alquist would spin in his grave if he heard you say that. He'd as soon cut off his left nut as let a red Indian in the family."

"Oh, now that's a pleasant image, so soon after lunch," Joanie said.

"Sorry about that. No, it was my dad, Harry. Half Chickasaw."

Mally was puzzled. "So, your granddad must have done it after all. I mean, not the surgery, but let your father in."

"Not on your life," Randy said. "When Virginia married Harry, Granddaddy cut her off without a cent. But then I came along and melted the old man's heart. Well, kind of."

"How's that?"

"Well, he didn't really leave anything to Mom," Randy said. "Just the played out oil wells and useless properties, like this one. He put all the good stuff into a trust for me that starts paying out when I turn eighteen." He spat out the stub end of the straw. "Nope, if Mom hadn't married Harry, she'd've had quite a fortune on her own, and she'd've had her pick of the crop around here, such as it is. Instead, she picked Harry." He stared at the horizon. "Don't ask me why."

Virginia decided to do the laundry after all. On some other day she might have just gone with a pocket full of quarters down to the laundromat and gotten the whole load dried at once, but the almost spring-like air lured her outside despite herself, and line drying would save those quarters for later. She stepped out on the back porch with a basket of damp clothes and was pleasantly surprised by the warm sunlight and freshness in the air. She walked to the clothesline, its four arms strung with plasticized cord like an inverted cat's cradle, and started pinning up the sheets.

"Good morning, Virginia," came a voice from across the alley.

She looked over and saw Mrs. Oldfield holding a cardboard box. "Morning, Clara," she said, turning back and pulling a shirt out of the basket.

Mrs. Oldfield crossed the alleyway. "I wasn't sure you were at home today," she said.

"Well, looks like I am," Virginia replied. The clothespin in her teeth gave her a good excuse to be terse.

Mrs. Oldfield patted the box in her arms. "I was wondering if you might take some of these tomatoes off my hands."

Virginia looked at her with some surprise, and then at the tomatoes. They were nice, beefy ones. "Thanks," she said.

"I know things have been slowing down some at the plant and I thought things might be getting a little tight."

"It hasn't quite come to that, Clara. We don't need charity."

"Oh, no, I didn't mean that," Mrs. Oldfield said. If Virginia hadn't known better, she would have said Clara was becoming flustered. "It's just . . . well, I should have pulled those tomato plants up weeks ago, and now I've canned more than I could possibly eat."

She *was* flustered. Virginia regretted being short with her. "Thanks," she said. "I'm sure we'll find a use for them."

"There was one other thing," Mrs. Oldfield said.

Of course there was. But she had already decided to be nice, so they may as well have it out. "It's a fine day, Clara," she said. "Speak your piece."

"Well, it's Randy."

"What about him?"

"Not him, exactly. His driving. The way he comes through the alley, here. I'm not sure he realizes what a hazard it is."

Virginia felt her color rise. It didn't help that Mrs. Oldfield was right. "He's always been a bit spunky," she said. "Do you reckon it's gotten worse of late?"

"Well, no, to tell the truth, it hasn't. Not *worse*. But with Reverend Jacobs living now in the little house . . . He doesn't move as quickly as some, you see."

Virginia nodded. "I get your drift."

"I know you've done the best you can, raising him practically on your own. It would be a lot easier with a man around to reign him in."

Virginia smiled. Now, this was the Clara Oldfield she knew how to deal with. "Be careful what you wish for, Clara," she said, giving her a wicked wink. "Lord knows who you might end up with as a neighbor."

She got the flushed and confused reaction she was hoping for, but before she could enjoy the moment, Randy's car pulled into the alley. When it failed to make his signature skid and pulled to a quite respectable stop beside the granny house, she gave Clara Oldfield a smug smile.

Mally got out and leaned into the window on Joanie's side. "I just want to say I really had fun today," he said to the two of them. "The most fun I've had since I moved down here. Thanks."

"Sure thing," Randy said.

"We'll do it again, sometime," Joanie said.

Randy looked at her. "When?" There was that challenge in his voice that Mally had noticed when he and Joanie were talking.

She answered him back in the same way. "The first pretty day of spring."

"There aren't any pretty days in spring in Oklahoma," he said.

"All right, then," she said, "the first clear day, then."

Randy looked at Mally. "Okay?" he asked.

Mally grinned. "It's a date."

"Okay," Randy said. Mally backed away from the car and Randy put it in gear, popping back into character at the same time. "'Bye, now!" he drawled.

"G'bye!" Mally drawled back, waving extravagantly.

"G'bye! G'bye!" Joanie yelled, leaning out the passenger window.

"Now, you write when you get work, y'hear, boy?" Randy yelled from his side.

"Ah will, Poppa-daddy!" Mally hollered. "You give mah best to Aunt Sarie Bell and Annie, now, hear?"

"Aw right, aw right!" Randy honked the horn a few times as the car ambled slowly down the alley. "'Bye! 'Bye!"

"'Bye!" Joanie yelled, waving a handkerchief she pulled from somewhere. "Yoo-hoo! 'Bye! We'll send you pictures of the baby as soon as they's developed!"

Mally did his best *Beverly Hillbillies* imitation, waving frantically and hopping up and down. As soon as the car turned onto the street he dropped the act and turned around in time to see Mrs. Edom and Mrs. Oldfield staring at him in open-mouthed astonishment. He hurried into the granny house before he burst out laughing.

Virginia looked at Clara, who looked back at her with raised eyebrows.

"Well, don't look at me," Virginia said. She peered down the alley where her son's car had vanished. "Maybe I'll have a talk with that boy after all," she muttered.

52
52
52
52
RAIN 2020

Chapter 8

FATHERS

R ANDY AND JOANIE pulled up outside the Tibbitses' house. "That was fun," Joanie said, not wanting to leave the car and break the spell. "I had a real nice time. And it was really sweet of you to ask Mally."

"Y'know, he's not half bad when you get to know him," Randy said. "He's kinda fun."

"There, you see?" she said.

"If a tad strange."

She gave him a punch in the arm.

"Ow!" he said. "Thank you, very much."

"You are hopeless."

"Yeah, but you knew that already, so what's your excuse?"

For an answer, she leaned in and kissed him.

He nodded. "Good excuse."

"I suppose you have to go to work now," she said.

"Well, someone's gotta help your dad run the store."

"Right." She smiled. "Still, I hate to have it end. It's really been a most amazing day. Oh!" She suddenly pulled away from him.

"What?" he said, confused.

"A most amazing day!"

"Yes, it has been. Is that alarming?"

"No, it's just . . . did Mally give you the book?"

"What book?"

"Oh, shoot, now I've given it away. He was going to give you this book of poems."

"What for?"

"Well, I had a bet with him. He said he could get you to read a whole book of poems by Christmas."

"A bet?" Randy said, giving her a look. "Now who's hopeless?" She looked genuinely chagrined, so he pulled her over to him again. "That's okay," he said, "I've got excuses of my own."

He found the book in the back seat where Mally had left it, *100 selected poems by e e cummings*. The cover was a glaring purple and the title looked strange. He glanced through it. It didn't look like any poetry he'd ever seen. It looked like it hadn't been printed properly—nothing was capitalized or punctuated right. But he found the poem that began, "i thank You God for this most amazing day," and he had to admit it was good. It captured the day they'd had perfectly. Even the bizarre punctuation fit with their screwy play-acting. He'd have to sit down with the book and give it a try. It'd be just deserts if he could lose Joanie's bet for her.

But first he had to get to the Rexall, and not just to work in the stockroom. There was something he wanted to ask Mr. Tibbits.

The bell hanging from the door jingled merrily as he entered, reinforcing his jaunty mood. That came to an abrupt end when he saw Candy in the cosmetics aisle. She was trying on a lipstick that was way too red, even for her.

She looked up at him as he passed. "Hi, Rickie," she said.

He just nodded, said, "Hi, Candy," and continued toward the back of the store.

"Been keeping busy?" she called after him.

He stopped and turned around. "Busy enough."

Mr. Tibbits came in from the stockroom just then and headed for the prescription counter.

"Oh, Mr. Tibbits," Randy said, trying to head him off.

"Oh, there you are, Randy," Mr. Tibbits said, inspecting the label on a bottle. "How was the picnic?"

"Real nice," Randy said. "'A most amazing day.'"

Mr. Tibbits looked at him, puzzled. "Yes, isn't it. About the last we'll see of them for a while, I suspect." He returned to the prescription he was filling

"Uh, Mr. Tibbits," Randy began. John looked up and over the rim of his reading glasses. "I was wondering if . . . Football season is just about over—"

"Over? Not hardly. You've got the biggest game of the season this Friday."

"Yes, sir."

"Win against Holdenville and Croy brings home the conference. That'll be the first time in five years, you know."

"Yes, sir, I know. But after that, well, I won't have practice and there'll be more time. I was wondering if I might take on more work here."

John Tibbits put down the bottle. "Well, there's always more to do."

"And, sir," Randy swallowed hard, but what the heck, "I was wondering if it might be for a little more pay." John Tibbits just looked at him for a second. "Per hour," Randy added. He imagined Candy was looking at him, too, but he didn't break eye contact with his boss.

And after a fretful moment or two, Mr. Tibbits smiled. "Sure thing, son," he said, then he laughed. "We'll make a horse trader out of you yet."

Randy grinned. "Thank you, sir."

"Well," Tibbits said, "may as well get started. There's five crates just delivered from Ft. Worth. Put four of them in back next to the paper supplies, and open the fifth and bring the stuff out here."

"Okay," Randy grinned and practically hopped over to the storeroom. A most amazing day! He was on such a cloud he hardly noticed what he was stacking in the back room until he opened the fifth box and saw what it contained.

Christmas cards. Maybe there was some mistake; it wasn't

even Thanksgiving yet. He'd better check with Mr. Tibbits. He picked up the opened box and used his shoulder to nudge open the storeroom door.

Mr. Tibbits was standing just behind Candy, whose hand rested on the cosmetics counter, her head tilted up to look John Tibbits in the face. He was looking down at her, and his hand rested on hers.

Randy stepped back quietly, turned around, and backed loudly through the door, calling out, "Mr. Tibbits, I think there's been some mistake." Then he turned around and faced them.

John Tibbits was several feet away from Candy, his hands behind his back. Candy was engrossed in her compact.

"Are you sure this is the stuff you wanted me to put out?" Randy asked.

John walked over to him and glanced at the box. "Oh, yes. Yes, that's the stuff." He smiled broadly.

Candy was wandering over to the other side of the store.

"It just seemed a little early, is all," Randy said.

"Oh, no," John said. "You'd be surprised. Some folks around here consider it a duty to get every one of their cards out the day after Thanksgiving." He guided Randy over to the card racks, away from Candy. "You see?" he said. "I've already cleared out a space. Put up as many different kinds as will fit and put the rest down below." He slapped Randy on the back. "You know the procedure."

"Yup." Randy nodded but didn't move.

"Good," John said and nodded too. He also didn't move. "Then I'll just leave you to that," he said at last and went back to the prescription counter.

Randy watched him go. He didn't even notice Candy slip out the door until he heard the bell jingle merrily.

Virginia was waiting for her son when he got home that evening. Ordinarily, she might have spent the afternoon at the Dew Drop

Inn, but she'd seen enough and heard enough to reckon it was time to check in on her son. She had a whole line of questions ready when he came through the door, but was thrown off by the bags he was carrying.

"What's that?" she said.

"I'll get to that in a minute," Randy said. "First, I got news."

Oh, brother, she thought. *Here it comes.*

"I'm going to be working more hours at Tibbits," Randy said. "Mr. Tibbits is going to let me take on more duties. And, he's giving me a raise."

She wasn't expecting good news so she treated it like bad news. "But what about school?" she said.

"This'll be after school and weekends."

"And sports?"

Randy took a deep breath. "I'm not doing sports, Mom. Not after football." He reached into the bags—grocery bags, she now realized—and pulled out two packages wrapped in butcher paper. "They're not Porterhouse," he said, "but they're steaks. You won't have to worry about December any more."

She turned away from him and swiped a palm across her cheek. Then she drew in a deep breath, put on a light smile, and turned around to face him. "Well, then," she said, "I'd better get supper started."

Mr. Tibbits was right about the weather. It turned sharply colder on Monday, and by Tuesday brisk winds started stripping the trees of their leaves. It seemed that, having delayed for so long, the seasons decided to rush from summer through autumn into winter in a week, completing a kind of reverse creation in seven days. By the time Friday came around, the Croy Cowboys were hosting the Holdenville Warriors in an intermittent rain that felt very much like it wanted to be sleet. The town was not deterred, however, and turned out to pack the bleachers.

Joanie, Mally, and Joanie's friend Bobbie Littledeer were

among the huddled masses. It did not look good for the Cowboys, who were down eighteen to twenty with less than two minutes to go. But a series of tackle-defying runs and one Hail-Mary pass had driven the Cowboys to within twenty yards of the goal line and brought the crowd to their feet despite the cold.

"Why doesn't Ardmore call time out?" Bobbie asked. The rain had spattered her glasses, giving her a blotchy view of the game.

"Can't," Joanie said. "We used them all."

"Besides," Mally put in, "an incomplete pass stops the clock."

"How do you know he's going to pass?" Bobbie asked.

The game itself answered her question. The Croy quarterback fired the ball for a five-yard gain, but the clock kept ticking

"They're close enough to punt, aren't they?" Bobbie said. "Why don't they punt?"

"Field goal, Bobbie, not punt," Joanie corrected, her eyes riveted on the field.

"Maybe they're going for a touchdown," Mally said.

"But we could win it with a punt, couldn't we?" Bobbie asked.

Joanie shook her head in exasperation.

"Yeah," Mally said. "By just one point, but that's—"

He was interrupted by disaster. The Cowboys had tried another pass, but the Warrior defense was too solid. They rushed in and sacked the quarterback for a seven-yard loss. The Cowboys made no more progress, and Holdenville took possession on their own twenty-five yard line.

"Oh, this is hopeless," Bobbie moaned as Croy's defense took the field. "I'm cold and I'm wet and I can't see a thing."

"They'll just run the clock down," Joanie conceded as they all sat down.

But the Warriors had another idea—or at least, their quarterback did. In a fit of hubris (or perhaps to further humiliate their rivals), the Warrior quarterback faded back to pass. He didn't reckon on Red Conner, though, who blasted through the line and came charging at him. The quarterback cocked his arm and fired the ball, but Red's arm batted it and it shot straight up in the air. When it came down, it came down in Red's arms. The crowd was on its feet again. He had a seventeen-yard dash to make it to the goal line.

But just as he began his sprint, the struggling quarterback caught him by the heel. He stumbled, sprawled forward, and the ball popped out of his hands. A Warrior promptly fell on it and hunkered down, buried under a pile of uniforms from both schools.

That did it. Holdenville did the smart thing and sat on the ball for the next two plays until the clock ran out.

"Another fantastic season down the tubes," Bobbie said as they slouched down the bleachers. "Are you going home?"

"No," Joanie said. "I'm waiting here for Randy. He said he wouldn't be long."

Mally hung back.

Bobbie scanned the thinning crowd. "Well, there's my parents," she said. "I'd better get going." She shuffled off through the crowd.

"I'd better go, too," Mally said.

"Why don't you wait?" Joanie said. "I'm sure Randy will give you a ride. You don't want to walk home in this mess."

Mally looked up at the streaks of rain falling like lances through the stadium lights. "Thanks," he said. Then he looked at the field. "Hey, what's that?"

Down on the field, two Croy football players still lingered. One was kneeling with his head practically bowed to the ground, the other one was standing beside him, a hand on his shoulder.

Red huddled on the field, the hardening rain ticking against his helmet beside him on the ground. "C'mon, Red," Randy said gently.

His friend was holding his head in his hands and shaking. "I had it, I had it!" Red kept saying.

"Let's get inside, buddy," Randy said. "Take a shower, shake it off."

A tall man in a raincoat come onto the field and stood next to them—Red's father.

"He'll be all right, Mr. Conner," Randy said to him. "He just needs to—"

"Thank you, Randy," Mr. Conner said dismissively. "I can take it from here." He turned to his son. "Get up, Richard."

Randy backed off. He looked toward the sidelines, where he saw Joanie and Mally waiting.

"Son, you're making a spectacle of yourself," Mr. Conner said, a little harder this time. Red continued with his face buried in his hands.

Randy leaned forward. "If you want, I can—"

Mr. Conner ignored him. "Richard, stand up!" he barked. "Act your age."

Red's face snapped up at that, came out of its cage to stare at his father. Randy had never seen such an expression on his face before. The rain pelted it with ice water, but it was steaming hot. He looked angry and betrayed and helpless all at once.

Mr. Conner turned to Randy. "Your friends are waiting for you," he said. "I can take Richard home."

Randy backed away, then turned and joined Joanie and Mally. But he felt badly all evening about leaving Red on that cold, friendless field.

The storm grew worse overnight, covering the entire state with a slick sheet of ice. There were downed power lines and centennial oaks snapped in two and any number of roadside fatalities—among them, Marcus Longacre's father, whose worn-out Dodge was found wedded to a bridge abutment on the road from Napier Corners. From the looks of it, he had been in an awful hurry to get home.

As the weather grew colder, Randy started giving Mally rides to school on a regular basis.

"Are you sure you don't want to drop me off a couple blocks away?" Mally asked.

"What for?"

"I mean, you know, those guys . . ."

Randy waved away the notion. "Aw, let 'em think what they think."

Mally got to be such a regular visitor at the Edom's, even on Saturdays when Randy was at work, that he and Randy's mother struck up a friendship. The benefits were mutual. Mally enjoyed Virginia's racy stories and her frank opinions about people—so different from his grandfather's diffidence and Mrs. Oldfield's cryptic Bible quotations—and Virginia got to pump Mally for details of her son's life she wouldn't have dared ask Randy herself. It was from Mally that she got the full story of the picnic on the hill.

"It's a nice little spot, isn't it?" Virginia said, cleaning up after a Saturday breakfast of coffee, toast, and last year's not very successful lemon-lime marmalade. "Too bad it'll never amount to much as a farm. But who knows?" She started filling the single-well sink. "Croy's growing. They just put that subdivision in five years ago and it's already filling up. Maybe the next big boom will be out in that direction."

Mally handed the plates to her. Breakfast here was sparser than the ones he usually served Grandfather, and he thought those had been pretty meager. "You gave up a lot to be married," he said.

"Oh, not so much as you'd think. I'd've given up more by playing by the rules. Besides, I got what I wanted. Or what I thought I wanted, anyway."

"Why did you do it, go against your folks and all?"

"For spite, I guess. No, not really. I guess I saw more in Harry than most folks did."

Mally got the towel that hung on the refrigerator door and started drying the dishes. "Did you think you'd change him?" he asked.

"Harry Edom?" Virginia snorted, which was her way of laughing. "Good Lord, no. I knew what I was getting into there."

"So you knew it wouldn't work out."

Virginia stared into the space above the sink. "Sometimes you get attracted to things, to people, even though you know it's not gonna turn out right. Sometimes, that pull is so deep, so alive, and it pulls you right from your middle, right where you don't have any defenses, and there's nothing you can do but fall right into it up to your neck and holler." She looked down and pulled the plug out of the drain. "Sometimes, that's enough." She leaned back against the sink and lit up a cigarette. "Sometimes, that's all you get."

Mally finished drying the dishes in silence, then returned the towel to its rack and sat down. Virginia was looking at him, but he was getting used to that.

"You're a deep kid, you know that?" she said. "Like your father."

"Did you know him?" he asked.

"Yeah," she said and sat down across from him. "Though he was a hard guy to figure out. Kind, yet sorta distant. A perfectionist when it came to his music. I like to think we were friends, but nobody knew him really well, except your momma. I think she's the only one really tried."

"What happened to him?"

"Didn't she tell you?"

"I thought for a long time that maybe they were married at first but got divorced when I came along."

Virginia looked shocked. "What on earth gave you that idea?"

Mally shrugged. "Well, there's my name. There's a verse in there, in Malachi, 'The Lord hates divorce.' I thought maybe they named me that because of it."

Virginia frowned, looking angry. "Oh, no, sweetie," she said. "You mustn't think that. It wasn't anything like that. Your folks wouldn't shame you like that." She patted his hand. "Your momma surely wouldn't."

He looked her in the eye. "So, what happened?"

She withdrew her hand. "She never told you?"

"No one ever mentions my father's name," he said. He was surprised by the bitterness in his voice. "All the time growing up, I never heard it. I knew it, of course. Andy Simms. Simms, not Jacobs. But no one ever talked about it, or him. That's why I got to thinking it must be something shameful like that, like divorce, or that he was already married, or he ran off before I was born, or maybe because I was born. And then Mrs. Oldfield said—"

Virginia got up. "Don't you believe a single word that old bag tells you, hear?" She paced the tiny kitchen and waved her cigarette in the air, seeming to have an argument with herself. Finally, she said, "Oh, I shouldn't be telling you this, but somebody's got to." She sat down at the table again and looked him in the eyes. "Your daddy died before you were born. It was an accident, a real tragedy. It happened right here in town. He and your momma were out riding in his car late one night and—and there was an accident."

"What kind of accident?"

"Oh, Mally—"

"Please."

She looked at him and knew he wasn't going to back down. "A train," she said. "Your mother was thrown free and lived, but your father— Everyone was so upset. They took it really hard down at the church. Everybody loved him so." She took his hand again. There were tears running down his face. "So, you see, he didn't run off or leave you or divorce your mother before you were born or anything like that. It was just an accident. And not his fault, either. Everyone says that. That crossing should have had a signal, but it didn't and it still doesn't." She stubbed out her cigarette. "Even after all that, they never fixed it. Typical."

Mally thanked her quietly, and inwardly drank in the details.

Three days before Christmas, Joanie and her mother and little brother made a last shopping trip around the square. They all had different motives for stopping in at the drugstore. Joanie was hoping for a chance to chat with Randy, who was now working so many hours they barely got to see each other during the week. She knew her mother was looking for some last minute gift wrapping. Lord only knew why they had to drag the Bean along, except that they didn't dare leave him at home. He'd ransack the house for presents for sure.

Her mother picked up one of the few remaining boxes of Christmas cards. "I swear this is the same design that's left on the shelf every year. Lord knows why your father orders it. Nobody ever buys it."

"Maybe its the same box, year after year," Joanie said. "You should buy it and put it out of its misery."

"And bring it home to roost? No, thank you. I'm just after a bit of ribbon and some Scotch tape."

Joanie looked around the store. Kyle was conveniently ensnared by the comic book stand and seemed to be in no immediate danger of setting the store on fire. She saw Randy behind the register. "Um, if you want me, I'll be over there, okay?" she said and left before her mother could answer.

Ruth just smiled and shook her head. She looked at the card again. Annoyed and perspiring elves were trying to shove a sketchy Christmas tree into a sack under a sleeping Santa. She had no idea why.

"Good afternoon, Mrs. Tibbits," Mrs. Oldfield said, cruising toward her down the aisle. Mally followed behind, looking like one of the disgruntled elves.

Ruth smiled politely. "Good afternoon, Mrs. Oldfield, Mally. And Merry Christmas to you both."

Mrs. Oldfield handed a small box to Mally. "Malachi, would you have Mr. Tibbits gift wrap this please? Thank you."

Mally suspected that gift wrapping was done by the store staff, not the pharmacist, but he wasn't about to argue the point and miss his chance to escape.

Randy was ringing up a sale when Joanie walked up to him. He flashed her a big grin. "Hi."

"Hi," she said. "Been promoted, huh?"

"I'd hardly call it that," he said. "I always thought Christmas was fun, but from behind here, it's pure hell on wheels. This last week I've had to stay past closing an hour-and-a-half, two hours each night."

"Oh, poor baby."

"Maybe not so poor," Randy said. "Your dad pays me time and a half."

"Well, maybe you'll buy the store soon and Daddy can retire." She turned around and said, "Hey," as Mally walked up to them.

"Hey, yerself," Mally said, then turned to Randy. "Excuse me, sir, but do you think I might be able to get this gift wrapped?"

"But of course!" Randy gestured expansively. "You are looking at the Wizard of Wrapping-dom."

"Excellent!"

"And may I ask if this is to be on your account, sir?"

"Ah, no. On that of my employer." He turned to Joanie with mock deference. "A kindly old widow, name of Oldfield."

Joanie nodded sagely.

"Ah, yes," Randy said. "I know her well. And what color do you think might be to her liking—red and green? yellow? pink?"

Mally looked over the assortment as if he were selecting a cheese by its smell, then he shook his head. "No, none of these. Do you have something in black?"

They settled on a dark green paper—close enough—and thin white ribbon teased into curls. "Like frost on a window," Joanie said.

"Do what?" Randy said.

"Never mind," she said. "Hey, what are you two guys doing Christmas Eve? I mean, the afternoon of."

"Well," Mally said, making a dour face, "me and Grandfather

have been invited up to the Big House for supper. Seems the Widow Oldfield has something special cooked up for us."

"What'll that be?" Joanie asked.

"Haven't the foggiest. Stuffed lizards and sauerkraut, most like."

"Mmm, yummy," Randy said, handing over the finished package. "Your father the slave driver has us working until four," he said to Joanie, "but after that, nothing much. Mom and I are going to have a quiet Christmas at home." He turned to Mally, "We've given the servants the night off."

"Most generous of you," Mally said and bowed.

"So," Joanie said, "why don't the two of you come over to my place, you know, later, after you get off work, Randy. We could exchange gifts then."

Randy grinned. "Sure," he said. He'd have to buy one real quick, but he could swing that.

Mally looked uncertain. "I'm not sure," he said.

"Your grandfather will be up at Mrs. Oldfield's, right?" Joanie said.

"That's just the thing," Mally said and looked at them with a sickly smile. "I'm not sure I trust the two of them alone."

"Oh, gross," Randy said. "I don't even want to think about that."

"Oh, come on," Joanie coaxed. "It'll be fun. Better than watching wrinkles grow."

Mally laughed. "Okay."

"Terrific!"

Mally grinned and headed back to the aisle where he'd left Mrs. Oldfield. He heard her before he saw her, one aisle over, still talking to Mrs. Tibbits.

"Joanie has certainly grown into a fine young lady," Mrs. Oldfield was saying to Ruth. "Reminds me of you, a little bit."

"Why, thank you," Ruth said.

"Been seeing quite a bit of Randy Edom lately, hasn't she?"

"They have taken a shine to each other,"

"Yes," Mrs. Oldfield said. "You know, they say like father,

like son. I certainly hope the same isn't true for sons and mothers."

Mally stopped in his tracks. He was on one side of the card rack, they were on the other. They hadn't seen him. He crouched down and pretended to inspect the few remaining Christmas cards.

"What do you mean?" Ruth said.

"Well, you certainly must know how Virginia Edom conducts herself about town," Mrs. Oldfield said.

"I haven't made it my business to know how Virginia Edom conducts herself," Ruth said. "I do know her son has always been polite and respectful to me and my daughter."

"That's a comfort. After all, she is a pretty young lady, as I've said."

"And as I've thanked you for."

Mrs. Oldfield persisted. "I just hate to see her make the same tragic mistake, that's all."

"And what mistake might that be?"

"I was just suggesting—"

"I know how to look after my own family, Mrs. Oldfield."

"I'm quite sure you do," Mrs. Oldfield said. "But I seem to recall a verse that says a woman can be the moral standard for her—"

"I know Scripture quite well, Mrs. Oldfield. You needn't quote it to me."

"I just thought perhaps a fresh perspective . . . I know I'm not telling you anything you don't already know."

"Then why bother speaking at all? I also seem to recall a verse about women and silence and how they might profit by it."

"Please don't take offense—"

"My husband will not be hounded into an early grave," Ruth Tibbits said. "Good day, Mrs. Oldfield."

Mrs. Tibbits rounded the corner and headed for the cash register. Mally didn't think she saw him—in fact, he didn't think she saw much of anything in front of her at the moment. He grabbed a box of Christmas cards for an alibi and came around the corner.

"Well, it's about time," Mrs. Oldfield said as he walked up to her.

"I thought these—" Mally said, holding out the cards.

"Oh, for heaven's sake, no, Malachi," She snatched them from his hand and put them back on the shelf. "Not those ugly things."

Randy locked up the store at 4:01 PM Christmas Eve and hurried home to wash and then pick up Mally before heading over to Joanie's. His mother was in the living room when he got home. He shouted a "Hi, Mom," and was headed for the bathroom when she called out to him.

"Randy, would you come in here a minute?"

She sounded serious so he went in right away. "What's up, Mom?" he said. "Something wrong?"

"Sit down, son," she said.

She wasn't smoking, he noticed, and there was a paper folded up on the coffee table. He sat next to her on the sofa, a frown beginning to form.

She smiled and waved her hand. "No," she said, "there's nothing wrong." She looked at him steadily. "We've been through a lot, kiddo," she said, "and sometimes it seemed like we were just two kids growing up at the same time. And sometimes, I want to tell you, it felt like I was pulling the whole world around on my shoulders, all by myself."

Randy opened his mouth to speak but she held up a hand.

"But not lately," she said. "You've really pulled your weight around here. And I know it hasn't been easy. I know you've had to give things up, like basketball, and hanging out with the guys," she gave him a lopsided smile, "and girls."

He blushed and looked away.

"I don't have much," she said, "but I thought it was time I gave up something, too. Something that showed you I trusted you and appreciated what you've been doing around here. And even if it's nearly a year till you turn eighteen, there's something I want to give you that tells you that, in my eyes, you're already a man."

She pushed the papers toward him.

"What's this?" he asked.

"It's the deed to the old farm, that little place on the hill outside of town," she said. "It's in your name, now."

"Mom," he said. "Mom . . . " and he couldn't think of anything else to say.

She sidled over to him and gave him a hug. "Now, you wash up and get going," she said. "You don't want to keep Mally and Joanie waiting." He got up and she swatted him on the butt. "And be back by 6:30. I've got a real dinner planned."

He grinned down at her. "Spanish rice and beans?"

"Oh, get out of here before I snatch that deed back!" she said.

All the lights were on at the Tibbitses' house, including a grandly decorated blue spruce in the front room. The combination of fresh pine and supper cooking was enough to make your stomach growl, but Randy and Mally were amply stuffed with cookies to take their minds off it. Kyle had been banished to his room from some unspeakable transgression, which was just as well. He would not have understood why Randy, Mally, and his sister were about to open their presents when he would have to wait a whole two hours and a dinner besides before he got his hands on his.

Mrs. Tibbits brought a plate loaded with Mexican tea cakes into the living room.

"Oh, please, Mrs. Tibbits," Mally said, "I couldn't eat another bite."

"Bring them right over here, ma'am," Randy said.

"After all those ginger snaps?" Joanie said.

"Now, dear," Mrs. Tibbits said, "that's what they're for. Why don't you three go ahead and open your presents for each other?"

She looked hopefully at the front door. "I don't know what's keeping your father."

Mally was reaching for a tea cake but stopped.

"You said he made a delivery over to Liddle," Joanie said, looking at Randy.

"Uh, yeah," Randy said, his words a little muffled by powdered sugar. He turned to Mrs. Tibbits. "He really should be along any minute now. He left around two and told me to lock up at four."

Ruth smiled. "Well, you go ahead anyway. I'll bring y'all some hot cider. He probably just got to talking with somebody and forgot all about the time."

They sat in a circle on the floor and Joanie played Santa Claus, handing out the gifts. It was a short stack, just one present each. That had been Joanie's scheme: she and Randy had gone in together to get Mally's present (so Randy wouldn't feel all weird about buying another guy a gift), and she and Mally had gone in together to get Randy's present (so Mally wouldn't have to stretch his budget buying two). She was on tenterhooks wondering what the two guys had gotten for her. She hefted the small rectangular package in her hand.

Randy ripped into his present, ribbons and paper flying in all directions, but Mally just sat there, cross-legged on the floor, holding his and staring into space.

"You'll find out quicker if you take the wrapping off," Joanie said.

"Huh?"

She pointed. "Your present."

"Oh," Mally said. "You know, I feel funny."

"What?" Joanie said. "Doesn't your family open presents on Christmas Eve?"

"No, it's not that," Mally said. "I mean, no we don't, but that's not why I feel funny. I feel like I *should* feel funny, but I don't. It's the first Christmas I've spent away from my mom. I should feel kinda sad. But instead, it's like I've been doing it this way all my life. So it feels perfectly natural. And that feels funny." He turned to Joanie. "That make sense?"

"Not a whit."

Mally nodded. "I didn't think so."

"Oh, wow!" Randy said, opening an intricate box. "A watch!"

Joanie grinned and Mally said, "Joanie thought you'd be running the store soon."

"So you'd better run it on time," Joanie added.

"Thanks, guys."

Joanie went next. Her small package proved to be a book. "Ohhh," she said dreamily, "*Sonnets from the Portuguese*."

"You can thank Mally for that suggestion," Randy said. "I didn't even know you spoke Portuguese."

"It's not *in* Portuguese, silly, it's—" then Joanie caught the twinkle in Randy's eye and stopped herself.

Randy grinned. "Gotcha," he said.

Mrs. Tibbits came in with a tray of mugs. "Here we are," she said and placed the tray on the coffee table. The front door opened and they all turned to the hall as a blast of cold air entered the room, followed by John Tibbits. "Hi there!" he boomed cheerily.

"Daddy!" Joanie called.

"Hey, there, Princess." He took his coat off. "Boy, it's getting cold out there. It'll snow for sure."

"There's some hot cider out in the kitchen," Ruth said. "I'll get it for you."

She began to head for the kitchen but John intercepted her. "No," he said, "I'll take mine in the dining room." He grinned at the young people in the living room. "Nice to see all of you again. Merry Christmas."

Randy and Mally chorused "Merry Christmas" back at him and watched him follow his wife into the dining room.

Joanie looked at her friends in consternation. "Well, don't just sit there," she said. "Mally, you're next, and yours is the largest."

"Where were you?" Ruth's voice came from the other room. "I was worried."

"Over to Liddle," John said. "Didn't Randy tell you?"

"For three hours?"

"The roads were a little slick."

Mally picked at the ribbons and tape delicately, trying to save the paper

"Don't be so timid," Randy said. "Rip right in."

A loud voice rang from the dining room: "I don't have to tell you where I am every minute of the day."

Joanie's face fell. "Uh-oh."

They all waited a moment, then Mally ripped through the rest of the wrapping paper in a display of enthusiasm. He was genuinely amazed at what was revealed: a star atlas. "Wow," he said.

"I remember how much you missed looking at the stars with your friend," Joanie said.

"I didn't even know they made such things," Randy said.

A door slammed loudly. The friends sat in silence another moment, looking at their presents and not each other.

Joanie sighed and hung her head. "Look, guys, maybe you should be going. I'm sorry."

Mally reached out to her. "It's not your fault," he said.

"I thought at least on the holidays . . ." she said.

Randy scooted over and gave her a hug. "Well," he said, "we had a nice time, anyway."

Randy and Mally were silent most of the ride back. Finally, Randy said, "Do you think she knows?"

Mally looked at him a moment. "Knows what?"

"About her father," Randy said with a quick look at Mally.

Mally sighed. "No. I think she just thinks her parents argue a lot lately. I don't think she knows why." He looked at Randy. "I didn't think you did, either."

He shook his head. "I didn't at first. I guess I didn't really want to. But then I saw them in the store." Mally looked at him. "Mr. Tibbits and Candy Sullivan."

"Oh," Mally said, "so that's who. Oh, jeez."

Randy shook his head again. "You'd think he'd be more careful, with me working there and all. I bet it's her fault, mostly. She just eggs him on."

"It's gotta be him some, too," Mally said. "It can't just be one-sided."

Randy frowned. "Yeah. I guess you're right."

They rode in silence. As they turned onto Choctaw, Mally said, "You think we should tell her?"

Randy thought about it, opened his mouth to speak, then changed his mind. "Naw," he said, "It's a family matter. Between her mom and her dad."

Mally looked at Randy for several seconds, then turned and looked out the window. The car cut silently through the night, light snow and blowing dirt ticking on the windshield. They said nothing more until they arrived, then just muttered, "See ya's."

Randy's mother had been cooking up a storm in his absence. He could smell the roast pork and something sweet—yams in brown sugar, maybe—as he crossed the back porch. For the first time in several months, he felt better about coming home than about being anywhere else.

He stepped inside and came to a sudden halt. Virginia was sitting at the table in a tight knot, pulling on a cigarette. A warning flashed from her eyes. There was someone else in the kitchen, a man sitting with his back to the door. He turned around like a cat stretching to look at Randy as he entered and a big smile spread over his face.

"Hello, son," he said. "Merry Christmas."

Chapter 9

THE PRIDE OF YOUR HEART

R ANDY STOOD IN the doorway. "Hello," he said.
Harry raised his eyebrows. "Hello? Is that all?" He turned
to Virginia. "What've you done, turned him into a zombie?"

His mother crushed out her cigarette. "He's probably gone
into shock. Like the rest of us," she said.

His dad turned back around. "Well, don't stand there, blocking up the door. Come in, come in, sit down."

Randy eased over to the table and sat down warily.

"Bet you thought it'd be a long time before you saw me
again, eh?" Harry said.

"It's been a long time," Randy said.

"It's been four years, Harry," Virginia said. She got up from
the table and began setting out the dinner plates—three places,
Randy noted.

"Has it?" Harry asked. He turned and grinned at his son.
"Ginnie tells me you've made varsity on the football team."

"Yeah, I did," Randy said. "Our last game was a couple of
weeks ago."

"Sorry I missed it," Harry said. "That would have been real
nice, to see my boy out there on the field." He stretched expansively as Virginia started serving supper. "They was just blasting
the cut through the hills then, though, and I was real busy. Hey,"
he leaned forward with an eager expression, "you remember
when me and you tried clearing those stumps out on the farm?"

Randy had to smile. "Yeah," he said.

"Two of you nearly blew up the whole county," Virginia added with a snort.

"That was nothin' compared to what we did to them hills," Harry said. "I tell ya, that turnpike's gonna be a marvel, a real marvel."

With supper before them, the reunion gradually grew more relaxed and social. Harry told them more stories about working on the turnpike; Randy told his dad some of the highlights of the football season; Virginia griped about lazy management and the cut in hours out at the paper products plant. Over a surprise dessert of apple dumplings (when did his mother have time to make those? Randy wondered) Harry volunteered that he was on holiday "break" from the Oklahoma Transportation Agency for about a week.

Randy shot his mother a glance, but she was just getting up to clear the dishes. "So, what are you going to do, then?" Randy asked.

"I thought I'd stick around here a bit," Harry said. "Get reacquainted with my boy."

"He doesn't turn eighteen till next year, Harry," Virginia said from the sink.

Randy saw his dad's face fall and the glint leave his eyes.

"That's a little hard, Virginia," Harry said quietly.

"Well, it's been a little hard around here," Virginia said. "Especially without the support."

Harry nodded. "I aim to fix that," he said. "This is good money they're paying me. You'll get the support payments regular again, you'll see. And the alimony, too."

"The alimony can go to hell," Virginia said. She turned around and looked at him. Something flickered across her face, like she was ashamed to let him see her like this. She softened. "But the support will be welcome."

"Where you gonna stay?" Randy asked.

"Don't know," Harry said. "They was all booked at the Claremont." He chuckled. "No room at the inn."

Virginia laughed out loud at that. "If you're the Virgin Mary," she said, "I hate to think what that makes me." She leaned against the sink and lit up a cigarette. She took a thoughtful drag and said, "Why don't you stay here?"

Harry looked at her, thunderstruck, then looked at his son and raised his eyebrows.

Virginia saw that. "On the sofa, lummox," she said and swatted him with the dish towel.

When her back was turned again, Harry leaned in and stage-whispered to his son, "It's the miracle of Christmas."

The snowfall had been barely enough to frost the lawns and alleyways. By the time Mally woke on Christmas morning, it was already steaming from the rooftops and sidewalks. Nevertheless, Mrs. Oldfield judged it hazardous enough to offer to drive Reverend Jacobs to services at Mt. Hermon. She even offered to take Mally the extra six blocks to St. Elizabeth's, an act of Christian charity, Mally thought, that must have been at war with her anti-Papist sentiments. He thanked her at the door and said they would get back to her directly, and she marched primly back up to her house, stepping carefully in the footprints she had made coming down.

"You'd think I broke my legs last summer, not my wrist," his grandfather said with a chuckle.

"Why don't you take her up on it?" Mally said. "It's Christmas, after all. Letting her do something for you would be like giving her a gift."

His grandfather smiled. "You've a sharp eye, Mally," he said. "How about you?"

"I think I'll walk," he said, turning away and looking out the window. "I kinda like the way the snow has brightened everything up. It'll all be gone by the time Mass is over."

His grandfather looked at him standing at the window a while but said nothing.

Randy slept longer than he meant to. His bedroom was just off the kitchen, and the smell of bacon and coffee tickled his senses awake. He slumped out of bed and entered the kitchen still in his underwear. His mother was at the stove, pouring grease from the skillet into a jar.

"Whatcha makin'?" he asked.

"Breakfast," she said, cracking some eggs into the skillet. "What's it look like?"

Randy glanced at the clock on the stove. It was nearly eleven. "Looks like lunch," he said.

"Yeah? Well, I didn't see you up with the cows, either."

Randy sat at the table and rubbed his face, trying to wake up. He glanced at the doorway to the living room, wondering if talking about last night would make it any more real. "Is he still in there?" he asked.

"Yep. Sleeping."

A bear-like "Aw-r-r-r" came from the living room just then and a crooked smile crossed Virginia's face. "Well, anyway, was," she said.

"What's he want?" Randy asked.

Virginia turned and frowned at him, but the frown passed into a shrug. "He says he's doing fine, that the OTA's got him signed on till spring."

"You believe him?"

Virginia poked at the eggs. "No reason not to."

"That'd be a first."

Virginia turned to him, eyes flashing. "Now just one minute, buster," she said. "What I think of him, that's one thing. But you still treat him with respect, you hear?"

Randy nodded, not looking at her. "Yeah."

"He's your father. He may not be much, but he's all you got."

"Yeah."

She waved the spatula at him. "And put some clothes on, will ya? It's Christmas, for Christ's sake."

Randy headed back to his room, snagging a piece of cooling bacon from the stove. His clothes lay scattered where he had dropped them the night before. He sniffed his undershirt, decided it was fit for wear, and slipped into it, holding the bacon in his teeth. The socks were past their prime, though; he fished a fresh pair out of the top drawer of his dresser. He crawled into his jeans and was thinking about a shirt when he noticed his letter jacket lying on the floor. He picked it up and was headed for the closet when a bunch of papers fell out.

"What's that?" a voice asked from the doorway.

Randy turned to see his father in bluejeans, plaid cowboy shirt, and a bolo tie standing in the doorway. Randy scooped the papers up from the floor. He had meant to show Joanie and Mally the deed last night, but they'd never gotten around to it. "It's nothing," he said. He shoved it under the socks and closed the dresser drawer.

"That's your letter jacket, isn't it?" his dad asked, coming into the room.

"Yeah." Randy held it out for him to look at.

Harry spread it open, looking at the pins on the large "C" on the front. "So," he said, "that one'd be for football, right?"

"Right," Randy said, smiling.

"And the other?"

"Track."

"Not basketball, huh?" Harry said, smiling wanly. "Me, neither. Track, though. I was good at that. The 440. Didn't get no letter, though." He smiled at his son. "I'd've liked to see you win that."

Randy blushed and put the jacket in his closet.

"I wish I'd been around more, son," Harry said. "I mean, what man wouldn't want to see his kid grow up? But you know how things are."

"Yeah, sure," Randy said.

"Harry?" Virginia called from the kitchen. "Get your coat on. We're going out."

Both men turned at once and said, "What?"

"You heard me, Edom," came the reply.

Harry and Randy filed into the kitchen. Randy's mother was already dressed in her camel coat. "But it's Christmas, Virginia," Harry said.

"We've got things to talk about," she said.

"So do me and my boy, here," Harry said.

Virginia cocked her head and raised one eyebrow.

"Okay," Harry said, "I know that look." He turned to Randy. "Hate to leave you all by your lonesome—"

"There's breakfast on the stove, Randy," his mother said. She turned to Harry. "Are you coming or not?" she said and headed out the front door.

Harry shrugged helplessly at Randy and hurried after her.

The kitchen was suddenly quiet. Randy could hear his father's truck start up and pull away. There was enough breakfast—or lunch or whatever—for three people on the stove, but Randy wasn't hungry. He went back into his room and pulled on his letter jacket. He picked a battered basketball out of a heap of clothes in the corner and went out the back door.

The snow was just patches hiding in corners and shadows by now. The alley was scarcely wet where it had melted. He bounced the ball a couple of times on the packed cinders in front of the pole and shot a few baskets. The ball made an almost metallic sound on each bounce, an empty ringing. He looked across the alley. Would Mally be home? Or off at church? He turned and took another shot at the basket and missed. Probably off at church. Like everybody else.

Mally hadn't actually been to Mass since his second month in Croy. St. Elizabeth's was a few blocks north of the town square, no farther than the high school, really, so it wasn't the walk that kept him from going. He'd never been strongly attached to the faith, that was all. It had been his Aunt Margaret's idea to raise him a Catholic despite his mother's antipathy toward organized religion. It had been Margaret who enrolled him in St. Albert's, where he remained a perpetual outsider by virtue of his mother's refusal to participate in any of the rituals that would have bound him to the Church or normalized him in the eyes of his classmates. His short stint on the freshman football team hadn't helped either.

One sunny October Sunday, miles away from Aunt Margaret in both body and spirit, he approached the doors of St. Elizabeth's as High Mass was about to start and just kept going past the parish church and on to the vacant lot with the abandoned Conoco station behind the hospital. He felt no great tearing away, nor had he any real fear of imperiling his immortal soul— though his intuition kept him from mentioning the change in routine to his grandfather.

Sunday mornings became his secret time, when he wasn't his grandfather's caretaker or his landlady's handyman or his schoolmates' peculiar chum or target of convenience. While the rest of Croy was safely closed up in their separate congregations, Mally roamed the back streets and outskirts of the city and down its alleys, where he discovered the exposed details of family life not visible from the street-facing porches. He explored most of the abandoned buildings in town, from the empty house on the corner to the roofless church lurking like a beached ship in a tangle of cottonwoods on the edge of the White Horse. He tested locks on chain-link fences and snuck in through carelessly closed side doors. He crept quietly through the Sunday stillness of the court house until he found the trap door to the belvedere and looked out over the rooftops and steeples of the town. He'd roamed as far as the farm house on the hill where they'd had the picnic, and he'd peered in through its dusty windows at the small barren rooms with an odd feeling of hope.

And so on this Christmas he knew just where he wanted to go. He entered the Santa Fe right-of-way where Choctaw crossed the tracks and headed north. He passed the water tower and the ever-cycling oil pump. He crossed Marlow and Chickasaw and Osage streets in the center of town, where the signals had recently been replaced with gates that swung down their flashing lights twice a day. No street crossed the tracks north of Osage, for there had once been a rail yard on this side of town. The steel had been pulled up long ago and nothing was left beside the main line except the ties, still embedded in the earth where nothing but the meanest weeds saw fit to grow. He passed the building he called "the Depot" because it still had a sign nailed to its side, the word "CROY" decipherable only in the difference in how the wood had weathered. He passed "the Tool shed," full of rusting and incomprehensible machinery. He passed the long, low building with boarded-up windows and a concrete ramp at one end—still on his list of sites to explore— and came finally to the last street to cross the tracks at the northern edge of town.

He stood there a while and looked at it, this transition point, with the town laid out in neat rectangles behind him and the prairie rolling away before him, where Post Street on his left became Tyrola Road on his right as it crossed the tracks and hooked northeastward toward the Shawnee Hills, the only crossing in town unguarded by a signal.

He knew of the cemetery, too, on the other side of the road, and had found the marker with his father's name. There was nothing distinctive about it. He had read everything he could lay his hands on in the city library about what had happened that night, and he had paced out the site of the accident, the place in the ditch where his mother had been found, even found some glass and twisted metal along the tracks that might have been relics of the fatal crash. Or they might have been mere random bits of trash. They didn't speak to him, or whisper his name, or tell him the truth. Unlike the town, they didn't bother to lie.

After a while, he turned around and started walking back

along Front Street. He saw no one except Marcus Longacre, who, in black leather jacket and blue jeans, was furiously and repeatedly kicking the door to a wooden shed that seemed about to collapse. "Fucker!" he shouted into the crisp Christmas air with each kick. "Fucker! Fucker! Fucker!"

Virginia stirred her coffee and looked out the window, a cigarette burning idly in her hand. Harry was in the restroom, washing his hands. He'd said he hadn't had time before they left the house, but that was fine. It gave her time to collect her thoughts.

They'd pulled into the Denny's on the south end of town. Virginia knew the cafe would be open, even today. She knew all the spots around Croy where you could get a cup of coffee or a drink any hour of the day or night. Yep, she was a real treasure trove of useful facts. Now if she could just get them out of her mouth without jumping down Harry's throat.

The girl with the menus and water glasses came by and gave Virginia a cheerful "Happy Holidays" before returning to her post behind the cash register. That greeting struck Virginia as a tad odd. "Happy Holidays," not "Merry Christmas." Was Croy turning cosmopolitan?

She looked at the blond teenager—she assumed she was a teenager, though Lord knows everyone was beginning to look like a teenager to her these days—and was further intrigued when a black boy, also in a Denny's uniform, joined her behind the counter. Virginia looked around the restaurant. Not a single head turned to marvel at this great wonder. Black and white children were working side by side as if generations had not died striving to prevent that very thing. "The miracle of Denny's," Virginia muttered to herself.

Harry came back from the washroom just then and slid into the booth across from her. "Well," he said, "here I am, all bright and shiny."

Virginia tapped her cigarette on the side of the ashtray.

"Look," she said, "I don't know how to put this any way that don't sound harsh, but I need to say it and you need to hear it."

"You were always straight with me, Ginnie," Harry said. "There's no need to pull your punches now."

She took a drag on her cigarette and looked at him squarely. "It's great that you're working again and it's great you had time to come visit us."

Harry smiled. "So far, so good."

"Shut up," she said. "I said it's great and I mean it's great for Randy. But you can't just come waltzing in and out of his life. If you're going to be around, then be around. Don't get his hopes up one minute and then disappear the next. And don't you be coming around if it's just to butter him up to hand over his money the minute that trust fund kicks in."

Harry looked away and seemed to be holding back his words. Finally, he faced her. "Boy, your Daddy really did a number on you, didn't he?" he said. "Even dead, old Lerner's managing to tell you I'm no good for you or for Randy, that I can't even take care of my own boy without picking his pocket."

"Harry, I've been through too many of your get-rich-quick schemes not to smell one a mile away."

"Virginia—"

She cut him off. "You say you're working for the OTA now?"

"Sure am."

"For how long?"

"Till March."

"Then what?"

"I got plans."

"Do they include us?"

Harry looked out the window.

Virginia stubbed out her cigarette. "You see, now? That's just what I mean. Randy's turning into a real neat kid and I don't want you screwing that up."

Harry nodded. "Fair enough." He looked her in the eyes. "How about you?"

"What about me?"

"How about me waltzing in and out of your life? You got any feelings about that?"

Virginia tried to shake off the question. "I'm not concerned about me."

"I am," Harry said.

Now that stumped her.

"I know I ain't been the best, or the most constant provider," Harry said. "But I meant it, what I said last night. You're going to see regular payments, and you're going to see all that back alimony, too. I mean it this time. It's going to take me a while to swing it, but I'm going to do it."

She eyed him askance. "If you say, 'Trust me on this,' I swear to God, Harry Edom, I'll kick your ass so hard you'll be spitting shoe polish."

"No," he said soberly. "Don't trust me. Watch me."

And she did, all through their Grand Slams with the weird little Christmas touches in the garnish. He talked and joked and told stories about the near criminal stupidity of his crew foreman, and she still wasn't buying it. When they went to pay the bill and he said, "I'll get it," she softened a little, but there was still a touch more suspicion in her "Thanks" than gratitude. But then, just as he was holding the door open for her to leave, she turned and looked back at the two kids behind the counter.

"Look at them," she said, nodding in their direction.

"Hmm?" Harry said, not quite sure what he was supposed to be looking at.

"You'd think they'd been doing that all their lives. They probably have no idea what we went through. No idea how hard it was to do something as simple as that."

"That was the whole point, wasn't it?" Harry said. She turned to look at him. "They shouldn't have to know."

A look of frustrated amazement spread over her face. "God damn you, Harry Edom."

He shrugged and looked baffled. "What?"

"Just when I think I've got you pegged and stowed away you go and say a thing like that."

"Like what? I swear to God, Virginia, I don't know what you're talking about."

"Yeah?" She eyed him closely. "Well . . . maybe neither do I," and she turned and walked out the door.

He followed her out thinking maybe—he didn't know how, but just maybe—he'd finally won her over.

The week between Christmas and New Year's seemed to come from another world. The days were bright and windless, the sky a fierce deep blue. By the calendar, the nights should be getting shorter, but as far as Mally could tell, they were just getting colder and darker. He wore sweat pants, gym shirt, and socks to bed to stay warm. He had a few yearning thoughts about the flannel nightshirts he used to wear, but for some reason they seemed part of an irretrievable past now, the boy he used to be. Frost made filigrees on the window in his bedroom, and when he held the curtain aside, the light from the streetlamp on the corner shone through the ice and fractured into glittering points. The stars, too, looked like sparks, the night so cold they barely twinkled.

"What . . . !"

The voice cut through the darkness of the house. Mally did not move. Had he really heard it, or had he fallen asleep and dreamed for just a second?

"What have you to do with me?" the voice called again in the darkness. Mally was awake for sure now and scared stiff.

The voice came a third time, his grandfather's voice, shouting from the living room, "The pride of your heart has deceived you!"

Mally leapt out of bed and ran to the living room. His grandfather was sitting bolt upright on the sofa bed, his thin white hair in wild disarray, the covers flung to a pile on the floor.

"Grandfather?" Mally said, approaching the bed.

His grandfather wasn't looking at him, wasn't seeing him, was somewhere else, seeing something else. "For the violence done to your brother Jacob, shame shall cover you, and you shall be cut off forever!" he shouted.

Mally was terrified. There was no phone in the house. Should he run up to Mrs. Oldfield's? In the middle of the night? He stepped forward hesitantly and knelt beside the bed. "Grandfather," he said, trying to sound calm. He cautiously reached out and took the old man's hand.

He turned to him then and looked at him, though he still seemed to be coming from somewhere far away. "You should not have looked upon the day of your brother," he said, "in the day that he became—a stranger."

Mally found that he was crying. "Grampa," he said.

His grandfather's eyes looked deep into his. "What have you to do with me, O man of God?" he said. He gathered Mally in his arms and hugged him to his chest. "Have you come to call my sin into remembrance, and to slay my son?"

Mally wrapped his arms around his grandfather's waist and cried.

"Oh, Malachi," his grandfather said, his voice now his own again. Mally looked up hopefully. His grandfather was searching his face. "They made me keeper of the vineyards," he said, "but my own vineyard I have not kept."

All the energy seemed to go out of him then and he sank back down on the bed. Mally gathered up the covers from the pile on the floor and pulled them over him. He could see tears tracking down the old man's face. "It's okay, Grampa," he said. "It's all right."

He stayed beside him for a long time, perhaps an hour, in the cold, dark house. Every once in a while he thought he heard a sob, and he would murmur, "It's all right, Grampa, it's all right," and pat the old man's hand.

Randy listened, leaning against his car in the alley, shifting his basketball from hand to hand. "Does he remember anything about it in the morning?" he asked.

"I can't tell," Mally said. "I try to ask him, you know, in a sort of indirect way. But I don't want to embarrass him."

"And it's happened again?"

"Once or twice."

"And he never says a word about it?"

"No." Mally kicked at the gravel in the alley.

Randy shrugged. "It could be anything," he said. "Maybe you should talk to your mom about it."

Mally shook his head. "Her last phone number's been disconnected. I could write to her agent, I guess, but what would I say? 'Dear Mother, Gampa's quoting Scripture in his sleep. Please advise.' That's why she left here in the first place."

"Maybe he's just having nightmares."

Mally shook his head and leaned against the car next to Randy. "I can't help but think he's trying to tell me something. Maybe my being here is making him remember things. It seems like I'm remembering things, too."

"Really? Like what?"

"Like living by myself. Or practically by myself."

"You weren't by yourself in the city, were you?"

Mally shrugged. "No. There was Aunt Margaret." And for a while there had been Mr. Anderson, but he thought he shouldn't mention that. "My mom was barely around when I was a kid, always off working. And now she's off somewhere else and I'm here. It all feels familiar. I keep getting shifted from one person to another, like nobody knows what to do with me, like it's all my fault, somehow. "

"I know how you feel," Randy said.

Mally looked at him.

"No, really," Randy said. "I remember when my folks split up. I remember hoping for years they'd get back together. And then when they didn't, I thought it was my fault. But that's stupid. It's all stuff *they* did, not us. Sure, we've got to live with it, but that doesn't make it our fault. I mean, I've got plenty enough to worry about that *is* my fault without taking the credit for my folks, too."

Mally thought about that while Randy spun the ball around in his hands. "I guess you're right," he said. "At least for you, it seems to be working out some."

"How's that?" Randy asked.

"Well," Mally said, "your folks are back together, sort of."

Randy frowned and looked at the house. "Yeah, I guess they are, sort of. I didn't think it would last at first, but he's here most weekends now." He turned back to Mally. "And I'm not so sure it's a good thing, really. It makes the house feel—I don't know—crowded. And don't *that* make me feel weird." He shook his head. "Ain't they something, though? Parents. You can't get ahold yours and I can't get away from mine."

"Yeah," Mally said. "I wish they'd grow up."

Randy laughed out loud and then sprang away from the car. "Hey," he said, "wanna play a game of horse?"

"What's that?"

"You never played horse?" Randy said. "Oh man, those Oklahoma City boys must be really backward. I'll show you."

Mally got only as far as "H" in the first game, but he got better as they played.

Chapter 10

She Being Brand

T HE NEW SEMESTER brought a shift in classes and Mally
found he'd been moved from the upperclassmen's PE to
the freshman and sophomore class, which met after lunch and
before his algebra II class. A few months ago, such an abrupt
change would have thrown him into a panic. Now it seemed
merely logical, and after weeks with the juniors and seniors, he
found none of his new gym mates remotely threatening—or
even, for that matter, interesting.

Coach Tucker alone was in charge of the underclassmen
boys' PE, Coach Ardmore being off in a classroom somewhere
teaching "health." Tucker ran a more structured class than
Ardmore did, and the boys got to learn the fundamentals of
games more complex than dodge ball and touch football. They
started with volleyball. Coach Tucker surprised Mally by making
him one of the team captains and putting him in charge of picking the rest of his team. Mally picked sturdy and quick boys, not
necessarily the ones in extracurricular sports. At the end of the
two-week intra-class tournament, his team, the Nads, had beaten
the G-Men and had the best win-loss record. Mally had jammed
a finger in the next-to-last game and sat out most of the final, but
joined in the celebration when his team won, jumping up and
down and hollering "Go Nads!" with the rest of the boys.

"All right, all right," Coach Tucker had said, standing stoic
and unmoved at the side of the court. "This ain't a circus, you
know."

Tucker also coached the wrestling team, which met after school in the balcony overlooking the gym where the basketball team practiced. The collapsible bleachers were pushed against the wall and two large red rubber mats were rolled out over the finished concrete. The boys would pair up and the coach would give them pointers about an escape technique or a particular hold, and then they would practice on each other.

Red had difficulty concentrating during practice matches. He kept expecting Randy to show up. After all, this stupid sport had been his idea. He'd been paired with Marcus Longacre this afternoon, which seemed really dumb. Marcus might weigh as much as he did, but Marcus was thin and long, not bulky like him. Marcus crouched on hands and knees on the mat and Red knelt beside him, making sure his own knees were behind his opponent's, his arm draped just so over Marcus's back and wrapping around his belly, and his right hand gripping Marcus's arm just above the elbow.

On the basketball court below them, Red could hear the guys running wind sprints.

Coach Tucker gave a short blast on his whistle.

With a movement so quick he couldn't follow it, Marcus had Red flat on his back. Red squirmed and tried to push down with his arms to pry his shoulders off the mat. He kicked out with his legs but Marcus just spread his own legs wider and leaned into him. In a minute, Red was exhausted and his shoulders sank to the mat. He was pinned.

Marcus was grinning down at him, his eyes glittering.

"How did you do that?" Red said in wonder, raising himself up a little. "I'm way stronger than you."

"It's not all muscle," Marcus said. "Sometimes it's speed. And sometimes," and here he leaned into Red again, forcing him back down on the mat, "it's leverage."

Red looked him in the eyes. "Show me," he said.

Mr. Hansen was turning red, but since he always turned red when he talked, it was a little hard to tell whether he was delighted or apoplectic. Mr. Tibbits had no idea why the man hadn't died of a stroke years ago.

"I can't tell you how delighted I am," Mr. Hansen said, putting Mr. Tibbits's mind to rest. "Most of the other parents don't seem to want to get involved these days."

"Not at all," Mr. Tibbits said. "The band does a terrific job and I'm sure they'll do well this year at state. I want to be along to see it."

"Well, thank you again," Mr. Hansen said. "We can always use another chaperone."

"There's one other thing," Mr. Tibbits said.

"Oh?"

"Joanie told me about the accommodations last year."

Mr. Hansen turned an impossibly deeper red. "Well," he said, "Enid is not exactly your metropolitan center." He was desperately hoping Mr. Tibbits wasn't referring to the argument he'd gotten into with the flag and rifle corps from Marlow at three in the morning. Those darned kids had been making a hell of a racket and deserved a good talking to, but maybe he had gotten a little carried away with his language.

"No," Mr. Tibbits was saying, "you don't get much of a choice around Enid. But I think we could do better."

Mr. Hansen spread his hands. "I can't argue with that, but—"

"Now, I know it's traditional for the band to raise its own money for the state tournament," Mr. Tibbits said, "and I support that. I think it's a good idea for the kids to learn how to earn their own way. But I was wondering if, once they *had* earned their own way, we might give them a little boost."

"Boost?" Mr. Hansen wasn't following Mr. Tibbits at all.

"Yes," Mr. Tibbits said. "I know of a place, right off Interstate 35, with much better accommodations than—last year's. The difference in price is not all that much. I was wondering if, once the band met its goal, I might supplement the total."

Mr. Hansen was dumbfounded.

"With enough to pay for the better lodgings," Mr. Tibbits concluded, just to make his point clear.

"That's . . . that's fantastic, Mr. Tibbits," Mr. Hansen said. "That's the most wonderful thing I've heard in—oh, I don't know. It's just wonderful! Fantastic."

Mr. Tibbits rose from his seat across from Mr. Hansen's desk in the band annex. "Good. Then it's settled," he said. "I look forward to March."

Mr. Hansen came around the desk to shake his hand. "Thank you," he said. "You can't know how much this means for the kids."

Mr. Tibbits just smiled and left.

Mr. Hansen leaned against his desk. What did Joanie Tibbits play? Oh, yes, clarinet. And a sophomore. That meant another two years after this. He was sure he could make her first chair by then. Visions of new band uniforms danced in his head.

Mr. Tibbits's charitable impulses began at home, as Mally and Randy found out a few weeks later. They were in Randy's back yard playing horse one Sunday afternoon when a bright red and white Malibu convertible pulled into the alley. They stopped and stared, their mouths agape.

"Joanie?" Mally asked.

"None other," she said, grinning broadly behind the wheel.

"Where in the world . . . ?" was all Randy could get out.

"My Daddy gave it to me," she said. She gave the horn a toot. "Ain't she a beaut?"

"Is it new?" Mally asked.

"Yep," Joanie said, grinning even more broadly. "Well, practically. A show model."

Randy grinned conspiratorially at Mally. "*she being Brand—*" he began and fired the ball to Mally.

"*—new,*" Mally quoted back at him, "*and you know consequently a little—*" and shot the ball back.

"*—stiff,*" Randy completed and the two of them laughed.

"What on earth?" Joanie asked.

"Well, what are we waiting for?" Randy yelled, running around to the passenger side and hopping in. "Let's give her the juice!"

"Good!" Mally yelled, leaping into the back seat. "To the Public Gardens!"

"I have no idea what you two are talking about," Joanie said, laughing, "but I don't really care!" She gave the accelerator a nudge and kicked up a few stones.

"Hey!" Randy yelled. "That's my trick!"

And they were off down the alley. They headed toward Main Street and Herman's. It was early March and the air was still cool, especially in the shade, but there was no point in riding through town in a convertible unless you had the top down.

"This is terrific!" Mally yelled.

"You mean he just drove it right up to the house without telling you?" Randy asked.

"Yep," said Joanie. "Just dropped the keys in my hand, gave me a hug, and said, 'Happy Birthday, Princess.'"

"It's some fine car," Mally shouted.

"I've got some fine Daddy!" she shouted back. She turned to Randy. "It sure beats that old heap you drive around in."

"Hey," Randy said, "don't knock the Dream Machine. She's got plenty of good miles left in her."

"Uh-huh," Joanie said. "About ten, I'd say, on the outside."

Mally leaned forward so he wouldn't have to shout himself hoarse. "It better be more than that," he said. "It's gotta take us to Lake Ouichita and back."

"You two still going on that hare-brained camping trip?"

"Yup!" Randy and Mally said in unison.

"Huh," she said. "Listen to the cuckoos sing."

"Hey," Randy said, "how's Mally ever gonna be a real cowboy if he doesn't spend a night out on the range?"

"Lake Ouichita is not out on the range."

Randy shrugged. "Close enough."

"Well, at least I won't have to worry about you falling into the clutches of Miss Candy Sullivan while I'm on the band trip."

"She's going, too, isn't she?" Mally asked.

"Yep. I think we're even sharing a room, Lord help me."

"Aw, you've got nothing to worry about with her," Randy said. "I wouldn't get within ten feet of her if you paid me."

Joanie laughed. "Well, you're going to have a hard time avoiding that, and you *will* be getting paid for it."

"What?"

"Daddy's hired her on as an assistant at the store, just like he did you. She'll be starting as soon as we get back."

Randy looked at Mally anxiously.

"Do you think that's such a good idea?" Mally asked.

"No," Joanie said. "I think it's a terrible idea. But I'll be back as soon as she is." She gave Randy a teasing look. "So just watch your step, mister."

Randy swallowed and looked at the passing houses. "Yeah," he said.

They passed Herman's and Joanie made a point of honking and waving. Mally waved, too, then regretted it. The only person he made eye contact with in the parking lot was Red Conner leaning against Al's car. Even at a distance, Red's eyes looked like two lumps of coal.

Randy was lying on the trunk of his car in the late afternoon, leaning against the rear window and looking up the e e cummings poem he and Mally had been fooling around with earlier. The sun was setting and he liked the way the orange light warmed up the page, even if it had no effect on his hands.

"Saw you earlier today," Red said.

"Jeez, Red!" Randy said, nearly falling off the trunk. "I didn't hear you come up."

"Saw you drive by Herman's in that flashy car," Red said.

"What? Oh, yeah. That's Joanie's new car. It's something, ain't it? Did Al see it?"

"Nope, he was inside. Did you see me?"

"No," Randy said, shaking his head. He didn't really remember going past Herman's

"Figured," Red said. "Whatcha reading?"

Randy showed him the cover of the book, wishing again it wasn't such a lurid purple. "Book of poems," he said.

"What? Poems my behind. Let me see that."

Red made a grab for the book but Randy pulled it out of reach. "No, really," Randy said. "Some of these are pretty neat. Listen to this, 'she being Brand—'"

"What the hell is this?" Red said.

Randy didn't know what to make of the look on Red's face. It was flushed and his fists were clenched. He looked like he was about to fight. With him? About what?

"What the hell is this?" Red repeated. "Poetry, and moonshine and roses, and that little jerk hanging around you all the time. Where the hell have you been?"

"I took that job over at Tibbits," Randy said. "I'm putting in more hours now."

"I know *that*," Red said, getting madder. "I mean, where the hell have you been? You didn't go out for basketball and you didn't go out for wrestling. I'm out there all by myself."

Randy was beginning to get ticked off himself. "I told you," he said. "I took on some extra hours at Tibbits. Extra pay."

"But why?"

"That's my business, Red."

"No, but why? Why didn't you tell me? You used to tell me stuff. We'd plan all our stuff together. Always." Red slumped, the fight gone out of him. "Oh, Jesus."

Randy looked at him. "Are you drunk?"

Red laughed humorlessly. "No. It's not legal to drink. Not till you're eighteen. You know that, Big Man."

"As if that ever stopped you."

"Or you."

"You are drunk."

"Nuh-*unh*. Smell my breath."

Randy leaned in. A sharp odor clung to Red's jacket and clothes and stung his nose. "Good God, Red," he said, backing up, "what is that stuff?"

"It's all perfectly legal. You can get it by the case." He suddenly brightened. "Hey, I bet *you* really *can* get it by the case. Right there at Tibbits. Just say you're building something. A model airplane, like." He spread his arms out and ran in a little circle. "Wheee!"

Randy got scared and angry at the same time. "Jesus God, Red, that stuff'll rot your brain. Who put you up to this?"

Red stopped his airplane act and smiled at him. "Longacre," he said. Then he started chuckling. "Boy, they sure named that one right. He's one lo-o-o-ng acre. Lotsa leverage."

"You gotta stop doing this stuff, man. I'm serious."

"Oh, now he's serious. Wooo-hooo. Serious."

"Really. I don't like this shit."

Red frowned at him. "Aw, just mellow out," he said. "It's fun."

"I'm serious, Red. I don't want you coming around here when you're high on that stuff."

"What?"

"I don't want you coming round here when you're sniffing glue."

Red held stock still. The color came back into his face again and he started breathing short. "You don't want *me*? Coming *around*?" Red suddenly exploded, his arms flying in all directions. "Screw you! Screw you and your prissy little friend and that snotty bitch!"

Without thinking, Randy pulled back and belted him one in the face. The punch caught Red off balance and he suddenly sat down. The shock of the blow nearly knocked Randy over, too. Plus it hurt like hell. "Jesus!" he hissed, holding his hand and shaking it.

There wasn't a mark on Red's face, but he looked like he'd been crushed from the inside. He got up slowly, keeping his eyes on Randy. Then he turned and walked away down the alley without a word.

Randy wanted to call out after him, maybe catch up with him, talk it out, but his hand was beginning to swell. He was going to have to wrap it in ice or something or it was going to be useless. He headed for the house. On the back porch, he looked down the alley again, but Red was gone.

He returned the book of poems to Mally the next day, handing it over to him in the hall during lunch hour. "Sorry I didn't finish it," he said. "I guess you lose that bet with Joanie."

"Aw, that's nothing," Mally said. "Did you like 'em?"

Randy shrugged. "They were okay, I guess."

"But you liked 'she being Brand,' right? I thought you would."

Randy looked over his shoulder. "I gotta go now," he said. "I might not be able to give you a ride after school."

"That's okay," Mally said. "I'll hitch a ride with Joanie. What'cha do to your hand?"

"It's nothing," Randy said, "see you later," and walked off down the hall.

Mally looked after him, puzzled, but he needed to get to his locker before gym class, which he was actually looking forward to, so he didn't have time to think about it much.

Randy took up his place on the stairwell with Al and Tom. He was hoping Red might be there, but there was no sign of him.

"Have you driven it yet?" Al asked.

"Driven what?" Randy said.

"The Malibu!"

Randy shook his head. "Not interested."

"Well, do you mind if I try?"

Randy gave him a look.

"Hey," Al said, eyebrows flying up, "I just want to borrow the car, not the girlfriend."

"Speaking of borrowing," Tom said, "are you done with that book of cummings poems?"

"Which book of what poems?"

"He's been carrying it around for months, lame brain," Tom said.

"I borrowed it," Randy said. "I gave it back."

"Oh," Tom said. "Huh."

"What's with the hand?" Al said.

"Nothin'," Randy said. This was getting on his nerves. He pushed off from the wall and muttered, "See ya."

"What's with him?" Al asked after he left.

Tom crossed his fingers and arms and smirked.

It took Al a second. "Oh," he said at last, then he smiled and nodded. "Way to go, Randy."

His father was just about the only person who didn't ask Randy about his swollen and bandaged hand, but coming from a long line of fighters and rowdies (two brothers in jail, one dead) he probably didn't need or want any explanations. They were walking along out at the farm, silent for a while, strolling up the hill till they got to the top and looked down on the town.

"You come out here often?" Harry finally asked.

Randy shrugged. "Once in a while."

"I used to come out nearly every week just to stand up here and look at it all, pick my fights, dream my dreams." He looked at Randy. "Your mother was one of them."

Randy smiled. "One of the fights or one of the dreams?"

Harry laughed. "Both! She was somethin.' Still is." He picked a stalk of new-growth wild barley and stuck it in his teeth. "Folks used to fault me for not farming this place, but hell, we never did get that orchard cleared. 'Sides, it's too small and mean to turn a profit." He spat out the end of the straw. "Naw," he said, "it's wicked country."

"I don't see what business it is of theirs, anyway."

"Damned straight," his father said. "I'm not gonna let the high and mighty citizens of Croy tell me what I can and cannot do, what dreams are fit for them and what's fit for me. They're good at that, here, killing dreams."

Randy looked at him askance. "You've got a new one, haven't you?"

Harry laughed and shook his head. "You are just like your mother, I swear."

"But you do, don't you?"

"Yup."

Randy waited a little, smiling at him. "Well?"

Harry turned away from him a moment, then spun around to face him. "Alaska!" he said.

"What? Wildcattin'?"

"Nope. Nothing that chancy. A sure thing, proven field. And the wages up there is sin, Randy, pure sin. Why, in one month's time . . ."

He stopped and the light seemed to go out of his face. "Aw, who am I kiddin'? Look, your momma made it pretty clear I can't pitch this at you, so just forget it."

"Forget what?"

"Nope," Harry said and he turned and started heading back down the hill. "It's no good."

Randy tagged after him. "Come on, Pop. You can spell it out. It's not like I'm buying it or anything."

"No, no," Harry waved his hand at him, not turning around. "I've got to raise the money myself. Gotta pay off that judgment and raise enough to get me outta here. But once I'm there, boy, look out. I'll make old New York Alquist look like the Yankee piker he was."

"Sure you will, Pop."

"You can count on it. Hell, you can bank on it."

They had reached Harry's truck. As he swung open the driver's door, Harry stopped, looking back at the old house.

Randy looked at the house, too, then at his father. "What?"

Harry rubbed his chin. "Look," he said, then paused as if not sure how to say what came next. "There might be some things I need, things I need so's I can raise the money. But I need a place to keep them. I can't keep them in my room in Tulsa and I don't want them lying around the house here in Croy, so I was thinking maybe I'd just stash them out here on the farm. Maybe you could look after them for me, make sure nobody filches them."

Randy shrugged. "Sure, why not?"

"Thing is," Harry said, "this being Ginnie's land and all, I don't want her to find out about it, see?"

Randy smiled at him, feeling pretty smart. "I don't see why she would," he said.

Harry grinned. "That's my boy," he said. "What she don't know won't hurt—"

"You."

Harry stopped, open-mouthed, then laughed. "You got that straight," he said, and they climbed into the truck. "Damned straight."

It was a cold day, more like late fall than early spring, but Mally was upbeat and feeling adventurous. He didn't feel like going straight home after school. Instead, he walked north along the railroad tracks, looking for something to catch his eye. He'd been to the crossing a half dozen times since Christmas, but there was nothing new for him there, so he walked along the abandoned ties to the long low building with the boarded up windows and the ramp. He scouted idly around the building, noting the features he'd seen before: the boards that loosely covered the windows on the long sides; the curiously featureless north wall, no doors, no windows, not even a break in the siding; a single door on the side facing the ramp, and a circular window high above it looking oddly ornamental on a building that was otherwise no-nonsense. That door had been solidly locked last time Mally had been by, but he gave it a try this afternoon anyway.

The knob nearly fell off in his hand and the door swung open. He fumbled the knob back into place and stepped inside, closing the door quickly behind him.

Once his eyes adjusted, he could see pretty well. Sunlight pried between the boards over the windows, slashing the main room with diagonals of light. The circular window high on the wall let in more light and made an oval of sun on the wall to his right. The window had long been a favorite for local target practice and wind whistled through the few remaining shards of glass, making the room drafty for all its being closed up. The main room was large and bare—just a few pigeon feathers and droppings, some broken glass, and scraps of ledger paper. The whole place had the sharp odor of rat urine.

The room was bare but not empty. There was a small table near the middle, and on it, something unexpected: a candle and matches. There was melted wax on the table. Mally dug his thumbnail into it. Recent.

The north end of the room was truncated by a low partition with a counter top and a half-door. He wandered over and let himself in through the half-door. On the floor of the small, office-like space beyond the partition was another surprise: a mattress. Was someone living here?

There were built-in cabinets on the inside of the partition. Mally was just about to make a search of them when he heard voices coming up the ramp. He looked around in a panic. There was no way out of the building except through the door he'd come in through, and no way out of the office except back over the partition, which would just put him out in the open in the main room. He might crouch here behind the partition, but he noticed a door to his right, beyond the mattress—a closet, maybe. There was a gaping hole where the doorknob had been, but he hoped that would make it easy to open. He dashed across the spongy padding and ducked inside just as the outside door opened.

He couldn't see them, but he could hear them, and he recognized one voice at once. "It sucks," Red Conner said angrily, and the other boy agreed. Then they talked a while in voices too low to make out words. Finally, the other boy said, "Here we go," and then they were both quiet a while.

It was cramped and dark in the closet and Mally was beginning to get cold from lack of circulation. He also thought he smelled something pungent and acrid. It made his eyes water. He hoped the boys would leave soon.

"So, do you wanna?" the other boy asked.

Red muttered an answer he couldn't hear, and then he heard their feet shuffling across the wooden floor. He hoped they were leaving and brought his eye to the hole in the door to check. He flung himself back almost at once. They weren't leaving, they were coming into the office! He backed away in the dark and bumped against something hard. It teetered behind him. He turned around quickly and grabbed a wooden frame wrapped in canvas tied with rope. Whatever was inside was heavy and would make a hell of a racket if it fell over, but his hands steadied it and it rocked gently and quietly back into place.

His heart was racing a mile a minute. What should he do if they found him here? He could—what?—tell them he was just snooping? Or maybe pretend to be asleep?

They weren't getting any closer, weren't heading for the closet. Judging by the sounds, they were on the other side of the office from him, over by the mattress. They weren't talking, just making enough small noises for him to know they were still there.

Then he heard something that nearly turned him to stone. He stared into the dark, not breathing, not thinking, getting suddenly so hot he started to sweat. He had to look, but he couldn't look. He had to. He leaned forward ever so slowly and silently and brought his eye to the hole.

The two boys were standing on the mattress. Red had his back to the wall and was leaning on it, his eyes closed. Mally could only see the back of the other boy's black leather jacket and bluejeans. He was leaning against Red, but off-center. His right hand was inside Red's pants, which were unbuttoned and unzipped. His hand moved methodically up and down.

Mally pulled back from the door but kept that part of the scene centered in his field of view. Red began breathing faster and the other boy was whispering encouragement. Suddenly, Red cried out and jerked. The movement freed his jeans, which went sliding down to his feet. His dick freed, the other boy's hand wrapped more tightly around it. It spat once, twice, three times, then Red grabbed the boy's hand to keep it from jerking. "Oh, shit," he said, "oh, shit." His breathing slowed and he slumped slowly to the floor, still leaning against the wall, his legs sticking out in front of him.

The other boy undid his belt and fly and knelt down, straddling Red's legs. He leaned forward, bracing himself with his hands on the wall. Nothing happened for a while.

"Hey, c'mon," the boy said. "Help me out here."

"I can't," Red said.

"Ya did last time," the boy complained. "What's with you, anyway?"

"I'm not . . . I'm not . . ." Mally couldn't make out what Red was saying. He sounded like he was choking.

"Well, screw you, then," the other boy said. He reared up on his knees then, completely blocking Mally's view of Red.

The other boy's jeans were sagging down around his legs down to mid-thigh. Mally could see his buttocks below the line of his jacket and his balls hanging between his legs. The guy licked his hand and then spat into it and reached down in front of himself. Mally could see his arm moving freely up and down, then the elbow tightened to his side and only the forearm was moving, jerking in an accelerating rhythm. The guy's hips began to buck slowly, his butt contracting with each forward thrust. Mally felt his own hard-on tighten against his pants. He felt if he moved a single muscle, he would come. Then the other boy cried, "Shit!" and his back arched and his head jerked back three, four times, his black hair flying.

Then it was quiet, the only sound was the guy in the leather jacket, breathing in and out with deep, ragged breaths. He sank back on his heels and stayed there a while. Another sound came from the room, a small sound from somewhere on the other side of the kneeling figure.

The guy with the leather jacket shook his head then. He hitched his pants back up around his waist and stood up. Mally heard the zipper and the metal jingle as the belt was buckled. The guy took another look at Red, slumped on the mattress. "Man," he said disgustedly, shaking his head again. Then he shrugged his jacket back into place on his shoulders and left.

A beam of sun slanted across the room, making a bright diagonal bar across Red's face. Mally could see the thick, glistening trail on his forehead, his chin. As he watched, two smaller trails crept out of Red's eyes and down his face.

Mally did his best not to breathe. He didn't know how long he would have to stay there—all night if he had to. It didn't take that long, though. Red eventually got up, wiped his face on the inside of his letter jacket, and left. Still, Mally waited until the sun had gone down and it was good and dark out, even though it was getting cold. He sure as hell didn't want Red to be hanging around outside and see him come out. He'd have killed Mally for sure.

Chapter 11

The Ordinances of the Heavens

J OANIE ARCHED AN eyebrow. "Didn't I warn you?"

"Yeah," Randy said, "so you're right all the time. So what else is new?" He scratched his head. "Thing is, we were going to drive it to Lake Ouichita."

"Well, how much does an alternator cost?"

"It's not the cost, it's getting the dang thing." He drummed his fingers on the cafeteria table. "I suppose we could put the trip off a week. But Mally's been real excited about it and I've been . . ."

"What?" Joanie said, getting ready to look cross.

"I've been a little stand-offish lately," he said. "I don't want him to think it's his fault or that I'm trying to back out or anything. I was kinda looking forward to it, really."

Joanie finished her lunch thoughtfully. "Tell you what," she said at last, "why don't you take my car?"

"Really? But you've had it less than a month."

"And I'd better still have it when I get back. No hot-rodding and no blazing trails across the prairie."

Randy raised his right hand. "I swear."

"Besides, I won't be using it while I'm on the band trip. We all get to ride in the splendor of one of Croy Consolidated High School's finest chariots."

"Would that be the one with or without the square wheels?"

Before Joanie could snap back an answer, a commotion broke out behind them in the cafeteria. They turned in time to see Marcus Longacre and another boy square off over by the windows.

Mr. Noyes was rushing forward, arms outstretched, "Now boys, boys," he was saying in a high-pitched wheedle. They were paying him no attention but were as rigid as rat traps ready to spring, Marcus with a chair in one hand. Just as Noyes reached them, the other boy spat and the fight ignited. The chair went flying but missed hitting anyone. It was followed by Marcus himself, who launched himself at the kid, who came out of a crouch fists flailing. Caught in the middle. Mr. Noyes, either out of good instincts or cowardice, crumbled to a heap between them, covering his face and yelling, "Don't hit me! Don't hit me!" The sight so shocked and embarrassed the boys that they both just stood there, looking at the pathetic figure.

"All right, all right," came a big, booming voice. It was Coach Tucker, striding through the cafeteria like a colossus. Both boys slumped in defeat, knowing there would be no fight now. Another teacher came out of the teacher's lounge, smelling of cigarette smoke. "The two of you, to the principal's office, now!" he ordered and marched them off, steering each boy by an elbow.

Coach Tucker leaned over the still huddled figure of Mr. Noyes. "It's okay now, Ernest," he said softly, reaching out a hand.

Mr. Noyes kept one hand over his face but reached out with the other and slowly got to his feet. Coach Tucker led him to the door of the teacher's lounge. As they passed, something slid partway off Mr. Noyes' head and down over one ear.

"Did you see that?" Joanie whispered. "What was that?"

"I think," Randy said, "Mr. Noyes wears a toupee."

It was a change in fortunes for Mr. Noyes, though hardly for the better. Students no longer referred to him behind his back as "that old fairy." Now, he was known as "Wigsy."

Ruth stood in the doorway of the bedroom while John got his things together. The shirts were neatly folded on the bed, waiting to be packed. There were more than enough of them for a three-day band trip.

She came in and sat on the bed, her hands folded in her lap. "John," she said.

"Yes, hon," he said, carefully folding his suit into the suitcase.

"I want you to think about this," she said.

"About what?"

"You know what I mean."

"You mean the trip?" He laid the shirts on top of the suit. "I'll only be gone three days, four at the most if that meeting works out." He straightened up. "It's just to Enid, Ruth. It's not the end of the world." He turned to gather his socks.

"It might be," she said, staring straight ahead.

"Hmm?"

"It might be the end of the world." He turned around to face her. "Don't make this difficult, John."

"Make what difficult? What are you talking about?"

"Where you're going, who you're staying with, afterwards."

John spread his arms and smiled. "A bunch of pharmaceutical salesmen?"

"Don't." Ruth got off the bed and turned away. "Not to my face. I've been quiet up till now because, well, because of Joanie and Kyle."

John frowned, looking baffled. "Look, Ruthie, I don't know what crazy idea's gotten into your head, but I made a promise to those kids and the school. I even paid for a better hotel."

She faced him. "Do you think I don't know that? Do you think I don't know which hotel, and how often you've been a guest there?"

The color drained from his face, then he suddenly got very busy closing the suitcase and locking it up. "I'm going to be late," he said and lifted the suitcase off the bed.

"Don't go," she said. "Up till now, it's been little things. Just little things that I've been willing to forgive and forget."

He took a step toward the door. "I don't want to talk about it."

"Then we'll be the only two people in Kennsing County who don't talk about it!"

His face went beet red and he gripped the handle on the suitcase hard enough to turn his knuckles white. "I will not stand here accused by gossip in my own home!"

"If you do anything, anything at all in that hotel, and Joanie finds out about it, you might not have a home to come back to!"

He stared at her, eyes furious, but could think of nothing to say. His anger and shame propelled him forward, trying to get out of the room, but she caught him by the arm in the doorway.

"You think about it, John Tibbits," she said, low, intense. "I gave you Joanie and Kyle. You've always wanted more, but I did give you two wonderful children." She let go of his arm. "Has anyone done you any better?"

He flew down the stairs and didn't even notice the front door as he flung himself out of the house.

"So, you, too, huh?" Randy said as Virginia checked the stuff in her purse one more time.

"Yup," she said. Outside in the truck, Harry honked his horn. "I guess it's a general evacuation of the city." She gave him a serious look. "You be careful on that camping trip, hear?"

"Sure thing," he said.

"And mind your driving."

"If I let anything happen to that car, Joanie will kill me."

"Well, she'll have to stand in line." There was more honking outside. "I wish to tarnation he wouldn't do that. He'll give Clara Oldfield a heart attack for sure." She suddenly smiled at him, shy and lit up. "What do you think she'd say, knowing I was running off to Tulsa for two weeks with my own husband?"

"I don't think she'd know whether to speak for you or a-gen you. She'd be tongue-tied."

"Historic occasion. Hate to miss it." One more honk. "Gotta fly," she said and gave him a peck on the cheek.

Grinning, he watched her go, then turned to finish his own packing. He hollered across the alley to Mally to see how he was doing.

"Um . . ." Mally yelled back.

"Yeah, I figured," Randy yelled. "I'll be over to help as soon as I get the car."

He strolled down Choctaw and then up Main Street and around the square. The town really did look deserted. Tibbits was closed. There were fewer kids at Herman's. There were no notable cars, like Al's, cruising up and down Main. Except for the kids at the state band and choral festival, most of Croy's high school students (and many of their parents) were at the state basketball finals, either playing in it, like Al, or cheering the Rangers on.

Red had been right about that: the team had done really well this year, despite having neither of them on it. Randy chuckled. Maybe *because* of not having either one of them on it. And then he started thinking about Red again and he started feeling crummy. But what was he supposed to do? Red was being a complete butt-head. It's not like he started out wanting to pick one bunch of friends over another. And why should he? There was nothing so strange about Mally that Red couldn't get used to. Or the other way around, even. They could all do something together, a game of horse, maybe. Mally was getting good enough to make it interesting. Or maybe they'd just hang out somewhere.

Aw, who was he kidding? He couldn't see Mally knocking back a beer with the guys, or Red and Tom discussing the poetic use of punctuation (well, Tom, maybe). Either way, Mally ended up unconscious.

He came up on the Tibbitses' in this distracted state of mind. The car was parked at the curb. Randy checked the ignition and all the usual places, but didn't find the keys anywhere. Then he noticed Kyle playing in the front yard with a small tin box.

"Hey, Stinker," he called to the boy. "Your mom home?

Kyle squinted up at him. "She's over to the neighbor's."

"Huh." Randy looked around. Which neighbor's? Mally was waiting back at the house. "Did she say anything about the car keys?"

"In the mailbox."

"Thanks." He strolled to the mailbox and fished out the keys. He was headed back to the car when Kyle called out.

"Hey, we've got him now."

"Who's that?"

"The General." Kyle said. "We'll get him good this time. See?" and he held out his hand with the tin box in it.

Everything seemed to slow down as Randy's eyes finally focused on what the boy had in his hand. "Where," he said, then had to swallow, then started again, "Where did you get that?"

"Over yonder in the field," Kyle said and made a sweeping motion with his other hand.

Randy caught his breath and held out both hands. "Kyle!" he said. The urgency in his voice made the boy snap back around. *Too fast*, Randy thought, *too fast! I'm just scaring the boy.* "Kyle," he said, "I don't want you to move."

"What?" The boy looked at him as if he'd just spoken Chinese.

"Just—I want you to stand right there and not move." Randy inched closer to him.

"What's the matter?" Kyle asked in a small voice. "You're acting funny."

"What you've got there, in your hand, it's very dangerous."

Kyle looked at his own hand as if it held a cottonmouth.

"Now," Randy said, "I'm going to take it from you, okay?"

"Okay."

Randy stretched out his hand, which wasn't shaking, he was surprised to notice, and very carefully picked the small container off the boy's open palm. Then he breathed a big sigh of relief. "Don't you ever, ever pick up something like this again, do you hear?"

Kyle nodded vigorously.

"If you see something like this again, you tell your mom or your dad or some other grown up right away, okay?"

"'Kay."

"And don't touch it." He looked again at the tin of blasting caps in his hand. "Where did you say you found this?"

"Over yonder," Kyle said, and he pointed west, to the hill just outside of town, to the farm that was now Randy's.

"God damn that man," Randy said under his breath. Kyle looked at him wide-eyed. "You remember what I told you now, hear?" he said to the boy. Kyle nodded again.

Randy got in the car and headed out to the farm. Sure enough, there were signs that Harry had been out there. The rooms looked like they'd been swept and tidied up, which wasn't much like Harry, but one of the cabinets in the house had a new lock on it, and he could just bet what was inside. He cursed his father again and then found a safe place for the blasting caps, some-place where even curious little hands couldn't find them. Then he made sure all the windows and doors were locked and headed back into town.

"What took you so long?" Mally asked.

"Nothing," Randy said tensely. It was obvious Mally wasn't buying it, so he waved it away. "Just some business I had to attend to. Something I forgot I was responsible for. You ready to go?"

Mally gestured to the heap of stuff he had piled on the lawn. "Reckon so."

Randy looked at the pile and burst out laughing.

Candy bounced up and down on the bed, a motion that nauseated Joanie just watching her. "I'd've thought you'd had enough jouncing around after that bus ride," she said.

"Nope," Candy said. "I'm just getting started. Hey! Do you think they have room service here?"

"Beats me," Joanie said. Her bones were weary and her ears were buzzing from the bus engine, and her head felt like it was full of cotton. She just wanted to lie still for a while.

Candy squealed in delight. "Oh, they do!" she said, reading from a card beside the telephone. She picked up the receiver and dialed. "Quick," she said, "what do you want?"

Joanie moaned. "How about a brain transplant?" She flopped backwards on the bed on her side of the room.

"Um, a strawberry sundae, please," Candy said into the phone. "With two cherries. Yes. Room 217. Thank you so kindly." She hung up the phone and giggled. "I can't believe it! That was so easy."

Joanie rolled her eyes. She should probably be unpacking her suitcase or getting out her clarinet or something, but she didn't want to move.

"So, why didn't you ride up with your Daddy?" Candy asked, suddenly friendly and concerned.

"He wasn't coming here right away. He had a meeting to set up. For later. I don't know."

Candy smiled to herself. "This sure is a nicer place than last year's," she said.

"Anything would beat that dump," Joanie said. "Were you in a room next to Earthquake McGoon and his girlfriend last time?"

"No, can't say as I was."

"It was pathetic," Joanie said. "All night long. It sounded like she was being repeatedly stabbed with a short, blunt knife."

Candy found that distasteful and got up and paced the room. There was a knock at the door. With a little cry, she ran across the room and flung open the door.

A black man stood there holding a cloth-covered tray.

"Eee!" she screamed. "A jigaboo!" and she dashed across the room and into the bathroom and slammed the door.

Joanie couldn't believe it. She heard Candy lock the bathroom door. She turned to the waiter at the door, mortified. "She's—" she started to say. She got up off the bed and walked over to the door. "She's a little shy," she said. "And . . . backward."

The man's face looked like a one-man race riot. "Your sundae, miss," he said in a dead-even voice.

"Um, thank you," she said and took the tray. The man stood at the door a moment longer, then nodded and walked away.

Oh, jeez, Joanie thought to herself. *A tip. I was supposed to give him a tip.*

"Is he gone?" asked a voice from the bathroom.

"Yes," Joanie said, exasperated. "Your sundae's here. It's melting. Two cherries and all."

Candy came out and stood in the bathroom doorway. "I'm not going to eat that hateful thing," she said.

Ruth climbed the front steps of Mrs. Oldfield's house, then nearly turned around before getting to the door. But it was a warm day and she didn't relish the idea of walking back home without sitting awhile somewhere cool. She approached the door and hesitated again, then knocked. She wondered why she knocked. There was a doorbell right there. Was knocking more neighborly? More discreet?

Mrs. Oldfield opened the door. "Oh," she said, looking surprised.

"Good afternoon, Clara," Ruth said. "I was wondering if you might tell me where Pastor Jacobs is. No one seems to be at home at the little house."

"Oh, he's right inside, right here in the kitchen." Mrs. Oldfield hesitated before stepping aside. "Won't you come in?"

Ruth entered the cool, dim front room and followed Mrs. Oldfield back toward the kitchen. "I don't want to intrude," she said.

"Oh, no, it's no intrusion." Mrs. Oldfield stopped and turned around. "It's just that the little house gets so warm on days like these. So I thought the Reverend would be more comfortable up here. Just till the heat passes."

Ruth was surprised at how anxious Clara was to have her understand this.

"Who is it, Clara?" asked a voice from the kitchen.

"It's Ruth Tibbits, Matthew," Clara Oldfield said, and they proceeded into the kitchen.

It was a bright, sunny room, but the rest of the house, closed and curtained against the day outside, kept it cool. Rev. Jacobs sat in a wicker chair next to a small table that held two glasses and a pitcher of lemonade.

"It's good to see you, Pastor," Ruth said, walking forward and taking his hand.

"Just Matthew, now, Ruth," he said.

Clara took the opportunity of their greeting to whisk away one of the glasses. "Can I get you some lemonade?" she asked.

"Thank you," Ruth said, sitting at the table.

There was silence all around as Clara produced a fresh glass, stirred the pitcher, and poured.

"Yes, it's unseasonably warm," Clara Oldfield said, apropos of nothing.

"This lemonade is perfect," Ruth said. "Delicious after a walk across town."

"I make it straight from the lemons myself," Clara said. "Not too much sugar or it only leaves you thirstier."

Ruth looked at her lap.

"Well, I don't mean to be an ungracious hostess," Clara said, "but those roses aren't going to prune themselves. If you don't mind?"

"Not at all, Clara," Ruth said, trying not to sound relieved.

Mrs. Oldfield turned at the back door. "You call, either one of you, if you want anything. I'll be right there in the back yard." She grabbed a straw sun hat from a peg beside the door and left.

Now that she was gone, Ruth found she had run out of reasons not to say what was on her heart, but she still couldn't bring herself to say it.

"It's been a treat seeing Joanie come by now and then," Matthew Jacobs said. "I remember how you and John struggled for your first child, and now here she is, nearly grown up."

"Yes," Ruth said, smiling distractedly.

"And little Kyle? How's he—?"

Ruth started crying before he could finish the question. Matthew Jacobs sat silently, a frown on his face, as Ruth got out a handkerchief and quickly brought herself under control.

"Oh, I'm sorry," Ruth said. "It's just— I'm afraid I've done something very foolish, pastor."

He looked down briefly. "Just Matthew now, Ruth, just Matthew."

She smiled. "I could never call you that. You were my pastor when John and I met, and you'll always be that."

"Well, Brother Joshua is your pastor now, isn't he? Joshua Mathers?"

"No, we're at Antioch now."

"Well, then . . ." Matthew Jacobs spread his hands.

She knew what he meant. He was retired and she had her own church to fall back on. "I guess what I really need is an old friend."

"Well, I certainly qualify on the old part." He was smiling.

She smiled back, relaxing.

"So, tell me, Ruth. Something very foolish?"

She shook her head. "I think I've gone and accused John of something—something he may or may not have done, I don't know. And now I think . . ." Tears were filling her eyes again. "I think I've driven him away. I'm afraid he feels—unwelcome in his own house, in our home."

Matthew Jacobs looked away. "Oh."

"I know I should seek advice from my own pastor, but I know what he'd say. A wife's duty is to uplift her husband. He'd quote

St. Paul about me being a model and a guide, but I certainly don't feel like one. I'm angry and distracted and sharp-tongued. I'm more of a scourge than a guide."

"Still, you should ask him."

"Oh, what would be the use? If St. Paul himself were here and giving me advice I'd probably just want to wring his neck."

Matthew Jacobs stood up.

"Oh, I'm sorry," Ruth said. "But you always looked on the kinder side of Scripture. I was hoping—"

"There isn't a kinder side to Scripture. Scripture is scripture." He put his hand on his forehead. "I'm sorry, Ruth, but I really haven't got anything for you. Nothing of any use."

"But I'm sure you do." She stood and faced him. "I remember how you used to preach. You used to say, 'Christ is not the answer, but Christ *has* the answer. We still have to go looking for it.' You said that at Andy's service."

"That was years ago."

"But it's still true, isn't it? You haven't lost your faith, I can tell that."

"No. But perhaps I've lost my belief."

"I think I may have, too. Or I'm about to." She reached out and touched his sleeve. "That's why I came to you. You always used to say, 'Doubt is a gift. It makes us listen.'"

"I said that?"

"Yes. I remember it from Andy's eulogy."

"And did it do any good?"

Ruth shook her head, baffled. "I'm sorry, I—"

"I didn't change any hearts at that service, Ruth. I just shamed them, made them feel it was somehow their fault Andy was dead. That's why I lost the church. That's how I lost Susan." He walked to the sink and leaned against it, his back to her. "No, the real sin lay in me, in my thinking that I had some special grasp on the human spirit, on how every single one of us is tied to the Divine through it. But I didn't, really. I didn't embrace the human spirit, not Andy's, not Susan's, not my own. And certainly not my church's. Instead, I tried to get rid of my guilt by making it theirs."

He turned around. "Do you know for sure if John has done this terrible thing you think he's done?"

"No, I don't."

"Would it matter?"

Ruth was shocked. "Of course it would. It would change everything."

"Would it really?" He stood up straight. "Would it change you? Suppose you knew right now that it had happened. What changes? Does John? Does your love? Now suppose you know for sure it hasn't. Who's different now? Are you? What kind of love is that, that turns on and off at a word? What kind of love is it that looks only at our actions and not at the miserable, mixed up hearts they come out of?" He walked back to the table and leaned on it. "You've got a problem with St. Paul?" he said. "Then to hell with St. Paul! What's in your heart, Ruth? What's written there? Not in some book, but in your heart. Where is the love that does not change? If we can't find it there, we never will."

She clutched her purse, unable to speak. His face suddenly drained of color and his eyes softened, became watery. He sat down wearily.

"I'm sorry, Ruth," he said. "I can't help you."

The night had finally cooled down enough that they could lie out on top of their sleeping bags without being eaten alive by mosquitoes. What was left of the campfire had burned to embers, but the tang of smoke still hung in the air.

Randy opened a can of beer. "What'd I tell you?" he said.

Mally sighed contentedly. "I could live like this forever."

"Ha! Not the way you fish. You'd starve."

"I don't care. Everything's so peaceful out here. Even the stars seem closer."

"They're something, ain't they? Hey," Randy said, "wanna beer?"

Mally shrugged. "Sure."

Randy handed him a can and the church key. Mally looked natural enough opening the can. Randy smiled and lay back on his sleeping bag. "Hey," he said, "you really know the names and stuff like that?"

"Huh?"

"I mean, I can point out the Big Dipper, but that's about it."

"Ursa Major," Mally said.

"Huh?"

"Ursa Major is what astronomers call it. Means the Big Bear."

"No kidding? What else is up there?"

"Well . . . See toward the middle of the sky, a little east of middle, that almost half circle of stars? That's Corona Borealis. Means the Northern Crown."

"Oh, yeah. I think my dad pointed that out once, only he had some other name for it, some Indian name."

"Lots of different cultures call the same group of stars by different names. Every group of people likes to put their heroes in the sky."

"Show me one."

"Well," Mally searched the sky, "it might be a little early in the year, but we might see Hercules."

"Hey, that's my man," Randy said, raising his beer in a toast. "Strangled snakes and stuff as a kid. Where is he?"

"I don't know if—" Mally craned his neck around. "Yeah, there he is. See between the Crown and that bright star? It's a kind of an 'H' with a warped pentagon on one of the legs."

Randy didn't really see what Mally was describing, but he tried to look enlightened. Maybe another swig of beer would bring the stars into focus.

"That's my favorite part of the sky," Mally said.

"How come?"

"There's a spot in that constellation where, if you use a good enough telescope, you can see a whole handful of stars—and not just stars, but galaxies. A whole cluster of them. I had a friend who pointed it out once. He said that there were nearly a hundred in that one spot, and there are some clusters with a thousand or more."

"Stars?"

"No, galaxies! A thousand galaxies."

"Jeez," Randy said. He turned to look at him. "You really get off on this stuff, don't you?"

"Yeah," Mally said, settling down. "Just another way of being weird, I guess."

"No," Randy said, "I didn't mean it like that. There's something about it you like."

"Yeah."

"What?"

"Aw, nothing. You'd just say it's dumb."

"No, I wouldn't," Randy said. "Really."

Mally looked at him, then looked back at the stars. "Okay. All those galaxies out there—each one has billions of stars. And most of those stars have planets and worlds. There must be millions on millions of them out there. And with that many, there's just got to be life. A different kind of life than ours, maybe, but life. And they're out there—planets, nations, families. With all that, there's got to be a place for everyone, everyone alive. The right combination of people and landscapes, planets and stars and night skies, a home, a friend, a place where you can open up your heart and say anything and not worry about if it's the right thing or what people will say. A place with no shame and no loneliness."

Randy raised his beer can. "I'll drink to that."

Mally looked at him. "I didn't think . . ."

"What?"

"I didn't think you ever felt like that. I mean, you don't seem to."

"Pssh," Randy grunted. "Everybody feels like that."

"You could've fooled me."

"That's mostly what we do." Randy rolled onto his side and looked at him. "We fool each other into thinking we're each perfectly fine and happy, and inside, we're a wreck."

Mally looked at him and took a drink of beer—and choked on it.

"What'sa matter?" Randy asked.

"Beer's gotten warm."

"Chug it."

"Huh?"

"Chug it. You know, all in one gulp."

Mally looked at him dubiously, then brought the can to his lips. He threw his head back and finished it off in five big gulps, some of it running down his chin. He pitched forward then and wiped his mouth with his arm.

"Atta boy!" Randy cheered.

"God, that was awful!"

"You'll get used to it," Randy said, grinning. "Keep chugging like that and you'll be one of the guys in no time."

"No, I don't think so," Mally said.

"Sure you will. All you need is a little practice."

"For what? So I can fake it?"

"Everybody fakes it, at least a little bit. But that's half your problem. You don't even try."

"Try what?"

"To fit in."

"Suppose I don't want to?"

"Oh, come on."

"No, really. Do you really see me playing football with the guys?"

"Well, maybe not football. But some other sport—"

"Oh, yeah, great, like that's my problem. Not enough time in the locker room getting ragged on by a bunch of jerks."

"Hey." Randy pretended umbrage. "Some of those guys are *my* jerks."

"Sorry. But why should I bother proving anything to them?"

"Okay, fine. If you're so damned cheerful about yourself, be my guest."

"I am not 'so damned cheerful about myself.' I just know my limitations, that's all. I'm not going to fake it to make people like me. I tried that at St. Albert's. It didn't work. I'll never be one of the guys. I know it and I don't give a shit." He lay down on his bedroll.

"The hell you don't."

"Aw, shut up," Mally said, rolling over and turning his back to him.

Randy looked at him a moment. "Hey," he said. There was no response. "Hey!" Mally twisted around and frowned at him. "Want another beer?"

Mally smiled wanly. "Naw. Thanks."

Randy finished his can. "'I know my limitations,'" he repeated to the dark. "Jeez. Where'd you learn to talk like that, anyway? Catholic school?"

"Hey, don't knock a religious education."

"Or what? You'll beat me with your rosary?"

"I just might." Mally rolled around to face him. "I can already beat you at horse."

"The hell!"

"Oh, yeah? Who won three of our last five games?"

Randy thought about it a moment. "Stand up," he said, getting up himself and standing by the fire.

"What?"

"I said stand up."

Mally got to his feet warily. "Are you maybe one beer over your limit?" He was in his gym shorts.

"C'mere," Randy said. Mally took a step toward him. "Not way over there, sissy boy," he said. "Right here," and he pointed to the ground in front of him.

Mally flushed red but stepped grimly forward till he was

nose-to-nose with Randy. No, not quite nose-to-nose. Mally was at least an inch taller.

"God damn," Randy said.

Mally remembered the scene the day he first arrived at Croy Consolidated High School. Only now both of them were standing there in nothing but their underwear. And his heart remembered and his skin remembered, and with a terrible and ecstatic feeling he felt other parts of his body beginning to take notice, too. This time, he wasn't going to run away.

It was Randy who broke the spell. He turned back to his sleeping bag. "I'm going to need another beer," he said.

Mally took a deep breath and let it go. He turned away and went back to his sleeping bag, covering himself up. "You'll be pissing all night," he said.

"That's half the fun," Randy said and pitched him a can.

Mally was feeling a little woozy the next morning and stumbled more than once getting the camping gear into Randy's car.

"You all right?" Randy asked him.

Mally laughed ruefully. "Not really. I think I had two cans too many last night."

"You only had two."

"Exactly."

"You're not going to up-chuck on me on the way back, are you?"

"You'll be the first to know. Well, maybe the second."

Randy slammed the trunk shut. "Do you wanna stop on the way back for fried pie?"

"Now you're deliberately trying to make me puke."

"Well, if you take care of it now, we won't run the risk later. You know we gotta return this boat looking fine. And smelling excellent."

Mally shook his head. "I'm not that bad off, really."

Once they were in the car and on their way, the fresh morning air rushing in the windows dispelled the miasma in his head and stomach. It was too fine a day to feel sorry for yourself or take anything too seriously. They got on the subject of dating, Randy asking why Mally didn't have a girlfriend yet.

"I dunno," Mally said, feeling surprisingly at ease about the subject. "I never met a girl I could talk to."

"You talk to Joanie," Randy said.

"She's different." Mally looked at him. "Besides, she's stuck on you."

"Bull," Randy said, but he smiled. He thought a moment, then he asked, "How do you mean, she's different?"

"She doesn't put up a front," Mally said. "She doesn't play games with people."

"Like hell," Randy said. "She put on this big act of thinking I was a real clod ever since I can remember, and she really had her eye on me all the time."

"And you had your eye on her, I'll bet."

"What?"

"You two were made for each other."

"Where'd you get that?"

"How else did you notice she had her eye on you if you didn't have your eye on her?"

"She told me."

"Oh, sure."

"She did!" Randy said. "Besides, I noticed, that's all. A guy looks around and he notices things like that." He looked over at Mally again. "Do you really think she's stuck on me?"

"Oh, yeah. Big time."

Randy grinned even more broadly. "Yeah," he said. Then the smile faded. "I wish she'd come right out and say so, though."

"Say what?" Mally asked. "You go on dates, you make out and all." He looked at him. "Don't you?"

"Well, yeah," Randy said, squirming a little. "We make out. But not . . . you know."

Mally suddenly blushed. He hadn't really meant to get this deep into it.

"I mean," Randy went barreling on, unaware of his discomfort, "I think she might be the one, the one to . . . you know."

Mally was looking out the window on his side, avoiding Randy's eyes. "So, you never . . ." He both wanted and didn't want to be talking about this.

"Nope," Randy said with frank honesty. "Hard to believe, isn't it?"

"Well, yeah," Mally said, though he believed it at once. "I mean, the way you and the other guys talk—"

"That's all it is. Just talk." Randy glanced at him. "I'll bet not one of those guys—" He heaved a big sigh. "Shit. It's not like I don't try. All the girls I dated. But I don't know. I think I was always looking for something special. I mean, I don't just want to do it with anyone, just to get it over with. I want it to be someone special." He looked at Mally. "Do you think Joanie's special?"

Mally looked at him. His heart was sinking and he had a funny feeling in the pit of his stomach, but it wasn't from the beer last night. "Yeah," he said, "she's special."

It was impossible for Mally to feel glum about it, though. By the time they pulled into Croy, they were joking again. Mally was doing impersonations of some of the teachers at the high school. He had Coach Tucker's booming voice down pat, even his manner of speaking. "All right, all right," he mimicked, "this isn't a Chinese Opera."

"This isn't a Christmas pageant," Randy added.

"This ain't the Queen Mary."

"Do what?" Randy said.

Mally laughed. "Never mind."

They pulled into the alley and unloaded Mally's stuff from the trunk. "Help you out with that?" Randy asked as Mally hefted his sleeping bag on his shoulder.

"Naw," Mally said. "I can manage."

"Okay then," Randy said. "I'll dump my stuff at my house and return Joanie's car. Think they're back yet?"

Mally shrugged and smiled. It was kind of cute to see how eager Randy was to get to the Tibbitses'. He turned and walked around the corner of the granny house. There was a pile of laundry on the lawn, just outside the door to the granny house. He thought that was odd.

"Hey," Randy said, "guess this one." He pitched his voice high and nasal. "Now boys, boys!"

It hit Mally suddenly. That wasn't a pile of laundry. "Grampa!" he yelled. He dropped his gear and ran to the man lying in a crumpled heap outside their house.

"Didja get it?" Randy called out.

"Randy!" Mally yelled. "Come here! Quick! Please!" He turned to his grandfather, who was lying partly on his left side, his face turned to the earth. He took his grandfather's head in his hands and turned it toward him. There was a trail of blood just below his nose.

Randy came running up behind him and froze.

"I think he's fallen or . . ." Mally said.

"Oh, Jesus," Randy muttered.

"We've got to get him up, get him to a doctor," Mally said. He got under one arm and Randy got under the other. Together, they managed to get the old man to his feet, but there was no way they could walk him anywhere. He was dead weight.

"We don't have a phone," Mally said. "You'll have to use Mrs. Oldfield's. Run up there quick and call. We gotta get a doctor."

Randy let go of his side and was about to turn away when the old man's eyes flew open. He reached out and grabbed Randy by the arm, making him jump.

"When did we see thee hungry, or a stranger?" Reverend Jacobs said, looking into Randy's face. "Or naked or sick?" Then he staggered backward into Mally and the two of them nearly toppled to the ground.

Randy reached out and grabbed him by the shirt, keeping both of them upright. "You run," he said to Mally. "I'll hold him."

Mally let go and ran for the house. He pounded and pounded on the back door, yelling for help. He took one look back across the lawn and saw Randy and his grandfather sitting on the grass, almost like a pair of lovers, the old man's head cradled in Randy's lap. "Oh, Jesus," he whispered and started pounding on the door again.

Chapter 12

GAD FLY

R ANDY SAT ON the edge of the chair, rubbing his hands together. It was a hard chair, for all the carved rosebuds in the backboard and the finely curved legs. He felt like it must be some antique, and therefore fragile, and therefore he shouldn't be sitting in it, let alone fidgeting, and that only made him fidget more. Across from him, Mally slumped on the sofa with one hand on his forehead. Randy glanced down the hall to the doorway that led to the bedroom where they had taken Reverend Jacobs. The doctor and Mrs. Oldfield were in there now with him. He looked again at Mally. "What do you think he meant by that?" he asked softly.

Mally dropped his hand. "By what?" he said.

"'When did I see you hungry, or naked, or a stranger.'"

Mally sighed and leaned forward, his elbows on his knees. "Gospel according to St. Matthew." He frowned. "I've never heard him quote the New Testament before." He held his head in his hands. "I don't know. I don't know what it means."

The doctor and Mrs. Oldfield came out of the bedroom then, the doctor saying, "He's not to be moved. He'll have to stay here."

"That's for the best," Mrs. Oldfield said. "At least there's a telephone here in easy reach."

Mally got up. "Can I see him?" he asked.

"He's sleeping now," the doctor said. "He'll be all right till morning." He turned to Mrs. Oldfield. "You have my number at home."

Mrs. Oldfield nodded. The doctor headed for the door.

"Dr. Evans?" Mally said. The doctor turned around, but whatever Mally was going to ask flew out of his head. "Thank you," he said at last.

The doctor nodded and put on his hat and left.

Mally turned to Mrs. Oldfield. "I don't know what happened," he said. "He was perfectly fine when we left."

"Don't fret, now, Malachi," Mrs. Oldfield said. "There's nothing you could have done. It's in God's hands."

Mally looked at her sharply, then looked down and nodded. "I'll go get some of his stuff from the little house."

Randy jumped up. "Do you need help?"

"It can wait, Malachi," Mrs. Oldfield said. "I want you to sit for a spell. You've had quite a shock."

Mally nodded again and sat down.

"You, too, Randy," Mrs. Oldfield said.

"I . . ." Randy started. He didn't know what to make of this kinder side of Mrs. Oldfield. "I actually have to return Joanie's car." Mally looked up at him, panic in his eyes. "I'll be right back," he said.

"Will you be going past the pharmacy?" Mrs. Oldfield asked. "Dr. Evans wrote out a prescription. It isn't urgent, but it would be handy to have today."

"Yes, ma'am," Randy said, glad to be of some use. "I'll be back directly."

Mally watched Randy leave, feeling unable to move, unable to say anything.

Mrs. Oldfield still stood just inside the living room, watching him. "Can I get you anything?" she asked.

"No," Mally said. "Thanks." She moved into the room and sat on the chair across from him. "I'll take care of him," he said. "I'll come up and fix his meals and—"

"There's no need, Malachi," she said. "I can see to all of that."

His jaw stiffened. He supposed he should thank her, but he couldn't. He felt angry, not grateful—as if something had been stolen from him.

"Are you sure you'll be all right in that house all by yourself?" she asked.

"Yes, ma'am," he said. "I'll be fine."

Mrs. Oldfield looked down and smoothed her dress with her hands. "There's one more thing," she said without looking up.

He looked at her.

She raised her head and straightened herself as if she had unpleasant news to deliver. "You'll have to contact your mother."

Randy nearly ran right into Mrs. Tibbits outside the TG&Y as he bolted around the corner.

"Randy, what on earth? You look a fright."

"It's old Reverend Jacobs," he said. "He's had a stroke."

Her hand flew to her mouth. "Oh, dear Lord."

"Doc Evans has seen him and he says he'll be fine for now, but I've got to get a prescription filled and get back to Mrs. Oldfield's. Is the Rexall open? Is Mr. Tibbits back yet?"

Mrs. Tibbits looked confused and worried. "I . . . I don't know." He turned to leave. "Randy, wait!" she called out. "I'll drive you. I'm parked just behind vanDoozer's."

"No time, Mrs. Tibbits," Randy called, already sprinting down the sidewalk.

The running helped. He made it to the drugstore in record time. He tried the front door but it was locked and the lights were off inside. He dashed down the alley to the side door. It wasn't locked. He stepped in and went through the storeroom door into the store proper. It was cool and dark inside.

"Hello?" he called. "Mr. Tibbits, are you open?"

There wasn't a sound at first, but then a figure sitting behind the prescription counter moved. "What is it, Randy?" Mr. Tibbits said.

"I've got a prescription here from Dr. Evans," Randy said. "It's for Reverend Jacobs. He's had a stroke."

"Please," Mr. Tibbits said, rising, "bring it here."

Randy walked up to the counter and handed over the script. "They said it wasn't urgent, but that they'd like it filled today."

Mr. Tibbits read the slip of paper. "I wasn't going to open to-day," he muttered, then disappeared into the pharmacy.

Ordinarily, the prescription counter marked the boundary between Mr. Tibbits's world and Randy's and he wouldn't have dared to cross it, but his nervous energy propelled him forward, following Mr. Tibbits into the rows of boxes and bottles. "Mally and I found him when we came back from the camping trip," he said. "He was on the ground, just lying there."

"Was he conscious?" Mr. Tibbits asked, sitting on a stool to count out the pills.

"He spoke to us. Something from the gospels."

Mr. Tibbits shook his head. "Things change so fast," he said, "so fast." He typed up the label and taped it to the bottle. He started to hand it over, but stopped just as Randy reached for it. "Randy," he said. "I may be closing up the store for a little while. I may be going away."

"Oh," Randy said. "Well, gee. I was kind of hoping . . ." His eyes had adjusted to the dim light by now and he could see Mr. Tibbits looking up at him. Clearly, there was something wrong. "I thought the store was doing real well."

"It's not the store. I just need some time away. So, I'm sorry, but there won't be a job for you."

Randy thought for a moment. "I guess that means Candy, too."

"Who?"

"Candy Sullivan. I heard she was going to start working here, too."

Mr. Tibbits looked down. "No," he said. "Miss Sullivan won't be coming to work here. That's . . . She won't be—coming here." He held out the prescription bottle. "You'd better take this."

Randy took the bottle and almost didn't say anything more, but there was a look on Mr. Tibbits's face, a look like a lost man hoping to be found. "I don't think it's a good idea, Mr. Tibbits."

Tibbits looked at him as if he were a table that had suddenly spoken. "What?" he said.

"Something else happened while you were gone," Randy said.

"What are you talking about?"

"I caught Kyle playing with some blasting caps."

Mr. Tibbits rose from his stool. "Good God in heaven."

"It's okay," Randy said. "I got them away from him. But he could have gotten hurt. Real bad. I gave him a talking to about it, but I think you should, too. So I don't think it's a good idea, your going away. He needs someone around. Someone to look after him more."

Mr. Tibbits stood there looking at him for a moment. Then he looked down and nodded. "Thank you, Randy," he said.

"Sure," Randy said.

Mr. Tibbits turned his back and Randy left quietly.

Joanie arrived at the granny house the next morning to help pack a few of his grandfather's things into a suitcase to carry up to Mrs. Oldfield's. She tried to lighten the task by telling the story of "Candy and the Jigaboo," but Mally's spirits were difficult to lift.

"I really appreciate all you're doing," he said.

"Aw, it's nothing," she said. "Daddy's still gone on his buying trip and Momma's moping around the house like a ghost. I was glad to get out. Were you able to get ahold of your momma?"

"Not really," Mally said. "Aunt Margaret's going to try to call her agent. I had to talk her into getting the number from Mr. Anderson."

"Why'd you have to talk her into it?"

Mally waved his hands. "It's a long story."

"Hello?" came Randy's voice from outside. "Am I too late to help?"

"Of course," Joanie called back.

"Come on in," Mally said. "Joanie's pretty well gotten everything packed."

"Really?" Randy said. "Good."

Joanie eyed him. "If certain people didn't sleep till noon, they'd get in on a lot more things."

"All the more reason to snooze," he said. "How's your granddad doing?" he asked Mally.

"Better, I think" Mally said. "He's awake and talking. And making sense. Mrs. Oldfield got him to eat a little something last night. Mush, mostly, but he seems to like it. I wouldn't have eaten it."

"I hate to think of him spending the nights up there with her," Randy said.

Mally looked at him. "Well, he's not exactly *with* her."

"You should have seen her yesterday," he said to Joanie, "hovering over him like some sort of vulture."

"Randy!" Joanie said.

"Well, she was."

She gave him a look and cocked her head at Mally, hoping it would occur to him that references to picking over corpses were in bad taste.

"Oh," he said. "Sorry."

"It's all right," Mally said, "and not too far off the mark." He looked out the window. "Speaking of which . . ."

They all turned and saw Mrs. Oldfield coming across the lawn.

"She probably wants fresh clothes for him," Mally said. "Let's take them outside. I don't really want her in here, snooping around."

Randy picked up the large suitcase and Mally the small bag

of toiletries and the three of them stepped out of the granny house together.

"Oh, there you are," Mrs. Oldfield said. "I was beginning to wonder if maybe you'd forgotten."

"No, ma'am," Mally said. "Joanie here helped make sure I got everything."

"That's really kind of her," Mrs. Oldfield said. "Thank you, Joanie."

Joanie exchanged looks with the boys. She hadn't really done it for Mrs. Oldfield, but she muttered "You're welcome" anyway.

"Do you need help getting it up to the house?" Mrs. Oldfield asked.

"No, thanks, ma'am," Randy said, hefting the suitcase. "We can do fine." He started up the lawn, Mally following.

"Well, it's good to have friends, isn't it?" Mrs. Oldfield said. "Especially you, Joanie, considering all you're going through as well."

"What do you mean, Mrs. Oldfield?"

"Well, I'm sure your mother has her hands full. It was kind of her to spare you. And I'm sure prayer and community will get her through this."

She saw Randy and Mally stop and turn around, their mouths agape.

"I'm afraid I don't know what you're talking about, Mrs. Oldfield."

"Why, the situation with your father, dear. You and your mother have my full support, and little Kyle, too, of course."

"Uh, Mrs. Oldfield—" Mally started to say.

Joanie looked at the boys and back at Mrs. Oldfield. "I don't know what you're talking about," she said. "My father is away in Oklahoma City on business."

"Oh," Mrs. Oldfield said, looking back at Randy and Mally. "Oh, I'm terribly sorry, my dear. I shouldn't have said anything in front of the boys."

"Anything about what?" Joanie said.

Mrs. Oldfield started fussing with her hair. "Maybe you boys should take those things up to the house, now."

But instead, Randy put down the suitcase and started walking toward her, his arms outstretched.

"Anything about what?" she demanded.

"It's nothing, Joanie," Randy said. "Don't pay her any mind."

"What is going on here?" she said, getting increasingly frantic. "What's happened to Daddy?"

Mrs. Oldfield was backing up the lawn. "I thought . . ." she said. "But surely, when your mother threw him out—"

"She did not throw him out!" Joanie shouted. "You've got it all wrong." She turned to Randy. "Tell her." He just stood there, dumbfounded. She turned to Mally. "Tell her, you guys. My father is in Oklahoma City buying pharmaceutical supplies." She saw nothing, nothing from either of them. She turned and ran to her car.

Randy ran after her. "Joanie!" he called. "Joanie!" Mally started after him.

"I've got to go home," she said. She was having difficulty getting the key in the ignition. "I've gotta talk to Momma."

"Joanie," Randy said, trying to touch her, to calm her down. "Don't listen to her. She's got it all wrong."

"What has she got wrong?" Joanie said, desperate.

"It's all over. He said so himself."

"Who said so?"

"You're father. It's all over with him and Candy."

Mally stopped in his tracks, his hands over his ears.

Joanie froze at the wheel. "Who?" she said.

Randy stepped back, his mouth open.

She looked at him. "Who did you say?" She was deadly quiet.

"It doesn't matter anymore," Randy said feebly. "He told me it was over."

"He told you? My father told you?"

"Well, not in so many words," Randy said.

"So, what, the two of you just talked it out, man to man?" Joanie said, fire in her eyes.

"No," Randy said. "It was nothing like that." He turned to Mally. "Help me out, here, Mally."

Joanie turned to him now. "You knew about this, too?"

Mally said nothing but he couldn't look away from her.

"You knew and you said nothing?" Joanie looked from him to Randy and to Mrs. Oldfield, standing horrified on the lawn. "My God," she said. "My God but it's great to have friends!" She jammed home the ignition key and cranked the engine.

"Joanie," Randy said, reaching in to her.

"Don't you touch me!" she yelled. She was over cranking the engine and it was making a horrible grinding noise. "Don't you dare come near me! I don't ever want to see you, or hear you, or touch you ever again. I wish you were dead! Get out of my way!" And she tore out of the alley.

"What did I do?" Randy yelled, running after her. "God damn it, what did I do?"

Mally ran up to him. "Randy—"

"Screw you!" Randy yelled. He turned around and shoved Mally aside. "Get out of my face!" He bolted across the alley and up the stairs to his house.

Mally stood for a moment in the middle of the alley. He could still hear the sound of Joanie's car tearing over the gravel and Randy's curse ringing in his ears. Then he turned around and saw Mrs. Oldfield, standing like a pillar of salt in the middle of her yard beside the abandoned luggage. He walked up to her, his eyes locked on hers.

"I had no idea," she said in a small voice as he got closer. "I certainly wouldn't have—"

"*Refuse to enroll younger widows*," Mally said to her face, "*for they learn to be idlers, gadding about from house to house, and not only idlers, but gossips and busybodies, saying things they ought not!*" He picked up the luggage. "1 Timothy, Mrs. Oldfield. Chapter Five, verses eleven and thirteen." He hauled the luggage up to the house, scarcely noticing the weight.

Candy Sullivan sat on her bed with her knees drawn up to her chin. The room was glum and stuffy with the window shut and the curtains drawn, but she wanted nothing to do with the annoying springtime noises playing around outside.

The band trip had been a total disaster. First, she had to share a room with that simpering sophomore prig. She knew right then that there was something wrong. Joanie Tibbits was the last person she'd have picked for a roommate if she were in charge of things. And then that creepy bellhop came right into their room. Didn't they teach those boys manners anymore? Then, just as she had feared, John had lost his nerve. He never even called. She had constructed the perfect alibi, staying with her cousin Marsha and Aunt Flo and Uncle Bud till the end of spring break. Nobody would have thought to check which days she was there. All that wasted effort! She had been so clever. But nothing ever worked out. Instead, she had to spend two humiliating nights in that cheap hotel room and then ride home with the squealing band goonies. She heard their whispers and snickering the whole trip back, her trophy riding on the seat beside her so no one would sit next to her.

Her trophy with the silver columns and the eagles and the ruby red globe on top and the inscription, "Oklahoma State High School Baton Tournament, Second Place." Again.

There was a light knock at the door. She didn't answer, but in a moment, her father gently opened the door and stepped into the room. He sat down on her bed and for a while didn't say anything.

"You know, you're getting to be quite a young lady," he said when he finally spoke. "Your mother and I were just talking the other day how much you stood out from the rest of the kids who went on the band trip."

She kept her lips tight. She might as well let him talk.

"We were really wondering if maybe you hadn't outgrown the whole high school band thing," he said.

She turned her head on its side and looked at him.

"Maybe it's time to try something new," he said and looked at her.

"Like what?" she said.

"Well, Beth will be starting high school next year."

"So?"

"And she's been doing pretty well, practicing. Maybe it's time for her to take over in the twirling department. You know, time for you to sort of pass the baton."

He smiled weakly at his joke but she felt hot tears beginning to burn in her eyes.

"There's something else I want you to do with your time," he said. "Something for me."

"What?"

He reached over and patted her arm. "From time to time, I have to take business trips, trips where I meet other car dealers and folks like that. And it always helps to have someone along. Someone smart and bright to take notes, help me remember names, keep conversations going when we go to dinner. And it doesn't hurt none if she's pretty, too." He smiled at her.

Candy wiped away the tear that had nearly fallen from her eye. "Momma always went with you," she said.

"Yep," he said. "And we were quite a team. Sullivan and Sullivan. She'd dazzle 'em and I'd rope 'em in. But she's not interested in traveling around the state any more. We were kind of wondering if maybe you would be interested."

She sniffled a little. "Really?"

He nodded. "Really."

"I'd like that, Daddy," she said. "I really would."

Mally sat at his grandfather's bedside. The old man was propped up slightly on the pillows, breathing shallowly, apparently asleep. The chair Mally sat on was small and dark, and even though it had an embroidered cushion, it was as hard and unyielding as a church pew. It creaked as Mally shifted a little, trying to get the circulation back into his buttocks.

His grandfather's eyes opened and Mally was instantly alert. The old man looked around the room, his eyes wandering over to the window and resting there. He seemed to become gradually aware that Mally was sitting beside him and he turned to look at him. "Mally," he said.

"Hello, Grampa," Mally said with a smile.

"It's a beautiful day. You should be outside."

"I'd rather stay with you," he said.

The old man smiled at him, then looked off at the far wall.

"I've called Mother," Mally said. His grandfather looked at him quizzically. "Susan," Mally added. "That is, I called Aunt Margaret. She's going to try and get in touch with her agent."

His grandfather nodded. "Thank you, Mally."

He smiled a little self-consciously at that. "You've never called me Mally before," he said. "You always call me Malachi, you and Mrs. Oldfield."

"You don't really like Malachi, do you?" his grandfather said.

"Well," Mally said, "it's kind of formal."

"Do you prefer Mally?"

He shrugged. "I used to, but it sounds, I don't know, soft. It's not really a boy's name. I mean, maybe it is, but it's more of a little kid's name, a nick-name. I don't feel like that anymore."

"So, what name do you want?"

"I don't know." He shrugged again. "Some guys at school call me Jake. Maybe that."

His grandfather sighed. "I never told you, did I?" Mally looked at him. "About how you got to be Malachi. It's my fault, I'm afraid. Susan was very ill after you were born. She was in the hospital for several weeks. And she was unconscious at the time when they came around with the birth certificate." He seemed lost in the past for a moment, then he turned to look at him. "I'm the one, Mally. I named you Malachi. I'm sorry."

"It's okay, Grampa. I've gotten used to it." His grandfather looked at him and suddenly he was really there, just like he used to be, gentle, chiding, giving him that 'Are you really sure that's what you want to say?' look. Mally grinned. "Well, sorta."

His grandfather smiled.

But Mally was still puzzled. "Why him?" he asked. "Why 'the messenger of the Lord'?"

"It's right there in the book," his grandfather said. "in the very first message he brings the people. 'I have loved you,' says the Lord."

Mally thought about the verse, about the many times he'd searched for a clue. He recalled from memory, "And the people say, 'How have you loved us?'"

"Do you know why?" the Reverend Jacobs said. "Do you know why they didn't know the Lord loved them? Because they didn't believe it. They couldn't see his love because they didn't believe in it." He reached out and took Mally's hand. "Believe in it, Mally, believe in it."

Mally placed his other hand on his grandfather's. Maybe, he thought, maybe he was beginning to.

Chapter 13

His Hand by the Door

M ALLY FELT HE ought to be doing more to take care of his grandfather, but the old man slept most of the time. There was nothing to do and the house had a creepy silence to it. Now that he'd finally had it out with Mrs. Oldfield, she barely spoke to him at all, and that only made him all the more jumpy.

He couldn't find peace anywhere. He felt suffocated in the quiet darkness of Mrs. Oldfield's house and loose and unfocused in the granny house, rattling around it like a dried pea in a shoe box. He'd even stopped walking along the railroad tracks, having learned more than he really wanted to know there. He'd been up to the farm house a couple of times, but now he felt he couldn't go there anymore, either. Things weren't right with Joanie and Randy. Joanie wouldn't speak to him and Randy was being stand-offish and sullen. His hoped-for family had fallen apart just when he needed them most.

So he lingered after school in the empty gym, toying with a basketball, playing phantom games of horse. It helped burn off some of the tension.

He still had heard nothing from his mother.

Randy finally found the right alternator and installed it in the Dream Machine himself. It felt good, getting something solid accomplished. He decided to celebrate and drove out to Red's house to see if maybe he might want to come along. He didn't go round to the back door by the garage as usual, though. They hadn't really left things in a good way the last time he and Red had talked. So he rang the front doorbell.

It was quiet for a long time. Randy wondered if maybe he should ring the doorbell again or maybe just go away. He felt oddly exposed on the concrete slab of the front porch.

The door opened and Red stood there. He didn't open it all the way—he just loomed in the doorway, a kind of shadow behind the screen door. "What do you want?" he said.

"Hey, Conner," Randy said. "The Dream Machine is back in action. I was wondering if maybe you might want to take her for a spin."

Red looked off, then back at him. "I gotta stick around here."

"Oh," Randy said. "Well, maybe later."

"No," Red said. "I don't think so."

Randy put his hands on his hips. "This isn't about that dust-up we had, is it?"

Red opened the screen door and stepped outside, closing the front door behind him. The sun was beginning to lower in the west and Red seemed to take a moment to look at it, then looked the other way at the town. "Look," he said, "my Dad wouldn't like it, your coming around here now that he's gone."

"What?" This was the first Randy had heard that Mr. Conner had something against him.

"You know 'what,'" Red said. "Just because he's gone doesn't mean things have changed."

Now Randy was completely confused. "What do you mean, 'just because he's gone'?"

"Don't play dumb with me, Edom," Red said, looking him in the eye.

Randy didn't know what to do. He just stood there, looking back. A change came over Red's face. It went from impatient to angry, then from angry to just giving up.

"You don't know, do you?" Red said finally. He looked off toward the town. "Figures."

"What's going on here, Red?" Randy asked, genuinely concerned.

Red looked back at him. "My father's been arrested," he said. He spat it out like an accusation. "They set him up. The insurance company, the sheriff, the whole damned town. They were all in on it." He spat on the ground. "I can't wait to get out of this shit hole."

"Jeez, Red, I had no idea."

"Yeah," Red said.

"Well, it's not true, is it? He's gonna fight it, isn't he? You'll see. Your dad will come out of it okay."

"It doesn't matter. There's a lien on the house. The bank'll foreclose in a month. He won't even get a chance to have his say. Damn this place."

"You could move back into town. There's still your old place—"

"I don't give a rat's ass about Croy, or the Cowboys, or the whole damned state. I don't want to have anything to do with them. I'm telling Coach Ardmore to take my name off the trophies."

"What in God's name do you want to do that for?"

"Because it's phony," Red said. "It's fake. Everything we've done here, everything we have is fake. Fake home, fake money, fake friends. I'm tired of phonies." He looked off at the sunset again. "I'm joining the Marines."

Randy laughed, caught off-balance. "What, the Green Berets?"

"Maybe. If they'll have me."

"You're kidding." Randy grinned at him but Red wasn't grinning back. "Come on, Red. We used to make fun of that song. 'Fearless men who jump and die.' We used to laugh at that."

"Well maybe it's time people stopped laughing." Red thrust his face forward with such a look that Randy backed up. "Maybe it's time we stopped and took a look at what's happening to this country. Hippies and perverts running everywhere. Ardmore was right. We've been laughing it up, having a good time, while others have been doing the fighting and dying. It's time we pulled our own weight, stopped fooling around, being boys, started being men."

"You can't," Randy blurted out.

"Who's gonna stop me?"

Randy had said it before thinking of a reason, so he grabbed at the first one he thought of. "You can't join up till you're eighteen."

Red looked down at him like he was sorry for him. "I am eighteen, Randy," he said. "I turned eighteen last month. I've been a year ahead of you all along, ever since we came to Croy. Biggest mistake we ever made, coming here. This town just sucks you down and tears you up. I'm joining the Marines and never looking back." He turned around and opened the door to go inside. "Good-bye, Randy," he said and shut the door.

Tucker loomed in the doorway to the coach's office like a tree. It was enough to change the lighting in the room. Ardmore looked up from his copy of *Golfer's Digest*. "What's up?" he asked.

"There's something I want you to see," Tucker said. He turned and walked away, leaving Ardmore to follow him or not as he chose.

I wish to God he wouldn't pull that silent Indian crap on me, Ardmore thought. But he sighed and put aside the magazine and followed him.

They went to the gym, but not the direct way from the locker room. They went around to the stairs and up to the balcony, then out to the railing and looked down on the court.

There was a lone boy down there, dribbling and shooting, playing around. Ardmore didn't recognize him right away. The kid was doing lay-ups, hook shots, pretending to fake out an invisible opponent, just horsing around. Just when Ardmore figured out who he was, the kid sank a perfect swisher. From center court.

"Well I'll be dipped in shit," Ardmore whispered.

Tucker smiled. "Yup. I thought you would."

Bobbie Littledeer could hardly contain herself. "There's not a penny left," she said, clutching the bottle of rubbing alcohol she had supposedly come in to buy. "It's all gone. All those insurance payments, just vanished."

Joanie rolled her eyes and fingered the cash register keys. She supposed she should be grateful. The Conner's misfortunes had certainly taken the spotlight off her own family. She had felt like a slug with warts crawling down the school hallways the first day she came to class after finding out about her father and—oh, she couldn't even let the name enter her mind. She had gone to her locker the first thing that morning, grabbing a whole day's worth of books and notebooks rather than running the risk of running into that, into that—oh for heaven's sake, now the only word she could think of was "hussy," something Bobbie Littledeer would say, only she wasn't talking about that at all, just babbling on and on about Mr. Conner and embezzlement and how she and her family always kept their money "somewhere safe, not in a bank," as if banks had anything to do with it, and how when the End Times came they'd be safe and cozy, and Joanie could just imagine them and their three years' supply of canned peaches hidden away in a fallout shelter lined with Red Letter editions of the Bible and a secret stash of hooch for "medicinal" purposes.

"Are you going to buy that alcohol or not?" she finally interjected at random into the running stream.

It stemmed the flow. "Oh," Bobbie said, suddenly aware of the bottle in her hand. "Yes. And do you have Kaopectate?"

That ought to be real handy in the End Times, Joanie thought, and pointed down the aisle across the counter. As Bobbie went in search of the potion the bell jingled and saw Mally walk in, a slip of paper in hand and a basketball tucked under his arm. When he saw her behind the counter he hesitated then came forward.

"I was wondering if your father could refill this prescription," he said, presenting the slip of paper.

"I'll see," she said. "Daddy?" she called out. "Can you refill Dr. Evan's prescription for Reverend Jacobs?"

"In a minute," her father called from behind the prescription counter. "I've got two ahead of you."

She passed the prescription to her father and turned to Mally with smug efficiency. He looked dumbly back at her for a moment, then seemed about to speak when Bobbie came to the counter with her two bottles. Joanie rang them up and bid Bobbie a cheerful "Thank you and good day."

"Bye, now," Bobbie said, nodding in her direction, and since she couldn't ignore Mally standing right next to her, she turned to him and said, "Good afternoon, Malachi."

He bowed in a courtly manner and said, "Miss Bobbie," and looked up in time to see her blush and scurry out the door. He turned around to catch a wicked grin on Joanie's face which vanished as soon as he grinned back.

"I'm not talking to you," she said.

"So I noticed," he said. He looked around. "I was hoping to catch Randy."

"A certain someone has decided not to show up this afternoon, for no apparent reason," she said.

"Oh," he said, "huh."

Good Lord, she thought, *he's even beginning to talk like a jock*. "What's with the basketball?" she asked.

He looked at it as if it had suddenly materialized under his arm like an extra head. He shrugged. "Coach Tucker said I could take it home with me if I wanted."

There was another silence. "I'm still not talking to you," she said.

"Yeah, so I noticed. Some more."

She glared at him and then suddenly came around the counter and grabbed him by the arm. "Daddy?" she called out. "Me and Mally are stepping outside for a moment."

"Okay," her father called, "I'll be done here in a minute."

She dragged him by the arm out the door and around the corner of the building into the alley. "How could you?" she hissed at him. "How could you keep a thing like that from me?"

"Well what was I supposed to say?" he hissed back at her. "'Why don't you and me get together some night and do homework and, oh, by the way I think your father is screwing a cheerleader'?"

She looked at him tight-lipped. "No," she said, "not that."

"Well then, what?"

"I don't know. But you should have said something."

"I was too embarrassed."

"*You* were embarrassed?"

"Yeah. How do you talk about things like that?" He leaned against the stone wall of the building and bounced the basketball a few times. "I mean, parents aren't supposed to have sex, not even with each other, let alone screw high school students."

"Would you stop saying that?"

"Well, you wanted me to talk about it."

"Well, now I want you to stop!"

"I'm sorry! Forget it! Pretend I never said anything. Which, you know, I *didn't* . . . so . . ."

She shot him a dirty look, but he was staring off down the cobbled alley. The old train depot shone across Broad Street at the end of it, promising escapes that would never come. *He has troubles of his own*, she remembered. "Have you heard from your momma yet?" she asked.

"No." He shot the ball across the alley and caught it on the rebound. "Her agent says she's in New York on an audition. They're trying to track her down."

"At least your granddad's doing better," she offered.

"Yeah." That didn't seem to cheer him up any, though. "Mrs. Oldfield pretty much takes care of him now," he said. "There's not much I can do." He caught the ball again and looked down. "You know what today is, don't you?" he said, not looking up.

"No," she said, trying to think of something.

He looked up at her sideways. "It's the first pretty day of spring."

"Well, it's hardly that," she said. "There've been plenty of . . ." But then she caught the look in his eye, half teasing, half pleading, and she remembered. "Oh, no," she said, pulling away from the wall and heading back to the store. "Oh, no you don't. I'm not going back out there with that two-faced, double-crossing—"

"Aw, give him a chance, Joanie," Mally pleaded, following behind her.

"Why should I?"

"Because he likes you. And, yeah, maybe what he and I did—or didn't do—was stupid, but he really likes you."

"So?"

"And you really like him."

She wheeled around on him. "Now you listen here, Malachi Jacobs. I know who I like and who I don't, and I don't need you to tell me the difference. If he's so taken with me then he can just come right out and say so, and a heaping huge load of apology would be good for starters. He's arrogant, he's ignorant, he's self-centered and dim-witted—"

"And you really like him."

She clamped her mouth shut and glared at him. He just stood there and smiled and didn't seem to take the hint. "I think your prescription is just about ready," she said. That knocked his smile back a notch or two. She turned around and marched back into the store.

He stood at the top of Stonewall Alley a moment longer, then followed her, bouncing the basketball with a vengeance against the cobblestones, each ring of the ball covering a muttered word.

It wasn't really all that nice a day. It was way too hot, and this early in the year that meant the summer would be unbearable. What little air circulation there was in the granny house seemed to stop about half way down the hall to Mally's bedroom, which sat in a deep pocket of stifling heat by the end of the day. By the time night fell, he had given up all notion of sleeping in his room. He pulled out the sofa bed, stripped down to his under-shorts, and put the window fan in the open front door to suck what little cool night air there was in through the screen.

So he didn't see the car lights play across the curtains, or hear the wheels skid hitting the edge of the concrete pad, or the tiny sound the keys made hitting the ground. What brought him bolt upright on the thin mattress was the sound of a football slam-ming into the screen door.

"Touchdown!" yelled Randy.

"Jesus God!" Mally cried out.

"And the crowd goes wild!" Randy called from the dark.

Mally sprang to the front door, nearly tripping over the win-dow fan. Randy was dancing in a little circle in Mrs. Oldfield's back yard, his hands in the air. "For God's sake, Edom! You nearly gave me a heart attack."

"Well, I tried to be subtle," Randy said, stopping his victory lap. "I called out real gentle." He put his hands to his mouth. "Ma-a-ally, Ma-a-a-a-lly. Hey! Jacobs!"

"Shh!" Mally said.

"But subtle don't work on you. So I drop kicked you an invi-tation. Boom!"

"Will you shut up?" Mally pulled aside the fan and opened the screen door. "Get in here before you wake up the whole neighborhood."

"Oh, yeah," Randy said, walking toward him. "I forgot. We got sick people. Shhhhhh!"

Mally stepped aside as Randy entered the room. He was wearing his letter jacket but no shirt and he smelled like hay. He took a couple of steps into the room, then stretched his arms over his head and sighed contentedly.

"What are you doing here in the middle of the night?" Mally asked him.

Randy turned and smiled at him. "Can't get in."

"Huh?"

"I can't get in. I lost my keys and I can't get in. Nobody home." He smiled. "So, I figured, where can a best man turn to but his best friend?" He spread his arms expansively. "Buford, your Daddy's home!"

Mally glared at him. "Have you been drinking?"

Randy raised his right hand. "Absolutely. I swear to God."

Mally sighed and shook his head. "Look, it must be nearly midnight. What do you want?"

"I lost my keys. I can't get in."

"We've been through all that," Mally said, exasperated. "What are you—" He looked down at Randy's feet. "Where are your shoes?"

"Injuns don't wear shoes."

"You're not an Injun."

"Okies don't, neither," Randy said, sitting down abruptly on the edge of the sofa bed. "'Sides, you get better traction for a punt without 'em. Leather to leather."

Mally sighed and sat beside him on the edge of the bed. "You are a real mess, you know that?"

"I certainly do."

"You didn't show up at Tibbits all day. Where were you?"

"Hercules!"

"What?"

"Hercules—the Thorny Crown—the Milky Whatever."

"Joanie's been worried sick."

"Aw, screw her," Randy said, dismissing it with a wave of his hand. "Screw all that. I bet she hasn't said one word, not one word about me. She doesn't give a rap about me."

"Of course she does."

"Well, why doesn't she come right out and say so, then?"

Mally rolled his eyes. How many times was he going to have to listen to this junk? "You don't just come right up and blurt out 'I love you' to someone," he said.

"Why not?"

"Well, what if you don't feel the same way about her, huh? I mean, she's got her pride, Randy."

"*Pride?*" He got to his feet. "Hell, she's only sixteen. She's got the whole rest of her life to be proud."

"And what about you?"

"What about me?"

"Why don't you take the first step?"

"Why should I?"

"Pride."

"I am not proud."

"Oh, no, not at all."

"No, I'm not," Randy said and took off his letter jacket.

Mally looked at him. "What are you doing?"

"Hey," Randy said, "what happened to my shirt?"

Mally got up. "What are you doing?"

Randy looked at him seriously. "My son, there are some things that are hard to explain." He unzipped his jeans and let them fall to the floor. "I," he said, "am going to bed." And he flung himself past Mally and landed face down on the sofa bed.

"What? Here?" Mally said, panic rising in his throat.

"Ow," Randy said. "Don't you have a mattress on this thing?"

"You can't sleep here," Mally said. "You can't sleep here like that."

"Yer right," Randy said, his voice muffled. He rolled over and started kicking his feet. "Gotta get these damned jeans off first." He thrashed about but only got them snarled tighter around his feet. He tried sitting up a couple of times to reach them but toppled over sideways and grew immensely tired. "Aw, the pity of it all," he said and gave out a deep sigh. His legs relaxed and stretched out across the bed. He seemed to be falling asleep.

Mally stood at the foot of the sofa in a state of shock. His brain seemed to be completely void of thoughts. Finally, he knelt down and reached for the jeans. "Here," he said quietly, "let me help you with those," and he started to tug the denim over Randy's feet.

"Hey!" Randy said, suddenly awake and angry.

Mally froze.

Randy shook a finger at him. "No tickling."

Mally nodded slowly. "Right," he said and gradually extricated Randy's feet from the jeans. He folded them and laid them on the floor next to his letter jacket and got up. "I'll get you a pillow," he said.

Randy snagged his arm as he went past, catching him off-balance. "No, don't," he said and tugged. "Come sit here."

As he was already toppling in that direction, Mally tried to land on the mattress gracefully. Randy still held his arm.

"Y'know," he said, "I think you're the only friend I've got."

Mally looked down at him. "Naw," he said.

"No, I'm serious." Randy said, looking up at him. "The only real friend."

"There's Red."

Randy snorted. "That phony."

Mally's heart raced. Did Randy know, too? But no, there was no special animosity in his face, just a lost and confused look. "There's Joanie," he tried.

Randy squeezed his eyes shut, a pained look on his face. "She really cut me down, you know?" he said. "Really cut me flat."

"She was upset. She didn't mean—"

"Oh, yes, she did." Randy opened his eyes. "I may as well be dead and on the other side of the world for all she cares. I'm Judas as far as she's concerned. And she's right. I know she's right. I should've known better. I did know better. I did."

He looked like he was about to cry. Mally didn't know what to do. Should he try to hold him? Should he turn away?

"I really thought she would be the one," Randy said. "I really thought so. I've never been with a girl, and I really thought . . . you know?" He looked up at Mally again. "Have you?"

Mally looked at him, confused.

"Have you?" Randy asked again.

"Huh?"

"You ever been with a girl?"

Mally looked anywhere but in Randy's eyes, but then heard him giggling.

"Oh!" Randy said and put a hand to his face. "Oh, shit." The giggles turned into choked laughs. "Who am I talking to, any-way?" There were tears running down his face now, but they were tears of laughter. "I must be really wiped, huh? To be ask-ing—"

Mally got up from the sofa bed.

"Oh, hey!" Randy said, sitting up. "Don't go. Oh, jeez, I'm sorry. I didn't mean it that way. I didn't mean to be laughing at you."

Mally stood there in the dark, not moving. "It's okay," he said.

"Man," Randy said, "I'm screwin' up my life faster'n shit. Here you are, the only friend I've got, and I'm driving you away."

"No," Mally said. "Forget it. It's nothing."

"No, no," Randy said. "It's not. Hell, I'm just like my old man. Find people and tell 'em I love them, and then shoot off my mouth and drive them away."

Mally sat back down. "No," he said, "it's not like that."

"Jeez, I don't want to end up like him." He turned to Mally. "He's not a bad man, you know. It's just that his dreams never worked out. Things never lived up to what he expected. People, real people, weren't what he hoped they would be. They had their own little dreams and . . . and he could never fit them into his. And so . . . he'd leave them."

"Like he left you and your mom?"

"Yeah."

"Well, he's come back, hasn't he?"

Randy snorted. "Come back for my money."

"Says who?"

"My mom."

"She could be wrong."

"Virginia? Don't tell her that. He's just hanging around till he gets enough of a stake together. Then he'll be off again. To Alaska."

"Maybe he'll stick around this time. Watch you play ball come fall."

Randy shook his head. "Naw. I wish he would, but—naw. He doesn't give a damn about me. Why should he?"

"Maybe . . ." Mally hesitated. "Maybe because you're one of the people who turned out like he wanted. You turned out right." Randy looked at him but Mally couldn't meet his gaze. "At least, I think you did," he said.

Randy looked at him quietly a moment. "You really think so?"

Mally swallowed and got up the courage to look at him. "Yeah," he said. He almost choked on the word.

Randy looked away again. "You think he does?"

"Yeah," Mally said, "I think he does."

Randy laid back down and closed his eyes. "God, I hope so. I wish I could be sure." He opened his eyes. "I wish I were like you."

Mally had to laugh at that. "The hell."

"No, really. You notice things. You . . . you sort things out. I always feel better after talking with you. I wish I could do the same for you." He reached out and took Mally's hand.

Mally looked at him a moment. "Go to sleep, Randy," he said. "It's late."

Randy closed his eyes. "Can't. Too much in my head."

"Too much beer in your belly."

"That, too. Hey, why don't you tell me that poem again?"

"What? 'She being Brand'?"

"No, not that crazy stuff. That song. 'Sit under my tree and eat my apples.'"

It took Mally a while to sort it out, but when he did, he smiled. "'As the apple tree among the trees of the wood, so is my beloved among the young men,'" he said.

"Yeah, that's the one," Randy said, his body relaxing.

Mally gazed down at him and continued the Song of Songs:

"With great delight I sat in his shadow, and his fruit was sweet to my taste. He brought me to the banqueting house, and his banner over me was love. Stay me with flagons—"

"With what?"

Mally broke out of his reverie. He thought Randy had gone to sleep. "Uh, 'Stay me with flagons.'"

"What're those?"

"Big mugs, jugs."

"Of beer?"

"Yeah, I guess so. Or wine."

"So, in other words, get me plastered."

"Yeah, sure." Mally tried to get back into the mood. *"Stay me with flagons, comfort me with apples—"*

"'Comfort me with apples'?" Randy's eyes stayed shut but his brows knit together. "How're you supposed to do that?"

"Listen to the whole thing, will ya?" Mally took a breath.

"Stay me with flagons, comfort me with apples, for I am sick of love."

"Amen," Randy said and let out a big sigh. "I am sick of love, so let's get drunk. And eat apples. Amen to that, brother, amen." He let out another sigh and brought his hands together on his chest, dragging Mally's hand along with them.

Mally held very still. In a little while, Randy's breathing became very regular and shallow. He had fallen asleep.

Softly, Mally whispered:

"O that his left hand were under my head and that his right hand embraced me! I charge you, O ye daughters of Jerusalem, I charge you by the roses, and by the hinds of the field, that ye stir not up nor awaken my love until he please."

He slipped his hand out of Randy's but let it lay there on his chest, just above his abdomen. The moon had risen and was gleaming through the window beside the sofa. In its thin light, Mally could see the fine hairs that swirled around Randy's nipples and lightly covered his stomach. They rose and fell with each breath, catching the moonlight, and gathered into a faint crest just below his navel to draw a line downward into the band of his jockey shorts. The center of his chest fluttered rhythmically with the beating of his heart, causing Mally's fingers to jump slightly in response.

His breath and Randy's were in synch, but his heart was going nearly twice as fast. His hand moved slowly down Randy's torso, seeming to feel each hair as if it were a tiny spark of fire, rising with each inward breath, gliding with each exhalation. He could see the outline of Randy's cock inside the cotton, its dark curve starting just below the elastic band where his hand now rested. *My beloved put his hand by the hole of the door and I trembled within to receive him.*

He felt it before he really heard it, the rhythmic thunder of the wheels, heavy with freight. It drummed through the night, sounding along the riverbed of the White Horse, filling the town with a heart of its own. The rumble found its way into the pulse of blood in his temples, found it and matched it, grew, and made it its own. And when it gave voice to its need to keep pushing, pushing, with a cry at that first fatal crossing, he withdrew his hand. And when the signal arms swung down across the center of town, he got up and walked down the hall. And when the last cry of the 12:04 sounded loudest, closest, Doppler-shifting into a falling wail for a past long dead and a future that could never be, he was already alone in his bed and didn't see Randy's eyes flicker open and stare wide into the night and then slowly close again.

Chapter 14

COMING HOME

H E THOUGHT HE was home. The sound and smell of cooking bacon were familiar, but when he rolled over, he became acutely aware of a metal bar cutting across his back under a too-thin mattress. This was definitely not his bed.

Randy opened his eyes and was even more disoriented. The room was too long and too narrow and too . . . noisy. There were small sounds coming from behind him where there should be a wall. He propped himself on his elbows and looked around.

"Well, there you are," Mally said, standing in the small kitchen on the other side of a pass-through bookcase. He stood in shorts and a sleeveless undershirt in front of a two-burner stove with a spatula in one hand and a plate in the other. "Can you stomach breakfast or should I call the hospital?"

Pieces of the room slid together and began to introduce themselves. This wasn't his house. This was Mally's house, the granny house, and he was lying on some evil version of a bed in the living room. He closed his eyes and sank back down with a groan and encountered that too-friendly metal bar again. "Not the hospital," he muttered. "Maybe the morgue."

"I tried to stay as quiet as I could," Mally said, "but it's getting near to lunch and I was hungry."

Randy looked up again and saw that the small table had been set. There were two plates, two glasses with orange juice, even daffodils in a vase in the middle. "You shouldn't have gone through so much trouble."

Mally shrugged. "This? This is breakfast. Breakfasts I do easy." He put the plate, now loaded with bacon, on the table and turned back to the stove. "Any eggs? I'm making them now." He gave him a look. "We're fresh out of fried pies. Sorry."

Randy tested his inner being. There was certainly something afoot in his stomach, but he couldn't tell yet if it was hunger or nausea. "Um, better hold off on those. You got coffee?"

"Your mom lets you drink coffee?"

"Yeah. A real progressive."

"Nope. Sorry. We are a tea-total house." Mally looked up from the eggs he was scrambling. "Tea-total. Get it?"

Randy winced and said "Hah." He squinted around the room until he saw the chair across from the sofa bed. His letter jacket was draped over the back and his jeans were neatly folded on the seat, and on top of them lay his shirt. "Hey," he said, "you found my shirt!" He got out of the bed and picked it up as if it were a marvel.

"Aha," Mally said. "So you do remember a little of last night."

"I remember I couldn't find my shirt. Or my keys." He draped the shirt over his shoulders without buttoning it. "Where was it?"

"In your car."

"And my keys?"

"Sorry," Mally said, bringing the frying pan over to the table and dishing half the eggs onto one of the plates. "I guess you'll have to wait until it's midnight again so you can remember where you flung them. Re-enact the scene of the crime."

Randy tugged his jeans on and hobbled over to the table. Mally stood there with the frying pan half-full of scrambled eggs and looked at him with raised eyebrows. "Yeah," Randy said, gesturing to his plate. Mally shoveled the rest of the eggs on it. "Thanks," he said.

Mally sat down and began digging in.

"So . . ." Randy started. Mally looked up with a mouthful. "What did happen last night?"

Mally swallowed and took a drink of orange juice. "Well," he said, "you started out by kicking a field goal through my front door, there," and he gestured at the screen door.

Randy glanced over his shoulder. The screen did have a suspicious dent in it.

"And then you came in here, complaining about your keys and your shirt—"

"And my shoes?" Randy asked, noticing for the first time they were nowhere to be seen.

"Nope," Mally said, swallowing again. "You said Okies didn't wear shoes."

"*I* said that?"

"Well, actually, you said Injuns at first."

"I said *that*?" He hid his face in his hands.

"And then you bitched and moaned a little about Joanie."

Randy collapsed on the table, his head buried in his arms.

"And then you passed out. Kinda like what you're doing now, only more horizontal." Randy peered over his arms and Mally raised his glass of OJ in salute. "It was a stunning performance," he said. "The crowd went wild."

Randy sat up and shook his head, which was its own punishment. "I certainly can make an ass of myself."

"Well," Mally said, "anyone can if they try hard enough and they really, really want to."

There was a knock at the door. They both turned and looked at it and then at each other. Neither made a move to answer.

The knock came again. "Malachi?" Mrs. Oldfield's voice came through the screen. "Are you in there?"

A worried look flashed across Mally's face as he got up and went to the door. Mrs. Oldfield was standing on the other side, one hand shading her eyes. "What is it, Mrs. Oldfield? Is there anything wrong with Grampa?"

"Oh, no," Mrs. Oldfield said, hurriedly. "He's just fine. There's a phone call for you up at the house."

Mally was thunderstruck. Mrs. Oldfield was running messages for him now? But then he thought it must be his mother, getting in touch at last. "I'll be right up," he said, and turned back to grab his shirt.

"What's up?" Randy asked.

"I think my mom's on the phone," Mally said.

"No," Mrs. Oldfield called from the doorway. "It's Joanie Tibbits."

Randy and Mally looked at each other.

Mally turned to the screen door since it was obvious Mrs. Oldfield was in on this conversation. "Are you sure she wants to talk to me?"

"Yes. She said it was really important."

Mally stood there a moment.

"She's still on the line," Mrs. Oldfield prompted.

Mally looked at Randy.

"Well, don't just stand there," Randy said. "Go!"

"You sure?" Mally asked.

"Yeah, go, man. Git!"

Mally dashed out the door and up the lawn without so much as a "Thank-you" to Mrs. Oldfield.

Randy sat at the kitchen table watching him go. Mrs. Oldfield, with a shake of her head and a *tsk!*, followed after him. Randy turned back and looked at his plate of eggs and the bacon cooling untouched beside it. He got up slowly and stood for a moment in the quiet house, already beginning to fill up with the day's heat. A bird's solitary twitter came through the windows by the sofa, cutting through the silence. He walked over to the chair and picked up his letter jacket. He didn't want to carry it, though, so he put it on. It seemed heavy and stiff, like it didn't fit him any more.

He went out through the screen door and picked his way carefully across the alley, mindful of his bare feet. He started search-ing for his keys in the grass, hoping he wouldn't have to search the sharp-edged cinder driveway where he had (somewhat diagonally) parked the car last night. But the grassy area proved fruitless, so he got down on his hands and knees and looked under the car.

"Well, ain't that a pretty sight?" Virginia's voice called from the back porch.

He popped up on his knees. "Mom," he said. "I didn't know you were home."

"Looks like." She cocked her head to one side. "What's with the posture? Or are you having a religious experience?"

"Aw," Randy said, getting up and brushing off his jeans, "I dropped my keys last night somewheres around here. I've been locked out."

"Well, that explains a few things. Where'd you spend the night?"

He nodded over his shoulder. "At Mally's. When did you get in?"

"Oh, let's see." Virginia propped an arm on her hip and gazed upward. "The bus gets in about 10:30, and I took a nice long walk home . . ."

"Bus?" Randy asked. "Why'd you walk? Where's Pop?"

Virginia gave him a lop-sided smile. "Come inside and I'll tell you the whole sordid story." She turned around and went into the house.

Randy followed anxiously.

"I should have known something was up when he handed me that check," Virginia said. There was coffee on the stove and she set out two cups and poured them each one.

Randy sat at the table. "What check?"

"The alimony," she said, drinking her coffee standing up. "The whole she-bang, all fifteen hundred dollars of it."

"Well," Randy said, "he said he was gonna. He said he was getting paid pretty well."

"Yeah, that sounded pretty good, didn't it?" Virginia said. "And he presented that check last night with a big flourish, and I really fell for it. I didn't even stop to think how unlikely it all was." She put her coffee cup down with a shudder. "That bus was disgusting. Made me feel grimy all over. I'm taking a bath." She turned and went into the bathroom.

Randy took a sip of his coffee. He barely tasted it. He could hear the water running in the tub. "So, where's he now?" he yelled at the slightly open door.

"Who knows? Guadalajara, Cheyenne, New Brunswick for all I care."

"He said he was headed to Alaska. To an oil field there."

"Alaska? Hah!" Virginia's head reappeared around the door. "There isn't an oil rig in North America that would take him on. He's too old and too sodden." She ducked back into the bathroom. "And he's on the lam."

"What do you mean?" Randy said, getting up.

"Why do you think I took the bus? He wasn't in the motel room when I woke up. And the reason I woke up was because there was a gentle knock on the door. And guess who that should be?"

Randy stood silent in the kitchen.

"Some nice gentleman from the OTA. Seems a few too many things had gone missing from the job site." There was the sound of her stepping into the bath.

Randy got a sinking feeling in the pit of his stomach.

"I don't know what he was pulling," Virginia went on, "but it was some sort of scam, and they were on to him."

"He must have had money from somewhere," Randy said. "He can't have got enough just skimming parts."

"Whatever you say. But he hasn't been working the turnpike since mid-March. That's when they started catching on to him."

"He can't have had enough," Randy said, not loud enough for her to hear. He headed for his bedroom.

"You wanna believe I deposited that check right quick, though, as soon as I got into town. God knows if it's any good."

"He can't have," Randy repeated to himself. He was in his bedroom now, opening the top drawer of his dresser, pulling the socks out, tossing them behind him without looking.

"Oh, and I haven't told you the punch line, yet. When I went to check out, guess what? He hadn't paid the bill!" Her hoarse laugh echoed from the tub.

It wasn't there. Randy stared at the bottom of the drawer, all the socks gone, strewn across the bedroom, and the drawer was empty. "That son of a bitch," he said. "That son of a bitch." He slammed the drawer shut and ran out of the room.

"Pays me the money, then leaves me the bill!" Virginia laughed. "Now that's class. Hell, it's better than class. That's balls."

The house was silent.

"Randy?" Virginia called out. "Randy?" There was no answer.

Joanie's voice was agitated and excited over the phone. "You were right," she said.

"I was?" Mally said. He couldn't imagine about what.

"My father and I had a long talk, a real serious talk. And he said he was sorry for all the confusion and hurt he'd caused."

"He told you that? Your father?"

"It was really something. He's never talked to me before like that. He didn't, you know, say exactly what he'd done or anything, but he treated me like an adult, like someone he should apologize to, not just a kid."

"That's great, Joanie. So, things are patched up with him and your mom?"

"I hope so. I think this was part of it. And you know who brought him to his senses?"

"No."

"Randy Edom."

Mally was speechless.

"He said Randy gave him a good talking to," Joanie went on, "and it made him realize what his real responsibilities were, and how much he loved me and Kyle, and how he wouldn't want to lose either of us. Who'd've thought that lunk-head could talk sense into anybody?"

Mally thought about last night. "Well, you got me there."

"So now I'm really upset."

"Whoa," Mally said. "You lost me. You just said everything was okay."

"Oh, yeah, it is—here. But I mean Randy. He must think I hate him after the way I've treated him."

"Well, he did seem kinda—"

"So I've made up my mind I should apologize. Do you think I should apologize? I think so."

"Well, yeah, if you—"

"So I tried calling him earlier this morning but nobody answers over at his house—"

"Joanie—"

"—and nobody's seen him for days, and the last thing I said to him was I wished he was dead—"

"Edgewise—"

"—and if he's gone and done something—"

"Joanie, slow down. He hasn't gone and done anything. He stayed the night at my place. He's just fine. A little fuzzy-headed maybe, but—"

"You mean he's been over at your place all the time? Why didn't you tell me?"

Mally closed his eyes and rested his head against Mrs. Oldfield's kitchen wall. "Why don't you just come down here and talk to him?" he said.

"Do you really think I should?"

"Yes," Mally said. He really thought she should.

But when she arrived at the granny house five minutes later, she found Mally folding up the sofa bed, the remains of two breakfasts on the kitchen table, and no Randy.

"Where is he?" she asked.

"Beats me," Mally said, grunting the bed back into sofa shape. "But he can't have gone far."

"Why's that?"

"It's a long, dull story."

"Well, should we try over at his house?"

Mally shrugged. "Can't hurt."

They apologized profusely when Mrs. Edom came to the back door in a bathrobe, dripping wet.

"Oh, don't bother," she said. "It just makes my day complete, is all."

"We were wondering if Randy was at home," Mally asked.

"Well, he was," Mrs. Edom said, toweling her hair. "But he tore out of here about ten minutes ago."

They thanked her and walked over to Joanie's convertible. "Where else could he be?" she asked, leaning against the door.

"I haven't the foggiest," Mally said, shaking his head. "His car's still here, and he hasn't got his shoes."

"What?"

Mally waved the question away.

"What about Red?" Joanie asked of a sudden.

Mally squirmed. "Red and Randy—haven't been getting along much lately."

Joanie crossed her arms. "Well, can you think of a better idea?"

Miserably, he had to admit he couldn't.

They drove out to the subdivision where the Conners lived and Joanie parked in the cul-de-sac that crowned the hill. The high school lay in the valley below them. They might try there next.

But first, the Conners. Mally lost the toss and went up to the door, but he might as well have stayed in the car. Red spoke in monosyllables through a barely opened front door, and Mally, sweating bullets, did his best to keep it short. When he got back to the car, he had no news to report.

"Figures," Joanie said. "That lump was never good for much."

"Don't take it out on him," Mally said. "He's had a lot to go through lately."

Joanie looked at him sideways. "You're a strange one, taking up for him."

"I'm not taking up for him," Mally said defensively. "Just—there's no point in kicking him when he's down."

"He would you."

"Yeah, well, that's where we're different. Look, maybe we should go back to—"

A deep, chest-pounding boom cut him off, making them both jump.

"Lord God Almighty!" Joanie exclaimed, looking all around her, wide-eyed. "What was that?"

"Beats the crap out of me," Mally said. "Sonic boom?"

"No!" Joanie said, starting the engine. "Look!" She nodded across the valley, to the hill on the other side. A column of smoke and dust was rising from it.

"Hurry," Mally said softly.

Joanie had no scruples about plowing new roads through the prairie as she left the county road and drove through the waist-high grass up to the farm house. Debris rayed out from it in all directions. The windows were blown out and shreds of curtains flapped in the gaping holes. A curl of smoke drifted from the shattered chimney and the front door lay broken in two twenty yards from the porch.

They found Randy by the tree. He was not hurt. He was kneeling there, tears and dirt and sweat running down his face. He didn't look at them, but at the house.

"Damn it!" he screamed. "Collapse, why don't you? Why can't you just fall down?"

"Randy," Mally called out, running up to him. "What in God's name are you doing?"

"He did it again," Randy said, still staring at the house. "He screwed us again. It was all a put-on, a big joke. He used me. He used me, and then he ran out."

"Randy, the house—"

"It was rotten!" he yelled. "He was using it. Stashing the stuff he'd stolen in it. So now I've blown it up." He rose to his knees and shook his fists at it. "So fall down, damn it! Fall down or I'll burn you down! I'll burn you down and every last stinking twig of this farm. And then I'll get a bulldozer and rip out this god damned tree and level the whole damn hill!" He sank back on his heels. "And then maybe people won't come up here and fill their heads with a lot of stupid ideas and dreams."

"Jesus God, Randy, it wasn't your father," Mally said.

"What?"

"It wasn't your father that was coming up here. It was me."

"Mally?" Joanie said, creeping cautiously forward.

"It was me, you big dope. I was coming up here."

Randy looked up at him, confusion and anger knotting his face. "What in hell are you talking about?"

"I was fixing it up. Bit by bit, with stuff I found." He looked hopelessly from one of them to the other. "I was trying to make it nice. It was going to be a surprise. You know, for the next time we were up here, for our next picnic."

Joanie shook her head slowly. "Oh, Mally," she said. She looked at Randy. "Well, Edom, you really blew it this time."

Randy glared at her. "Oh, don't you start on me again. I've had it with your holier-than-thou attitude. Get out of here. I'm sick of you. I'm sick of both of you! Get the hell out of here!"

Mally's anger boiled over. "What the hell's the matter with

you?" he yelled at Randy. "Don't you push her away. Don't you push *me* away. Not after all we've been through. Not after last night. Don't you *dare* push me away."

Randy looked up at him.

"Oh, for God's sake," Mally said. He grabbed Joanie by the right hand and knelt down, pulling her with him. He grabbed Randy by the left and put their hands together. "I am not going through this again. Either the two of you patch things up or I've had it with the both of you." He looked at Joanie. "Do you love this idiot or not?"

Joanie looked at him, half startled, half angry. "Well, I wouldn't say—"

He gripped her hand more tightly. "I mean it," he said.

"Well, okay, then," she said and glared at him. Then she turned to Randy. "I guess I do. Sort of."

Mally turned to Randy. "And you?"

Randy opened his mouth but nothing came out.

"Come on, Big Man," Mally coaxed. "You can do it."

"Yeah," Randy said. "Sure."

Mally let go of their hands and sat back. "There, now. Was that such a terrible thing?"

Randy and Joanie looked at each other and smiled. Then Randy reached out and grabbed Mally's hand, causing him to start a little. "What about you?" he asked.

Mally stared at him.

Randy looked him in the eyes. "Do you love this idiot or not?"

Mally went pale.

Joanie reached out and took his other hand. "You do, don't you?" she said softly.

He looked at them both. He'd never been so frightened in his life. Then suddenly, he just let it go, let go of the fear and the hope and just held their hands. He looked at the ground and nodded. "Yeah," he said, "yeah."

"Is that such a terrible thing?" Randy asked.

Mally shook his head. "I don't know," he said. "Maybe it is."

"Mally," Joanie said, almost scolding, "why didn't you say something?"

"Why? What good would that have done? "

"We could . . . maybe we could've . . . helped."

He looked at her. "I don't need help," he said. He looked at them both and shook his head. "No. There's nothing you could have done—" and he looked at Randy "—sober."

Randy looked down and nodded.

"Would you kids like to tell me what's going on out here?"

They looked up and saw a large man standing a few yards away. The sheriff's patrol car was parked a little ways down the hill, its lights flashing.

The sheriff took a few steps forward. "We got reports of an explosion." He scanned the debris scattered around the field. "Pretty accurate reports, looks like." He turned back to the three high school students.

"It's okay, sheriff," Randy said. "I was just . . . clearing a little land and . . ." he trailed off.

"You got a permit for that, son?"

"Well, um . . ." Randy started again.

"His father's got the permit," Joanie said.

The sheriff looked at her suspiciously, then looked back at Randy. "This is you mother's property, isn't it?"

"No, sir," Randy said with more confidence. "It's my property."

Mally and Joanie looked at him as if he'd sprouted wings, which did not inspire the sheriff's confidence. He took off his hat and wiped his brow. "Well, I guess we'll have to sort this out later." He gestured at Randy's feet. "But first maybe we'd better get your feet looked at."

Mally and Joanie both looked down at them for the first time. Mally gasped and Joanie whispered, "Good Lord!"

Randy looked at them ruefully. "Could you guys maybe help me to the car? I don't think I can walk."

Mally got under one arm and the sheriff got under the other and they hoisted Randy to his feet. The three of them started for Joanie's car with her trailing helplessly behind them, crying and cursing in sympathy and anger.

Before they got to the convertible they were met by a deputy walking up the hill.

"Is one of you kids Malachi Jacobs?" the deputy asked.

Mally looked up from his burden. "Yes, sir," he said.

"You're wanted over at the hospital," the deputy said. "Your mother's looking for you."

The deputy rode with Joanie and Randy while Mally went with the sheriff. Mally's mind was going a mile a minute. Something must have happened with his grandfather, that's why the hospital called. He was pretty certain there'd been a mistake, though, and someone had thought that Mrs. Oldfield was his mother. Indeed, there she was in the lobby in a print dress he'd seen a dozen times and a small white sweater. He anchored his eyes on her and headed in that direction, determined to find out what was going on. But then the woman standing at the nurse's station turned around and suddenly the whole room swiveled and centered on her and he came to a halt. "Mom," he said. "You're here."

Susan Jacobs held out her arms. He hesitated a moment, then stepped forward and embraced her awkwardly, then pulled away. She smiled warmly at the large man who had followed her son into the lobby and held out her hand. "Susan Jacobs," she said.

"Marty Jackson, ma'am," he said, shaking her hand lightly. "Sheriff. Pleasure to meet you."

"Thank you, sheriff," she said. She gestured toward Mally. "You needn't have gone to all this trouble."

Sheriff Jackson paused just a moment, then touched his hat.

"No trouble a-tall, ma'am," he said and walked back to the entrance where Joanie and the deputy were walking Randy to a gurney.

Mally saw them come in and was torn. He should be trying to help Randy, but he needed to find out what was happening with his grandfather. He watched helplessly as a nurse came over and started asking Randy and Joanie questions.

Susan saw the look. She noted that the sheriff and deputy were still hanging around, too. "Who are they?" she asked, nodding in the direction of Joanie and Randy.

"Friends of mine," Mally said. "From high school."

"What's wrong with that boy's feet?"

"He's . . . in track," Mally said. A doctor came up and began picking bits of things out of Randy's feet. It looked slow and painful. He tried to put it out of his mind. "Where's Grampa?" he asked. "What's happened?"

"It's nothing," his mother said. "Why don't we go over there and sit down?"

They walked over to an area of the lobby where chairs covered in aqua plastic waited in long rows bordered by potted greenery that never needed watering. Mrs. Oldfield got up from one of the chairs as they approached, looking distressed but real in a sea of artificial comfort.

"Can I get you something from the cafeteria?" she asked Susan as they sat down. "Some coffee?"

"Please," his mother said without looking at her. She opened her purse and started looking for something.

"What's going on?" Mally asked.

"Nothing's going on," his mother said, getting out a handkerchief and daubing her face. "Your grandfather just had a little trouble breathing, that's all, and Dr. Evans thought it best that they bring him in here for observation."

Mally felt miserable. "He was fine this morning," he said, then he closed his eyes and put his head in his hand. "No, no.

That was yesterday. I didn't see him today. I usually do see him every day. I should have looked in."

His mother patted his hand. "Mally, sweetheart. Don't get yourself worked up. It's certainly not your fault. If anything, it's my fault. I should have gotten word to you that I was coming, but things were so hectic in New York, and then the flight down here and the drive. There just wasn't time. I probably gave him quite a start, walking in like that."

"So, you've talked to him?"

"Yes, and he was just fine. But then he started breathing rapidly and Mrs. Oldfield said we should call the doctor and . . . well, here we are." She smiled at him.

"Can I see him?"

"I don't know, sweetheart. Dr. Evans is in there now. We'll just have to—" She looked up and past him. "Well, maybe we won't have to wait after all. Here comes Dr. Evans now." She rose gracefully, a cordial smile on her face. Mally stood beside her.

"Mrs. Jacobs?" Dr. Evans said.

"Miss," Susan said, her smile not faltering.

"Reverend Jacobs is doing just fine," Dr. Evans said. "It was just a mild case of tachycardia."

"What's that?" Mally asked.

"It's just a sudden increase in heart rate," the doctor said. "It happens all the time to people. It means nothing."

"Can we take him home?"

"Now, Mally," his mother chided.

"I think, given his recent history, it's best to keep him here for overnight observation," Dr. Evans said. "I'm sure he'll be coming home tomorrow."

His mother turned to him. "There, now, you see? Nothing to worry about." She turned and smiled at the physician. "Thank you, Dr. Evans."

"You're quite welcome," he said. "Where can I reach you folks if I need to get ahold of you?"

"Mrs. Oldfield's," Mally said at once.

His mother looked uncomfortable. "Well, yes, Mrs. Old-field's, for now," she said.

"Come back tomorrow morning," the doctor said, walking away from them. "I'm sure you'll be able to take him home then."

His mother sighed and seemed to relax some. Then she turned to him and smiled. "Well, sweetie," she said, "I guess we've got a lot of catching up to do. What do you say we go get a bite to eat? The food in this place is dreadful."

Mally cast a glance at Joanie as he and his mother headed for the door. The doctor and nurse were wheeling Randy's gurney down the hall to the emergency surgery. "Call me" he mouthed at her. She nodded and turned and followed the gurney, holding Randy's jacket in her arms.

When Mrs. Oldfield returned moments later, gingerly holding a cup of hot coffee and a handful non-dairy creamers, there was no one left in the lobby at all. Even the sheriff's department had left, called away on other business.

After lunch, during which Susan told Mally all about her audition and call-backs in New York City, they drove back to Mrs. Oldfield's. Mally wanted to change his clothes, which were gritty and hay-covered and had an odd, acrid smell in them. She pulled up on Choctaw in front of the house and Mally scooted out and down the side yard. Susan got out more slowly. Mrs. Oldfield's car was back in her drive, she noted. She supposed she should thank her for all the trouble she had gone through, but she didn't really feel like confronting her right now.

She wandered around the house and into the back yard with its sloping lawn that ended in the small green house. She saw Mally disappear inside and she heaved a sigh. The mask of pleasantness and competence she had been wearing slid off, and the real worry and concern crept in, drawing a line between her brows and pulling down the corners of her mouth.

She had no idea what she was going to do next. She didn't even know where she was going to stay. She wouldn't stay in her father's room at Mrs. Oldfield's, which she was sure was going to be offered to her, and she couldn't stay in the granny house with Mally—too many ghosts.

The heat had moderated and Mrs. Oldfield's daffodils were dancing all along the edges of the lawn and beside the little house. Standing here looking at the garden and the lawn, she could almost imagine a long afternoon when she and Andy had lain on this spot and talked about music and wildflowers and whether there was a heaven and a hell. She had been shocking, the scandalous preacher's daughter, saying she was certain there was a heaven, but couldn't imagine a God so spiteful he would create a hell. That was before she knew where hell really was.

"Suzie-Q, is that you?"

She turned at the familiar voice. All the tension drained out of her. "Ginny," she said, "Ginny Alquist."

Virginia crossed the alley and the two of them embraced, smiles and tears mixing together. "Or is it Ginny Edom?" Susan said as they pulled apart.

"God knows," Virginia said, laughing. "I certainly don't. How long have you been in town? Though I suppose I should have known you had arrived when I saw the flashing lights."

Susan lifted her chin. "I still know how to make an entrance." They laughed again. "I just arrived this morning. Oh, it's been too long," Susan said and they hugged again.

"Well, I hope you've put the time to good use," Virginia said. "Are you burning up Broadway yet?"

"Not hardly. But I did just get back from an audition in New York."

"Theater?"

She shook her head. "T.V." Then she started laughing. "A soap opera!"

"You're kidding!" Virginia gave a deep, husky laugh. "What

ever happened to those artistic principals of ours? What was that slogan?"

In unison they shouted, "We were born to change the world!"

Virginia chuckled. "Too bad we forgot to change ourselves."

Susan smiled. "We're a long way from our wild days, aren't we?"

"Speak for yourself," Virginia said. "I'm still having a good time."

Susan looked at her.

"Well, yeah," Virginia admitted. "But a soap opera? What would Miss Burdell say now!"

"Maybe it's best she'll never know," Susan said, laughing.

They suddenly both fell silent.

"How long are you here for?" Virginia asked at last.

"I don't know," Susan said with a sigh. "It depends on how well father does."

"How's he doing?"

Susan shook her head. "The doctor says he's fine, but I don't know. He didn't look at all well. He looked like . . . Ginnie, it looked like he'd already been dying for a long time."

"Oh, no, I'm sure you're wrong, there, kiddo," Virginia said. "He was actually starting to perk up some. I think having Mally around gave him a real kick. He's quite the kid, you know."

"Really?" Susan seemed genuinely delighted.

Virginia cocked her head at her. "What are you going to tell him?"

"About what?" Susan said.

"Susan," Virginia said, impatience in her voice. "I had to tell him something. He wanted to know."

Susan looked at her, distressed. "What did you say?"

Virginia raised her hands. "I just told him about the accident," she said. "The same thing the papers said. That's all. He didn't even know Andy was dead. How could you not have told him that?"

"It's . . . complicated," she said. Saying it out loud made her realize how hollow it sounded.

"He was making up all sorts of weird stories by himself," Virginia said.

"Like what?"

Virginia shook her head. "Talk to him. He needs to know."

"What can I say? I don't want to lie, but I can't bear to tell him the truth."

"What's so awful about the truth?"

"Every time I tried to do something for Andy, I just ended up hurting him more. I don't want to do the same thing to Mally."

"Oh, that's not true. You were the best friend Andy Simms ever had. You showed all those busy-bodies and bigots how wrong they were."

Susan shook her head. "No," she said. "No, I didn't. And they weren't wrong. Oh, they were wrong to hound him and snicker at him and call him names behind his back. And the church was wrong to dismiss him. But what I did was worse." She turned to look at Virginia. "If you could have seen his face, Ginnie, you would have known. I didn't help him. I used him." She looked away, ashamed. "I took advantage of him when he was scared and alone and needed someone. And I did it just to prove a point, just to show them they were all just a pack of prejudices parading around as a religion." She turned to face her again. "How do I tell him that?"

Virginia stood looking at her a moment. There was the sound of a screen door opening and she turned toward the granny house. "Look at him, Susan," she said. "He even looks like Andy."

Susan turned and looked as Mally came through the door of the small green house. He straightened his shirt and set his shoulders, then looked like he didn't know what to do with his hands. He looked up the slope to where his mother and Virginia stood waiting and smiled and waved and started walking toward them.

Virginia was right. In his stance, his gestures, he was exactly like his father. But how could he have known that? He'd never seen Andy stand like that, never seen him fumble with his own hands, never been on the receiving end of that goofy half-smile.

"Talk to him, Susan," Virginia said. "He deserves to know."

She was able to give Virginia one last honest look before she put the polished mask back on again. Then she turned and smiled at her son. "Well, now, that's better," she said, putting her arm around him. "You even smell nice and fresh."

Mally blushed. "Good evening, Mrs. Edom," he said to Virginia with a nod of his head.

Virginia raised her eyebrows at the formality. "And good evening to you, young sir," she said.

It made him smile self-consciously. "Is Randy okay?" he asked.

Virginia shrugged. "Far as I know."

He blushed again. "I mean, his feet."

Virginia frowned. "What about his feet?"

Before he could answer, they were interrupted by Mrs. Oldfield coming out the back door, wearing a darker than usual frown. "They wouldn't talk to me," she announced to the three of them from the porch. "They said you should come to the phone." She was looking at all of them, so it was unclear whom she was talking to. She came down the steps unsteadily. "I asked them why, but they wouldn't tell me." She was clearly heading for Susan now, her arms outstretched. Susan started toward her, then walked quickly past her and ran up the back steps. Mrs. Oldfield seemed to be propelled by her own momentum, her arms still outstretched. She looked in Virginia's face and in Mally's. "They said they couldn't talk to me." She seemed to totter and Mally grabbed her hands to steady her. "Why?" she asked him. "Why won't they talk to me?" Tears fell freely from her face and she twisted around to look back at the porch, gripping Mally's hands tightly.

Mally looked up the slope of the lawn as his mother came through the door. She stood there on the porch, looking down at them, saying nothing. And he knew.

ANDREW
LEWIS
SIMMS

Chapter 15

ROLES

S USAN KNEW HOW to play this scene—the graveyard, the coffin, the mourners. She sat dignified but unmoved as Pastor Mathers gave the eulogy. It said all the right things, but it seemed distant, somehow. It didn't really talk about the man she knew, just the man all these other people knew. That surprised her: the number of people who turned out for her father's funeral. She was under the impression that her father had been pretty much cut off once he left the church, but many people seemed to remember him from his hey-day, more than fifteen years ago. Ruth and John Tibbits were there, even though they didn't go to the same church anymore. And the two kids she had first seen in the hospital, one of whom turned out to be Ginny's son, and the other Ruth and John's daughter. So, they'd finally had a child after all—two, apparently. She recognized deacons and other members of the church she hadn't seen in all this time and wondered if they recognized her, even as they came up and shook her hand and offered their condolences.

It was funny how all the history and all the faces came back to her, seemingly familiar, but then suddenly not. In her mind, these people had been vivid, clear, and implacable, like types waiting to be cast in some grand epic of Americana: how a mundane people wore out an entire continent. Now, they seemed to have all gone fuzzy, with unpredictable flashes of complexity she had never seen before. Mrs. Oldfield, for example, was crying quietly but openly. It was hard for Susan to keep her image of that woman fixed in her mind when she saw her like that, so devastated, so human. And Ruth and John seemed affectionate and shy with each other, as if they had only just started dating.

She didn't know how to play the next scene, the one where the people drift away and she was left alone at the grave site with her son. She was going to have to wing it.

The adults streamed away from the graveside. Virginia Edom and Joanie's mother and father walked ahead while Randy and Joanie stayed behind, Joanie to offer a word to Mally, Randy just to give him an awkward hug. Joanie noticed Mrs. Oldfield scurrying on ahead of everyone, hastening to set up the wake at her house, no doubt. Then she and Randy headed down the hill, too, but she hung back and caught Randy by the sleeve so they could have a moment together. He stopped and she nodded in the direction of the grave, where Mally and his mother now stood alone.

"What do you think she's going to do?" she whispered.

"About what?" he said in a normal voice.

She looked at him in exasperation. "About Mally. With his grandfather gone, he's got no relatives here."

Randy looked suddenly worried. "I hadn't thought of that."

"Do you think she'll take him with her to New York?"

"Jeez, I hope not."

They started walking again. Joanie kept glancing back at Mally and his mother, so she didn't know what prompted Randy to halt suddenly. She nearly ran into him.

"Oh, brother," he said.

"What?"

He nodded down the hill and she looked to see her parents and his mother about to reach their cars when another man came up to them. It was Sheriff Jackson.

Susan and Mally stood quietly for a moment. She was staring at the headstone but not really understanding why. Then it hit her. Both of them. They were both gone now. Her mother, younger than her husband by fifteen years, and nearly twenty years sooner in the grave. And now he had finally caught up to her. She'd never really thought of that before: how much of his life her father had spent without her mother, both before and after they met and fell in love and were married. All her life, she had thought of him as a rock, an immovable object, something you could cling to or avoid or ignore. Now it occurred to her that perhaps he had always been the one at sea, the one adrift, that maybe his spirit had always wanted an anchor and that now, at last, he had one.

Mally interrupted her thoughts. "Why didn't she come?" he asked.

Susan shook her head, not knowing whom he was talking about.

"Aunt Margaret," he said. "Why didn't she come?"

She took a deep breath and let it out. "I guess she never forgave him," she said. "She always thought it was his fault your grandmother left the Church. But it wasn't like that." She looked down at him and smiled. "My mother really loved the work. And she really loved your grandfather."

Mally looked at her, then at the gravestone and nodded.

They were quiet again. Then Mally said, "Are you going to go see it?"

She knew, this time, what he meant, but she couldn't answer.

"It's over this way," he said. He took her hand and led her gently. She followed along, almost empty of will, as if she were a balloon on a string.

It was a small grave, a small headstone. She had never visited it before.

As they came down the hill, Virginia saw Sheriff Jackson leaning against his patrol car. He straightened up as they approached and came forward to meet them.

"I'm sorry to intrude," he said, "but this seemed the most likely place to find all of you together."

"Ruthie," John Tibbits said, turning to his wife, "could you put Kyle in the car, please?"

Ruth gave him an odd look, but took the hint and herded the little boy off, who was beginning to itch and wriggle anyway.

"What is it, sheriff?" Virginia asked.

"We think we have a line on Harry, Mrs. Edom. He may have been sighted outside of Boise. The bank that floated him the loan based on that deed is going to press charges."

"What will they charge him with?"

"Hard to say. Fraud, most likely. Theft, too, if the OTA can prove he took material from their yards."

Virginia sighed and looked down, shaking her head. "I appreciate your telling me, Marty, but I really never want to see or hear of Harry Edom again."

"There's still the little matter of that incident out at the farm."

Virginia looked up, frowning. "They recovered the deed, didn't they? It really is Randy's land. I signed it over to him last Christmas."

"It's more serious than that, ma'am," Jackson said. "If those blasting caps were stolen from the OTA, Randy could be guilty of destroying evidence."

"Uh, no," John Tibbits intervened, "that's my responsibility. I told Randy to set those caps off. I had no idea they might be stolen. He just brought it to my attention that some kids had found them and they might get hurt playing with them, so I told him to get rid of them. I didn't think they might be stolen. I just thought they were a hazard."

"Still, he should have gotten a permit."

"That's my fault, too. I told him I had a permit, but truth is, I was going to get one and I . . . forgot."

The sheriff cocked his head. "Your daughter said it was Randy's father who had the permit."

John looked away, then back at the sheriff. "She was confused."

Jackson looked at him steadily. "Seems to be a lot of that going around," he said. He, too, looked away for a moment. "Still 'n all, it's the most succinct version I've heard to date. And it has the advantage of not involving the state boys."

"I appreciate that, sheriff."

"Don't thank me yet. There's still the matter of the fine for blasting without a permit."

"I'll pay that, too."

Virginia stirred. "That's real generous of you, John," she said, "but Randy knows the law as well as you do. He'll pay the fine."

"It's my fault," John said, turning to her.

"I don't want him getting off scot-free."

"How about I pay the fine and he pays me back? I'll deduct a portion from his paycheck each week."

"Fair enough."

"Okay, then."

Sheriff Jackson looked from one of them to the other. "Well, if the two of you are done negotiating, I guess my work here is pretty much done. Sir, ma'am." He touched his hat to each of them and left.

Holding the wake at Mrs. Oldfield's was awkward, but there was little choice. Susan had refused Pastor Mathers' offer of the church hall with just about the last bit of fight she had left. And it had to be held somewhere, for Mally's sake as much as anyone's. Susan noticed how his friends formed a little protective knot around him, as if shielding him from the clumsy attentions of the adults in the room. She wished she had a similar cordon around her. Even talking to Ruth and John, people her own age, she felt out of place. Then she spied Virginia out on the front porch swing, drinking something that did not look like fruit punch. She went out to join her.

"Thank you for coming," she said as she approached the swing. "I know how much you hate these church things."

"This ain't about church," Virginia said. "This is about you and Mally." She patted the seat beside her on the swing and Susan sat down. "How are you doing?"

Susan smiled, then looked down and shook her head.

"Hooch?" Virginia offered, holding out her cup.

"Oh, please," Susan said gratefully. She took a big gulp.

"I don't know how the widow gets by on nothing but bug juice and sherbet," Virginia said.

Susan shuddered. "I should never have come back. Things go wrong here, horribly wrong. No matter what I do or intend to do."

"That's just ghosts, honey, just ghosts."

"I'll be glad to get back to New York." She drank again and handed back the cup.

Virginia looked at her a moment. "You're not taking him with you, are you?"

Susan threw up her hands. "Well, I can't leave him here on his own. He's just a kid."

"So were you when you started out."

"Oh, yeah, right, and look how good that turned out."

"And he's not alone," Virginia said. "Look around."

Susan looked back in through the living room window. Mally and his two friends were getting up and heading toward the back of the house. Probably going outside. Good for them. She sighed. "I never knew how to get along here," she said.

"Mally seems to have figured it out," Virginia said. "You should have seen him when he first arrived. Outsider, awkward, not a friend in the world. Now look at him."

Susan gave another look over her shoulder. "Yeah, he's figured it out." She looked her friend in the eye. "He told me how much he'd figured out, when we were out there, at Andy's grave. He knew, Ginnie. He knew I hadn't been thrown from the car. Nobody told him. He just knew."

Virginia nodded slowly. "And the rest?"

Susan looked away. "I don't know. I think so."

"And he isn't upset?"

Susan shook her head. "He said he wanted me to know he didn't blame me. That I probably did the best I could."

Virginia gave a quiet laugh. "Kids. We think we're protecting them, and all the time they're protecting us." She gave Susan a sideways look. "It would be a shame to take him away now, just as he's setting down roots."

Susan bit her lower lip. "It's going to be a while before I get an apartment and get settled in."

Virginia nodded. "Probably at least a few weeks, till the end of the school year at any rate." She looked at her. "At least."

Susan twisted her hands and then looked at her. "Will you look out for him?"

Virginia laughed out loud at that. "I don't seem to be doing such a hot job with my own. But, yeah, I'll look out for him." She finished off her drink. "So, tell me about it."

"What?"

"The job, that soap opera."

Susan brightened. "Well, it's not like any soap opera you've ever seen before," she said. "It's set in a lonely town in New England, half of contemporary, and half done in period costumes."

"Really? Sounds fancy."

"And it's about vampires."

Virginia snorted. "That'll never fly."

Sometime later, Susan walked back through the house, looking for Mally. She passed through the crowd, her progress halted briefly as hands reached out and touched her, words were passed in low voices, small offers of help were made and graciously acknowledged. *And these are the same people*, she thought, *the same people who hounded Andy to death, who turned their back on my father when he lost his faith, who told me I would burn in hell because I wouldn't accept their shaming.* She shook her head. *Yet here they are when they think I need them. Who's the hypocrite, then—them for wanting to help, or me for needing it?*

When she finally got to the kitchen, she stood in the hallway just outside. The wake murmured and hummed behind her. She looked in at the yellow tiled counter tops, the spotless stove, the tin canisters of flour and sugar, and the old woman sitting at the table who might have been as self-contained and dust-free as the jars of tomatoes on the shelves. Susan had thought Clara Old-field would be in the front room managing the wake, soaking in the one moment when she and her home were finally the hub of some important to-do. Instead, she was in here, alone.

She stepped into the kitchen. "I wanted to thank you," she said.

Mrs. Oldfield stirred, looking startled, as if Susan had just accused her of something.

"I spoke with my Aunt Margaret," she continued. "She told me how you found my father and took him in, paid off the hospital. I know we haven't been on speaking terms since Andy died—"

"Susan, I—"

"—but I wanted to say thank you. I haven't been too big on Christian charity, at least not the way it's practiced in Kennsing County. But you really were . . . doing him a mercy. And I thank you."

Mrs. Oldfield folded and unfolded the handkerchief in her lap. "Saint Paul says it is best that widows not remarry," she said at last, "but if they burn, then it is better that they marry than burn." She took a deep breath and let it go. "I didn't burn. After Gerald died, there was nothing left in me to burn. Though I wanted there to be, I wanted so badly. When I saw couples to-gether, a young man and a young woman, I saw something precious, so fine, so fragile. Young people, they don't know, don't know how quickly things can change, how they can fall apart or rot from inside or just a sudden flash and they're gone.

A foolish fancy, a car gone out of control, a cancer. One minute, Gerald was here, and this house was warm and had a purpose, and the next minute, he was gone, and there was nothing that could make this kitchen anything but a tomb, a hollow space where someone wasn't anymore, where his voice wasn't ever going to speak again, saying, 'My, that bread smells good,' or 'Clara, is there any more of that blackberry pie?,' or 'Your love is what keeps me going, your faith is my life.'" She got up and went over to the sink and looked out at the back yard. "So when I see that young glow of happiness, that wonder in their eyes, I want to rush right up and build a wall around it, hide it away from the world, because the world will try to tear it from them, turn it rotten." She turned and faced her. "And when Andy told me what was in his heart, I knew it had gotten to him, too. He can't have meant it, Susan. I know he can't. What did he know of the world to say those things?"

Susan hung her head. "I thought so, too," she said quietly

"We all tried our best to save that boy."

"No," Susan said. "No we didn't. We all tried to change him. No matter what gifts he brought us—music, kindness, friendship—we all told him it wasn't good enough."

Mrs. Oldfield paced from counter to sink, touching the canisters and jars lightly, as if she could coax one more inch of orderliness from her kitchen. "It's my fault," she said. "He came to me first. Love the sinner, hate the sin. That's what I was taught. And that's what I believed. But I got too good at it, too good at hating the sin. And when I got around to loving the sinner, I found I had forgotten how. All I could do was pray and scold and threaten, until there was nothing left of me but bitter words and accusations." She turned to Susan. "Your father was the only man who saw otherwise, who saw something other than a crabbed old witch. You think I was doing him a mercy? He was doing me a mercy. And he was just beginning to help me . . . remember."

It was late in the day and all the mourners had gone home. Joanie watched Susan Jacobs cross the lawn from the granny house to Mrs. Oldfield's. Her black dress made her stand out crisply against the vivid green of the lawn, sharp-edged but elegant. Joanie could well believe she was an actress. There was a glamour about her that made you want to reach out and touch her yet kept you rooted to the spot. And where had she found such a dress on such short notice? Joanie knew all the stores in Croy by heart but even vanDoozer's didn't have anything half so fine. And there hadn't been time to get to Tulsa or even Oklahoma City and back. A costume, maybe?

She shook the speculations from her head and walked up to the door of the little house. She hesitated before knocking, not sure she really wanted to know but not able to keep her apprehensions in check. Too much was changing too quickly. She knocked.

"Come in," Mally's voice answered.

She opened the door and stepped inside. Mally was in the kitchen area, putting away some dishes. There was the smell of strong coffee. He turned and smiled at her, but it wasn't the full goofy grin she had been hoping for. *Well*, she thought, *there has been a funeral and all*. "How have you been?" she asked.

"I'm okay. A little weirded out, but okay."

"I saw your mom leave."

"Yeah." He sighed deeply. "She's gone up to Mrs. Oldfield's to pack her things."

Uh-oh, thought Joanie.

"She leaves tomorrow," he finished.

Better get this over with, she thought. "And you?"

"I get to finish out the school year. Then I join her in New York at the end of June."

"And next year?"

"She's leaning toward letting me come back. I got the impression Randy's mom had something to do with that."

Joanie breathed a sigh of relief and squeezed into a chair at the kitchen table, which really wasn't much bigger than a TV tray. So, it wasn't all falling apart after all. There was hope. Then it struck her what Mally had said. "Wow. New York. New York *City*. What'll that be like, living in a big city?"

Mally shrugged. "I lived in Oklahoma City for years."

She scowled at him. "I mean a real city." He shrugged again and turned to put some cups away. "You seem underwhelmed."

"I was kinda hoping to spend the summer here."

"Have you ever been in Croy in the summer? All the cool kids are off on vacation somewhere and there's nothing to do. And the weather, ugh."

"It can't be that bad."

"Are you kidding? It's like walking around inside somebody's mouth."

His grin reappeared. "No, I mean, you guys would still be here. You and Randy."

Joanie was secretly thrilled he was going to miss them but covered up by saying, "You won't miss a thing, really. If I spend one more balmy summer evening at the DQ I'll go balmy myself. Believe me, you're better off in New York." Mally got quiet again so she changed the subject. "Your mom is really going to be on television?"

"Yep. Looks like she really hit the big one this time."

"And we'll see her and all?"

"Well, sure."

"Wow. It's like a celebrity, right here in our town. She'll be famous. You'll be famous." There was that shrug again. "What's with you?" she asked. "The two of you didn't fight, did you?"

"No." He turned and looked out the window. "We talked about . . . We talked about my dad. About how he died."

"You mean the accident?"

"It wasn't an accident. It was deliberate." He turned to face her. "He killed himself."

"Oh, Mally." She didn't know what to say. "That's awful."

"It's just what I figured, anyway."

"Did she say why?"

"I know why. She didn't have to say. He was different. Tried to fit in but couldn't, no matter how hard he tried. He was always the odd one out, always alone, even among his friends. Which he could never believe really were his friends because he was . . . different. Queer." He swallowed. "Like me."

Joanie looked at him a long time. "You don't feel that way, do you?"

Mally flapped his hands in exasperation. "You know how I feel about Randy."

"No, that's not what I mean. I mean, you don't feel alone when you're with your friends, do you? When you're with me?"

"Well, no, but . . . " he trailed off.

Joanie knew about his long walks along the railroad tracks. A terrible thought occurred to her. "You're not thinking— Look, Mally, you're not ever alone. Don't you ever think of doing something like that."

He looked baffled. "Like what?"

"Like what your father did."

"Oh, God, no." He looked genuinely surprised.

"Good!" she said. "Because if you ever pulled a stunt like that, I'd kill you."

They looked at each other a split second then burst out laughing.They were so loud a dog down the block started barking. Mally collapsed in a chair across the tiny table from her.

"Naw," Mally said, wiping the corners of his eyes, "I want to change my life, but that would be a bit too much even for me."

"What? Why? What do you want to change?"

"Well, my name, for one."

"What's wrong with Mally?"

His face twisted. "Too many L's. And Malachi won't work. I mean, I love my grandfather—" He stopped short, then started again, quieter. "I loved my grandfather. But Malachi is no name for a kid."

"Well, what then?"

He brightened. "I'm thinking 'Jake.' Jake Jacobs."

"You're joking."

"No," he said, his voice rising defensively.

"Jake Jacobs," she repeated. "It's so . . . boyish."

He stood up, "Well, I think it's kind of manly." Joanie rolled her eyes, which she was glad Mally didn't see. Jake didn't see. Oh hell, she was never going to be able to call him that!

"And I am the man around the house now," he was saying, putting away the last of the dishes.

"Yeah, I guess you have the place to yourself. At least till the end of June."

"That's right. Think of the wild parties I could throw."

"Under the beady eyes of Mrs. Oldfield."

"Hey, you can stir up a lot of excitement with iced tea. Well," he gave her a look, "maybe not tea. Too stimulating."

She returned the look. "And maybe not iced. Ice cubes, you know."

"Hmm. Could lead to something stronger."

She took a breath and started the second question she had come to ask. "Speaking of wild parties . . ."

"What?" He sat down again. He looked so trusting, she hated pursuing it. But they were friends, after all. "Just what went on here that night?" she asked, trying to sound casual.

"What night?"

She cocked her head at him. "You know what night. That wasn't iced tea I smelled on Randy's breath when we found him. I thought for sure the sheriff was going to bust him."

"Yeah, he was pretty smashed."

"So . . . ?"

Mally arched an eyebrow, an expression she'd never seen on him before. "I'm not the kind to kiss and tell," he said.

"I'm serious," she said. He still looked at her. "You're . . . you're *not* serious. Are you?"

He laughed. "Don't get your face in a knot. Nothing happened. He was drunk when he got here and passed out right away."

"Right away?"

"Well, practically. And, no, nothing happened then, either. Or later. I'm not *that* kind, either."

"Good. I'd hate to have to scratch your eyes out."

"Well, my eyes and your nails thank you. No, you're his girl. I'm just his . . . friend."

"Great!" She curbed her enthusiasm. "I mean, it sucks for you, but great." And now she arched a brow. "Besides, I saw him first."

"Mebbe so," he replied smoothly, "but I've seen *all* of him."

"Oh! You're a pig. All men are pigs."

"Well," he said, getting up from the table, "it beats being the family dog." He looked out the window. Randy was carrying a bag of garbage out to the trash bin. "Speak of the devil—"

Randy slung the sack of trash into the can and slid the lid carelessly back on top. It slid off. He picked it up and felt like drop-kicking it clear across the alley—across the county, for that matter. His ears still burned from the tongue-lashing his mother had given him. His mother—not tough, sarcastic Virginia, but his *mother*. He looked back at the house. He couldn't go back in there again. He still had some pride left.

He slouched over to his car and hopped onto the trunk and leaned back, looking up at the sky. God, he could really use a beer right now. But that brought back his mother's hard words and he had to shut his eyes to block them out. He heard a screen door slam and looked up to see Joanie and Mally heading his way, looking downright conspiratorial. He sighed and leaned back. Whatever they were up to, he hoped they would get it over with quickly.

"So," Joanie started, "how's the county arsonist today?"

"Not arsonist," Mally chimed in. "Demolitions expert."

"Rag all you want," Randy answered. "I've heard it all, up one side and down t'other."

"Your mom?" Joanie asked.

"None other."

"She still upset about the farmhouse?" Mally asked.

"I guess you could say that, yes," Randy said.

"Well," Mally said, jumping up onto the trunk beside him, "it's not like you did all that much damage."

Randy shot him a look.

Joanie hopped up on the other side. The shocks complained a bit. "There is some good news today," she said.

"What?"

She nodded at Mally. "Tell him," she said.

Mally grinned. "Looks like you're stuck with me, at least till the end of the school year."

"Really?" Randy sat up. "That is good news. Then what?"

"I'll head out to New York City as soon as my mother gets her place set up. After that—" he shrugged.

"What?" Randy could see Mally looking at Joanie and Joanie looking at Mally. "What is it, you two?"

"Well," Mally said, "it's kinda up to your mom."

"My mom?" Randy exclaimed.

"Yeah. She kinda agreed to 'look after me,' whatever that means, so I could come back here and finish out high school."

Randy stared at him. "You're shittin' me."

Mally crossed his heart and raised a Boy Scout salute. "I shit you not."

Randy turned and looked back at the kitchen door. Joanie and Mally followed his gaze. Apparently, his mother had depths he knew nothing of. "Way to go, Virginia," he said softly.

Joanie turned back to him. "I'm sorry about your dad," she said.

Randy shook his head. "Harry didn't do anything we

couldn't've seen coming a mile away. I'm not sure Mom knows who to be madder at, him, herself, or me." He jumped off the trunk and walked over to the alley. "Me, I guess. I'm not so sure I'd argue." He kicked at the dirt.

"So, you're grounded, huh?" Joanie said.

He grimaced. "Yeah."

"For how long?"

"Twenty years to life, from the sound of it."

Mally hopped off the car and joined him. "So, what's the deal?"

"No car, except to and from school and my job. No—" he mimed opening a beer can.

"Oh, now that's cruel and unusual," Mally commiserated.

"And no hanging out," Randy concluded with a heavy sigh. "That's the one that really bites."

"Well, you won't be able to avoid hanging out with me," Joanie said cheerfully. She slid off the car and joined the boys. "Daddy's going to take me on as assistant as soon as school lets out. We'll see each other every afternoon."

"And you can't avoid me," Mally said. "What with all the 'looking after' I'll be needing."

Randy turned to look at Joanie. "So, it's you on one side of me," and he looked at Mally, "and you on the other."

"Yep," Mally said, putting an arm around his shoulder. "You're surrounded."

"No rest for the wicked," Joanie said, draping her arm around him from the other side.

Randy rolled his eyes to heaven. "My God," he said, "but it's great to have friends."

The Families of Croy

Randy's Family

Harry Edom – Contractor, oil rig worker, and past employee of the Oklahoma State Highway Department. Estranged from his wife, Virginia, and his son, Randy.

Virginia (Alquist) Edom – Daughter of the once-prominent Lerner Alquist, she gave up her prospects to marry Harry. Now a single mother to Randy. Mally's neighbor across the alley.

Randy Edom – Harry and Virginia's son. A junior at Croy Consolidated High School with hopes for a sports scholarship. Takes a job at Tibbits Rexall when money get tight.

Mally's Family

Reverend Matthew Jacobs – Retired pastor at Mt. Hermon Bible Church. Father of Susan and grandfather of Malachi. In declining health.

Susan Jacobs – Daughter of Matthew. Escaped Croy to pursue a career in theater, she keeps being pulled back to the town by her connections there.

Malachi "Mally" Jacobs – Son of Susan Jacobs and Andy Simms. Interests include e. e. cummings, astronomy, and figuring out what his growing interest in boys means.

Joanie's Family

John Tibbits, Jr. – Pharmacist and owner of Tibbits Rexall, which he bought from the previous owner in the 1950s. Husband of Ruth and father to Joanie and Kyle.

Ruth (Snepp) Tibbits – Wife of John and mother to Joanie and Kyle. She leaves Mount Hermon when Reverend Mathers take over, but misses the connection she felt there under Reverend Jacobs.

Joan "Joanie" Tibbits – Daughter of John and Ruth. The first person to befriend Mally when he starts at CCHS. Plays clarinet in the marching band.

Kyle "Bean" Tibbits – Joanie's younger brother and talented troublemaker.

Recurring Characters

Al Mattingly – High school buddy of Randy and Red, interested mostly in cars and basketball. Drinks some.

Andy Simms – Music minister at Mt. Hermon Bible Church when Reverend Jacobs was pastor. Friend and contemporary of Harry Edom, Virginia Alquist, John Tibbits, and Susan Jacobs. Mally's father. Dies when a train hits his car.

Clara (Whitlock) Oldfield – Widow of Gerald Oldfield, who drank away most of his inherited wealth. Landlady to Andy Simms, then Matthew Jacobs and his grandson, Malachi.

Henry "Hank" Ardmore – Head football and basketball coach and head of the P.E. department at CCHS.

Ida Lane Lancaster – Head librarian at Croy Memorial Library. Curator and guardian of books, periodicals, and other library materials.

Jedediah Tucker – Assistant football and basketball coach and head wrestling coach at Croy Consolidated High School.

Marcus Longacre – High school buddy to Red Conner and Randy Edom. Star on the CCHS wrestling team. Works for his uncle at Longacre Brothers Conoco.

Marsha "Candy" Sullivan – Drum Majorette with the CCHS marching band. Her father owns Sullivan's Auto Deals.

Richard "Red" Conner – High school buddy of Al Mattingly, Marcus Longacre, and Randy Edom. Talented fullback on the football team, looking for a scholarship.

Roberta "Bobbie" Littledear – High school friend of Joanie Tibbits, raised in a strict fundamentalist Christian family.

Samuel "Sammy" Anderson – Meteorologist. Friend and neighbor of Susan and Mally while they lived in Oklahoma City. Introduces Mally to astronomy and Susan to television weathercasting.

ACKNOWLEDGMENTS
FOR THE 2008 EDITION

The seed for this story was planted by Sally Taylor, who told me an anecdote about her high school days in Oklahoma one afternoon in the smoke-filled teachers' lounge at Benton Consolidated High School. The story has grown and changed so much since then that she would probably not recognize it if I did not acknowledge its genesis here.

The shape and depth of the story owes much to its early readers, especially Tim Learmont, Mike Overman, Remy Ceci, and Surajit Bose. I owe a special debt of gratitude to Tom Schmidt and the Gay Book Club of Palo Alto for reading the first complete draft; their questions, comments, and enthusiasm inspired me to keep going. Thanks also to my Oklahoma informants: Ed Rousar, Jeff Bowles, Debbe Ridley of the Marlow Chamber of Commerce, and Dr. Christine Pappas of East Central University. Although *Comfort Me* is a work of fiction, their input has helped keep it real.

I am indebted to Shawn Clements of Prizm Books for shepherding a nervous author through his first novel.

And finally, special thanks to Ken Goldman. Without his technical assistance, the typed manuscript of this novel would still be sitting in a ring binder at the bottom of a footlocker serving as a plant stand in my bedroom.

ACKNOWLEDGMENTS AND AUTHOR'S NOTE
FOR THE REVISED EDITION

I am indebted to Brett Waxdeck and Billy Jim Crawford for lending their photos and likenesses to the depiction of Mally in publicity, advertising, and cover designs. Their assistance helped make the 2008 edition a success, and their continued support is invaluable.

The keen and critical eyes of Dave Pederson, Judith Lancaster, and Steven Brook caught many minor errors and major gaffs that would have been embarrassing had they made it into print. Any remaining mistakes are entirely mine.

I always meant *Comfort Me* to be accompanied by another novel. *Comfort Me* would tell the story of three young people and how they found their way through the lies, prejudices, and mistakes of their parents' generation to find true friendship. Its companion novel, *If I Remember Him*, would tell the story of those parents when they themselves were young adults, revealing the choices and accidents that created the world in which their children live.

The project seemed straightforward enough, but the complexities of life, both for my fictional characters and myself, made it otherwise. Twelve years passed between the first publication of *Comfort Me* by Prizm Books and the final draft of *If I Remember Him*. In the interim, Prizm and its parent company, Torquere Press, ceased operation. All the while, the characters in both stories grew and developed. The geography, history, families, and alliances of the fictional town of Croy, Oklahoma became an intricate web of intergenerational aspirations and illusions, losses and redemptions. Inconsistencies crept in, names changed, locations shifted. And that, of course, required revisions to *Comfort Me* once *If I Remember Him* was complete.

But the history of a town, even a fictional one, is never complete. No matter how aware or ignorant a people may be of their past, no matter how firmly they hold to their histories, as long as they live they will continue to spawn new stories, new contradictions, new generations.

And so it is. Two more novels are planned for the Croy Cycle. They will follow Malachi "Jake" Jacobs and his friends as they mature and bring to completion what their parents started all those years ago.

About the Author

Louis Flint Ceci was a high school teacher of English and drama in Benton, Illinois; an assistant professor and chair of the Department of Journalism and Mass Communications at the University of Northern Colorado, Greeley; a commercial actor and freelance science journalist in the Denver-Boulder area; and a software engineer for several companies, including Skype, where he helped design and develop a user interface for the blind and visually impaired.

His poetry is published in *Colorado North Review* and *Impossible Archetype*. His scholarly articles on linguistics and poetics have appeared in *College English*, *Language and Style*, and *Literature in Performance*. He won the Gold Medal in the Poetic Justice Poetry Slam at the 2002 Gay Games in Sydney, Australia.

His short stories have appeared in *Diseased Pariah News*, *Jonathan*, and *Trikone Magazine*, and in the anthologies *Queer and Catholic*, and *At Second Glance: Gay City Volume 4*. He has twice been a finalist in the *Saints+Sinners: New Stories from the Festival* annual short fiction contest, and was inducted into the Saints+Sinners Hall of Fame in 2017.

He is an avid U.S. Masters swimmer and won two gold and three silver medals at the 2020 International Gay and Lesbian Aquatics World Championships in Melbourne, Australia.

He lives in Nevada City, California.a